MELISSA FOSTER

A novel

Megan's Way

Outskirts Press, Inc.
Denver, Colorado

Megan's Way

v2.0 R2.0

Outskirts Press, Inc.
http://www.outskirtspress.com

ISBN: 978-1-4327-4442-7

PRINTED IN THE UNITED STATES OF AMERICA

For Hilde Alter, my mother, who taught me that I could do anything I ever want to do by never giving up. For my husband, for believing in me even when I didn't believe in myself; and for my children, who have graciously accepted my nose in the computer and my fingers on the keyboard for far too long.

Prologue
Summer 1988

Megan and Holly ran, weaving their way through the crowds of the carnival and hollering to hear over the thick cheer that permeated the festive evening. Two teenage boys looked them up and down as they passed. Megan yanked Holly by her arm and pulled her into a long shadow cast by the colorful lights that illuminated a rickety roller coaster. They huddled together, giggling. A moment later, the roller coaster whooshed by, sending them scampering through the mass of carnival-goers, engulfed in uncontrollable shrieks of laughter.

A small red tent with a psychedelic sign that read "Psychic Readings! See Your Future! $3!" caught Megan's attention. She dragged Holly to the entrance, and they peered into the smoky gloom as they parted the curtain of stringed glass beads, which clinked and jingled as they were pushed to the side.

Holly pulled at Megan's sleeve, "Let's get out of here."

Megan distractedly shrugged off Holly's hand. She was mesmerized by the rush of the unknown, spellbound by the eccentric woman sitting within the darkened tent. A chill ran up Megan's spine. The woman looked into her eyes and beckoned her forward. Megan reached behind her and grasped Holly's hand, pulling her into the tent against her will. She reached into her pocket and, barely able to take her eyes from the old woman's, fumbled to count her money and then shoved six crumpled dollar bills into a glass jar that sat on a pedestal by the entrance.

The cacophony of the rides and the crowds seemed to fall away as a hushed stillness closed in around them, save for the crackle of the flickering flames dancing on their wicks. The girls' hands trembled. They were equally scared and excited by the mystical old woman shrouded in veils. Several bracelets clanked and dangled from her thick wrist as she motioned for them to sit around the small round table. They startled when the old woman grabbed their hands with her rough, plump fingers, then she slowly and dramatically closed her eyes.

Her hands tightened around theirs. The woman gasped a deep breath, and her body raised up and back, as if she were being pushed against the back of her chair. She held her breath, then let it out in a rush of air. Her hands fell open, releasing theirs. Her shoulders slumped forward, and her head followed.

Holly snapped her head in Megan's direction and mouthed, "What the hell?"

The woman opened her heavily-painted eyes, which grew wide and laden with concern, and stared into Megan's eyes. Megan felt riveted to her chair. The woman reached across the table and touched her hand, sending a jolt of energy up Megan's arm. Megan pulled her hand away, frightened. The woman whispered to her, "Ah, High Priestess, my teen querent. She will need you, and you will know."

Megan's legs trembled, her heart pounded in her chest. Her breaths came in short, clipped bursts. She and Holly turned wide, scared eyes toward each other. The woman moved her vision to the space between Megan and Holly. "Three of Swords pierce a heart. Against the background of a storm, it bleeds." She closed her eyes again, and whispered, "I see death." Her eyes slowly opened and she squinted, as if she were watching a scene unfold of a different time and place, her eyes darting without focus. Then seeming to recite, she intoned, "Blood or poison will come: Transformation—passage—truth."

The girls reached for each other's shaking hands. Holly's eyes welled with tears, her head visibly shook. Megan remained focused on each word the old woman said, unable to turn away.

The psychic turned those same concerned eyes to Holly. They glazed over with a look the girls could not read. Fear? Hatred? Understanding? She pointed a long, painted fingernail at Holly and hissed, "Judgment asks for the resurrection to summon the past, forgive it, and let it go." She lowered her hand and said, "One will be released," then quietly, under her breath, "and returned after death."

After a moment of panicked silence, the girls stood, sending their chairs flying askew. Then they fled, running fast and hard into the chaos of the carnival, caught in a frenzy of fear and hysterical laughter.

The psychic screamed into the night behind them. Her words trailed in their wake and echoed in Megan's ears for days, "With this spell, I empower thee. I empower thee!"

Chapter One
2009

Megan steadied herself against the cold porcelain sink, hoping the morning's nausea would subside and trying to strengthen herself for the tough decision that had been wreaking havoc with her mind lately, and the choice that lay ahead. The familiar *Tink*, pause, *Tink*, pause on her bedroom window drew her attention. A confused cardinal had repeatedly gone beak to glass in recent weeks, as though trying to rouse her. As she tried to calculate the number of times she'd also awakened to nausea, the familiar surge of bile rose in her throat.

She clung to the toilet as if it were a security blanket. The smell of last night's dinner still wafted in the air, sending her body into convulsions of dry heaves. *Great*, Megan thought as she grasped her stomach. She looked up at the ceiling, *What the hell am I going to do now?*

"Mom?" Olivia's voice carried down the hall. "Moom!" The single word stretched into two perfect teenage syllables.

Megan heard the drama in her voice and closed her eyes against her growing frustration. She knew that particular scream, the self-centered, in-a-hurry, where's-my-stuff scream. She did not have the patience to deal with Olivia's drama on this particular morning. She grabbed hold of the sink and pulled herself up. Her stomach lurched again, causing her whole body to clench. She prayed for some relief as Olivia's voice came screaming at her again.

"What!" she snapped back. She wished she could have been more patient with Olivia, but at that moment, she was overtaken by exhaustion, confusion, and anger. She wanted to kick something, to cry, to scream until she no longer had a voice—but her body was too tired to do any of those things. She had to pull herself together and get through the day.

Megan rinsed out her mouth and averted her eyes from the sheet-white face that reflected back at her.

"Never mind!" Olivia yelled from the hall. Her voice carried lightly, the tension from a moment ago gone.

Thank God, Megan said to herself. She made her way back to her bed and lay down, pulling the blanket over her head to shut out the light—and maybe life—for a moment.

Olivia bounded into the room and jumped onto Megan's bed a few minutes later. "Come on. We're going to be late!"

The flea market! Megan stretched her small frame and lowered the covers, revealing her mass of dark hair and a feigned wide smile. "Okay, chill, I'm up. I can't believe you are, though."

Olivia laughed and made a beeline to her mother's closet. "C'mon. What are you going to wear? Can I wear one of your scarves?" She wrapped a silk turquoise scarf around her slim neck, and turned to see the effect in the mirror. A smile grew across her face. "Please? I promise I won't ruin it."

"It does look pretty on you," Megan managed, pleased that Olivia's earlier exasperation had faded.

"Oh, thank you!" Olivia wrapped her arms around Megan. She withdrew and scrunched her face, "Geez, Mom, you'd better get ready. You look awful."

Megan felt a pang in her heart. She had liked it better when Olivia had been ten years old and had believed that even at her worst she was still the most beautiful mom in the world—but Olivia was right, she did look like hell. She felt like hell, too, and was in no mood to be told how awful she looked. She pointed to the door, silently ordering Olivia out of her bedroom so she could shower. Olivia rolled her eyes and flounced out of the room. Megan turned and sighed, relieved to have a moment's peace. She walked past the piles of books she was considering reading, past the wicker hamper overflowing with dirty clothes, and across the thickly-piled shag rug that covered only the center of the hardwood floor. The changing of hardwood to cold ceramic sent a shiver through Megan. She closed the bathroom door and caught a glimpse of herself in the mirror. Fine lines defined the edges of her mouth, drawing the ends downward, making her cheeks appear dull and drawn. She raised her eyebrows, and deep creases streamed across her forehead. Her exhaustion was evident. The face that stared back at her looked closer to fifty than thirty-eight. She wondered where the supple skin of her youth had gone, and how it had changed so fast. She turned away in disgust, summoning energy for the day ahead.

The radio played lightly in the background as Megan and Olivia worked around each other to prepare their breakfasts. Olivia hummed.

"What are you having?" Olivia asked.

"The usual, probably," Megan smiled. "What are you having?"

"Cereal, same as always."

Megan picked up on the flat tone of Olivia's normally perky voice.

"Hm, I think I'll have toast, actually, with jelly."

Olivia stood with her back against the counter, bowl in hand, and watched her mother.

"Toast? That's it?" Olivia said accusingly.

"Yes, that's it," she paused, turning to look at her. "Olivia, is something wrong?"

Olivia stared into her bowl, her lips pursed.

Megan sighed and chalked up Olivia's attitude to being fourteen. "Sit with me," she said.

Olivia sat and desultorily pushed her cereal around with her spoon. The silence hung in the air, uncomfortable.

Megan tried to lighten the mood. "What are you looking forward to most at the flea market?" she asked.

Olivia's eyes lit up, but her voice remained flat. "Everything, I guess. I hope Joe is there with the wind chimes, and I want to get another pair of wraparound pants." Olivia's voice began to carry a happier tone, "Oh, and the jewelry! I guess all of it, really. How about you?"

Megan smiled. She knew the thought of shopping would lift Olivia's spirits. Megan longed to be one of the flea market vendors once again, and realized that in her current condition, that was not likely to happen. "I'm just looking forward to everything, you know, being with you and Holly, and seeing everyone from last year."

"When are you going to sell again, Mom?"

"I don't know, Liv," Megan's response was short. Her bowels rumbled with urgency. She went to the sink, turning her back to Olivia. *What am I going to do?* "Are you ready? We don't want to be late."

Olivia left her unfinished bowl of cereal on the table and flew upstairs in search of her shoes. Megan made her way to the bathroom, grabbing the bottle of Pepto-Bismol along the way. The pink, peppermint liquid had become like an old friend, soothing away her daily discomfort.

The tips of the flea market tents appeared in the distance, and Megan's heart beat a little faster. "There it is, Livi!" She smiled and turned to face her daughter. "Isn't it exciting? I can't believe it's been a whole year."

"Mm-hmm," Olivia grunted in pure teenage annoyance.

Megan rounded the bend into the field of parked cars, scanned the grounds for an empty parking spot, and glanced at her watch. *Why the hell am I always late?* She sighed, realizing that her life had become one late appointment after another but pleased that her stomach issues had subsided. She hastily pulled her Corolla between a conversion van and a Lexus.

Megan lingered for a moment, watching the people hurry through the parking lot. A sense of loss floated through her. The image of Lawrence walking up to her vending booth on that steamy afternoon so many years ago flashed in her mind. Her nerves tingled, a reminder of their immediate attraction. Quickly, she pushed the thought deep inside. *Can't cry over spilt milk.*

"We have to hurry," Megan said quickly. "Do you see Holly anywhere?"

She checked her hair and makeup in the mirror and scrunched her face in displeasure, oblivious to her daughter's silence. She twisted her hair into a loose bun with all the finesse of a bumbling plumber and secured it with the quick stab of a pencil. *That'll have to do.* She grabbed her patchwork bag and hurried Olivia out of the car.

Megan rushed across the field toward the tents. Olivia lagged behind. "Where did we say we'd meet Holly?" she asked, frustrated with the fogginess of her mind.

Olivia sighed heavily and spat out, "At the scarf guy."

Megan spun around. "What is *up* with you, Liv?"

Olivia looked down, unable to meet her mother's eyes. "Nothing," she said. A strained moment of silence passed between them before Olivia said, in almost a whisper, "What's up with *you*?"

Megan froze. *Oh, God. She knows.* "What?" she said, more than asked.

"Come on, Mom. I heard you this morning. You were throwing up again." Olivia turned away from her mother.

Holly's voice cut through the tension, "Meggie! Olivia!" Holly waved as she ran toward them, arriving out of breath. "I've been looking all over for you guys!" She embraced Megan. "Meg, have you lost weight?" She moved to hug Olivia.

Megan shot her a look that said, *Don't go there*. She forced a smile and put her arm around Olivia, ignoring Olivia's eye roll. "C'mon! Let's go see what they have this year!"

They joined the crowds, strolled past the entrance and into the large tents that housed the vendors. Megan lingered at the jewelry stands, drawn in by the bright gems and sterling silver. She turned toward the sound of Olivia's laughter, and watched as Holly and Olivia tried on sunhats that were wider than their bodies. A feeling of comfort and happiness embraced her, immediately followed by jealousy—or was it fear? She felt lightheaded and dizzy, and settled onto a nearby bench.

She thought of her previous years as a flea market vendor, the excitement of building her career and meeting the locals. She smiled at the memory of Olivia, toddling around the grounds, wrapped in a sweatshirt and gloves until the brisk Cape air settled and the sun rose. The end of the day would find them bundled back up as the sun set and they headed out to their usual dinner at Arnold's Clam Bar. *The years have passed so quickly*, Megan thought. *It's as if just yesterday Olivia was four years old and bursting with joy over new sights that only a four-year-old could recognize.* Even two years ago, at her last flea market as a vendor, Olivia had still delighted in the novelty of the staggering array of wares. Megan sighed, if only she had known then that she would not be a vendor again, she wondered what she might have done differently. She might have enjoyed each moment a little more, said goodbye to her regular visitors.

The flea market patrons hustled past. A stab of pain seared into her lower right abdomen, bringing with it the anxious memories of the long hard battle that she thought she had won—beaten, erased, never to rear its ugly head again. She remembered the fear and sadness that Olivia and Holly had worn like winter coats during that hot and hectic summer, the fatigue she had waded through as her treatments had ravaged her body. Her face tightened in anger. *Remission. Remission my ass! All remission really means is that the disease still lurks in your body somewhere, waiting to steal your life away.* She hated illness. She hated the silence of illness, the way it slithered inside of you, eating away your fortitude without so much as a hint that your body, your life, was about to morph into a weakened shadow of its former self, or be taken away completely. She hated the way she felt like a marionette, with no control over her own body. Sometimes, she even hated God.

Holly hooked her arm in the crook of Olivia's elbow and walked toward Megan, where she rested on a wooden bench. "C'mon, Olivia," she said conspiratorially, "let's go check out the clothes!" She winked at Megan, flashing her a friendly smile as she and Olivia walked away. "Your mom takes forever when she looks at jewelry." Holly yelled over her shoulder to Megan, "We'll meet you at the concession stands in forty minutes."

They faded seamlessly into the crowd, passing mothers and daughters that other women may not have noticed, but Holly desperately yearned for such a relationship. She watched the women's carefree glances, the confidence of knowing their daughters were right there beside them. Some women smiled at Holly—private smiles that spoke volumes about the shared secret pleasures of motherhood. Holly knew it was wrong to pretend as she did, but it made her happy. She was proud of Olivia, and she liked to feel like Olivia's mother, if even for a moment. At times like these, she was ashamed of her feelings. As effortlessly as happiness had enveloped her, her fraudulence tore it away.

"Holly!" Olivia said for the second time.

"What?" Holly said, pulled abruptly from her reverie.

Olivia cocked her head in question.

"I'm sorry," Holly said quickly, "I was just thinking about something."

Olivia shrugged and continued talking.

Holly remained silent. The sun beat down on her shoulders, bringing warmth and what should have been relaxation. Instead, her heart began to race and her hands tingled. A familiar anxiety coursed through her—the feeling that all eyes were upon her, as if every stranger saw into the recesses of her haunted mind, and they knew what she had done.

Just look at her, Holly thought. *How could anyone not see it?* How could I have done such a thing to Megan, to Olivia. Then, swallowing the desire to cry out and run, she asked herself, *How could I have done this to myself?*

Olivia tugged on Holly's arm, pulling her mind out of its panicked state. Holly breathed deeply and willed herself to believe that it was only her own fingers doing the pointing. The strangers were just that—strangers. They could not know the depth of the deceit that lay within her soul.

Olivia chatted on the ride home as if their earlier discord had never happened. She talked about her new scarf, and how it looked just like one that Megan owned. She wore her sun hat and inspected her new shirts and earrings. "Holly loved this on me. Do you like it, Mom?" she asked.

Megan glanced beside her and was astonished at how old Olivia looked with her hair swept back off of her face and held in place by the peach-colored hat. She fought hard to keep the tears that threatened at bay. She focused on the road and cleared her throat, willing herself to remain unemotional. "I love it, Livi. It's beautiful. You're beautiful."

"Thanks!" Olivia took off the hat. "Hey," she said, "who is Lawrence?"

Megan's eyes flew open wide, and for a moment, she sat in stunned silence.

Before she could form an answer, Olivia said, "Mom! Who is Lawrence?"

Megan feigned ignorance, "Who?"

"Some guy named Lawrence. Holly said he helped you start your career or something before I was born."

"He was a very kind man." Megan hoped that would be enough to satisfy Olivia.

"Oh, I thought he was your boyfriend or something," Olivia said. "Holly said something about you missing the boat with that guy or something."

Megan remained silent.

"Hey! I've always wondered, Mom, why *don't* you have a boyfriend?" Olivia asked.

Megan laughed, "A boyfriend?" she said. "Who has time for *that*?" she winked at Olivia.

Olivia shrugged, "Yeah, I guess, but you know I wouldn't mind if you had one."

"Yeah," Megan said, thinking about how she hadn't felt as though she'd missed out on much by not having a boyfriend, or boyfriends, for that matter. She'd been happy with her life with Olivia. "I wouldn't mind if you did, either," she quipped back at her.

They were almost home when Megan was enveloped by another rush of nausea. "Olivia, I need to use the bathroom. We'll stop at the farmer's market."

"Mom, I really want to get home. Can't you wait?"

"No, I can't!" Megan snapped. "It'll just take a minute."

"But, Mom, we're almost home," Olivia's annoyance was clear.

Bile rose in Megan's throat and she began to gag. She swerved to the shoulder of the neighborhood road and threw open her door.

"Mom! Are you okay?" Olivia was right behind her, caught between embarrassment and worry. She held her mother's hair back as Megan threw up on the hot pavement. "Mom?"

Megan's stomached emptied itself of the salad she'd had for lunch and the toast and jam that had been breakfast. She swallowed the acidic remains. "Kleenex, please, honey."

Olivia rummaged through the front seat of the car, tossing her mother's books and paints to the side until she found a clean rag. "Here, use this," her voice shook. "I can't find the Kleenex."

Olivia grew angry as she watched her mother. "You're sick again, aren't you?" she accused.

Megan looked at her through tear-streaked eyes and shook her head, *No*.

"Yes, you are! Why else would you be throwing up so much? I heard you this morning!" Olivia stomped to the car, her back to Megan. "I'm not a baby. You can tell me, you know."

"Olivia, I am *not* sick again." She looked at the pavement, her lie tasted as bad as the vomit. "I just ate something bad, that's all." She settled her shaking body into the front seat, avoiding Olivia's stare.

The car ride home was silent. Olivia's face was ridden with anger and mistrust, and Megan wallowed in her own miserable thoughts. The doctor's words played in her mind like a bad rerun, "We can try chemo again, but it's already metastasized to your bones. It will delay things a bit, give you a few more months, maybe." *Months? I need years, not months! Olivia needs me here. Olivia can't go through this again. It's not fair! God damn you!*

Olivia disappeared into her room and ignored Megan's calls to the dinner table, leaving Megan alone with her sorrow and confusion. Megan pushed her food around on the plate. Salmon, she sighed to herself. She had made Olivia's favorite meal with hopes of smoothing things over. She hated to waste food and forced herself to take a bite. She winced in disgust. Her medications made everything she ate taste like metal. She spat the salmon into her napkin. Her heart hung heavily in her chest. She hadn't realized that loneliness could cause such weight.

Megan endured a constant mental battle to make a decision about her treatments, and the angst with Olivia brought the battle full-on like a loud drum beating in her head. Her doctor had made it crystal clear that treatments needed to begin immediately in order to buy her any extra time, and yet, she remained undecided. Should she suffer through the harsh treatments that would slowly and certainly deteriorate her body and spirit, and ultimately end in her death? Or should she simply let her body go; allow her body to leave the Earth in the manner God had chosen for her, without delay, forgoing the interfering medications that would make her sick and unable to care for herself?

She could not bring herself to imagine the devastation that her death would cause Olivia. Instead, she guided her thoughts to dissecting her daughter's feelings toward her decision. Would Olivia ever be able to get past the fact that it would have been her choice to terminate treatments? Would Olivia hate her forever? Would she understand that it would break Megan's heart to watch her daughter's hopeful eyes, only to know the hope was useless? Would the pain and anguish of false hopes that the treatments would give Olivia just extend her inevitable torture? How could she choose to leave her daughter?

Megan was depleted, ravaged by the irresolution, yet she remained unable to escape her tangled thoughts. Her mind swam in circles, inevitably drifting to Holly. An overwhelming sense of loss and jealousy consumed her, and guilt pierced her heart. She loved Holly. She could think of no one else that she'd rather have raise Olivia than Holly and Jack. *Jack.* Megan couldn't even go down that road. She had enough anguish on her plate.

As evening turned to night, Megan felt smothered by her illness, as if it hovered around her, waiting to steal her last breath. Its vigilance was inescapable. She tried to distract herself. She attempted to paint, but her mind was a black hole. Her typical creativity lay dormant, stale. Reading was out of the question; each word attacked her in its own way. Living, *I won't be living anymore*. When, *There will be no when to plan for*. Mother, *What kind of a mother leaves her daughter?*

She sat on the couch until fatigue settled in. Then she made her way upstairs to Olivia's bedroom and listened at the door—silence. She peered into the dark room. Olivia was tucked into her blankets, still wearing her clothes from the afternoon.

Her sleeping face looked soft as cotton and smooth as water. Megan's eyes washed over her daughter's, which, even closed, she knew were green around the edges with brown flakes in the center. *Fields of lily*, the ophthalmologist had said. The most beautiful ones he had ever seen. She took in her upturned nose and her delicate pink lips, which had spread across her face through puberty, as if they were painted on, bringing with them a confidence that only a teen could posses and a seductive quality that Olivia herself had yet to become aware of.

Olivia's fine golden hair reached across the pillow in straight lines. Megan reached up and fingered the ends of her own chestnut brown hair. Once full of body and effortless bounce, it hung frizzy and limp against her sheer cotton nightgown. *It's so thin.* Megan remembered how she had always wanted hair like the other girls—the other women—straighter, thinner, and more manageable; the kind you could throw up in a pony tail and pull down without thought; the kind that cascaded over your shoulders and flowed with the wind. Now she'd give anything to once again have her thick mop of unruly curls. She laughed to herself as she remembered her mother's daily rant, *Brush your hair! It looks like "where's that hair going with that girl!"*

Megan's limbs ached from exhaustion. She lowered herself carefully behind Olivia, whose body settled naturally against her own. Megan draped her arm around Olivia and listened to her breathe, memorizing the simple sound of air being released from her daughter's lungs. She felt Olivia's heartbeat through her back, strong against her own fragile chest. She closed her eyes and willed her heart to dance to the same rhythm as Olivia's, reveling in the feeling of oneness, the closeness she'd always shared with her—the closeness she now had to let slowly slip away.

Moonlight crept in through the sheer curtains, and Megan carefully extracted herself from the warmth of Olivia's body. She padded to her bedroom, slowing only for a moment to ponder getting into her own unmade bed. Her body, however, had another destination in mind and carried her into the bathroom.

Megan caught sight of her reflection in the mirror. She wondered how her body could have betrayed her in this way. She ran her fingers along her right shoulder and traced her sharp, visible collar bone. She did not want to believe the signs her body was giving her. If she ignored them, she hoped that maybe they would go away and the whole mess could be chalked up to a miracle, or a mistake.

Megan's stomach heaved, pushing her hopes out of her body along with the contents of her stomach. She clung to the cold toilet and waited for the next retch to tear through her. Anger and helplessness stewed within her and flushed her cheeks. Every muscle in her body tensed. A chill ran down her spine. She clenched her eyes shut. *I cannot do this to Olivia! We cannot go through this again!* She shook her head to clear her mind, but the heart-wrenching decision to forgo her treatments remained.

Megan pulled herself to her feet with determination. She lifted her gaze to the medication on the shelf above the toilet, staring with both desire and angst. Seven pill bottles like the seven dwarfs: sleepy, nasty, nauseous, baldy, weepy, starving, and full. That's how they made her feel. She closed her eyes and reached for the bottles. Her hand shook as, one by one, each plastic container released a pill until all seven settled restlessly into her palm. She closed her fingers around them, recognizing each pill by their odd shapes and sizes, their sandpaper scratch or too-smooth texture. Megan hated the way they made her hand feel heavy and wrong. Her eyes closed again, her body swayed, the slightest of movements. She took in a quick and deep breath and brought the pills toward her mouth, hesitating for just a second beneath her nose. The pungent odor of the medicine, a mixture of metal and dung, hung in the air. Her stomach lurched again. Her throat impulsively closed. With a quick jerk of her hand she threw the pills into the toilet. Breath rushed out of her like a balloon emptying its belly, and she took several gulps of the cool night air streaming through her window. Tears sprang from her eyes as she flushed the toilet.

She watched the seven dwarfs swirl in the water and wash slowly down the drain, wondering for a split second if she'd done the right thing. She turned back to the mirror. Seeing horror in her eyes and a withering face that she did not recognize, she knew she had made the right decision. She accepted the tears that came from deep within her soul and wept into her frail hands. Her body became heavy, tired. She leaned back against the pale green walls and let her deflated body slowly sink down to the tile floor.

The early hours of dawn found Megan back in Olivia's bedroom, rocking in the same chair in which she had rocked Olivia as a newborn. She looked around the bright yellow room and remembered the squabble she and Olivia had had over the color. Megan had thought that light purple might be more soothing, but eleven-year-old Olivia had insisted on "the color of the sun." The breeze from the bay window blew the dragonflies that she and Olivia had spent three weeks creating out of wire, fabric, and paint. They moved in circular motions, as if they were flying rather than hanging by yarn.

Olivia's blanket shifted slightly with each breath, each

breath strengthening Megan's resolve to maintain her choice—the choice that she believed would hasten her death, thereby diminishing the suffering and agony Olivia would endure during a prolonged and fruitless battle.

"Mom?" Olivia said quietly from her bed.

"Mm-hmm."

"What's going on?" she asked.

"Nothing," Megan opened her eyes and whispered. "I just needed to be with you. I'm sorry."

Olivia sat up in bed. "Why? What's up? What did I do?"

"Nothing, honey," Megan said. "I just missed you."

"O-kay," Olivia said, laden with sarcasm.

Megan reached down and brushed Olivia's hair from her face. "I'm sorry if I woke you."

"You didn't." Energy crept into Olivia's voice, "What are we doing today?"

Megan had anticipated, even dreaded, the question. They spent most weekends together, shopping, gardening, or watching movies. There was a time that Megan had worried about Olivia's lack of desire to hang out with other girls her age. Teenage girls were supposed to do fun things with their friends, not their mothers, but ever since Megan's first bout with ovarian cancer, Olivia was reluctant to leave her side. Megan knew that if she was going to save Olivia from prolonged heartache, she had to put some distance between them.

"I don't really know, honey," Megan said, softly. She

looked at the pillows, the floor, anywhere but into Olivia's eyes. "I thought you might want to call one of your friends, go to a movie maybe."

Olivia stood abruptly. "No, thanks. What are we doing today?"

Megan shifted her legs under her body and got off the rocker, keeping her back to Olivia. "Well, I have some painting that I need to do, so you should find something else to keep you busy."

"Can I come with you?" Olivia asked, energetically.

"Not today, honey. Today, I have to do it by myself."

"But you always bring me!" Olivia pouted.

"I know," Megan said, as she peered out the window at the dunes in the distance, "but this time I can't. I'm sorry."

Olivia stood and adjusted her boxer shorts and t-shirt. "Well," she stretched her arms and carried her voice with them, "can we go shopping later for my new binder?"

"I don't know, maybe." Megan felt a pang in her heart. She'd lived her life taking extra care to spend time with Olivia, intentionally keeping her weekends free from other commitments. That was *their* time. Megan reveled in being a single parent. Raising Olivia had completed her in a way that she felt no man ever could. The thought of Olivia living her life without Megan in it was devastating.

Through her heartache she managed, "When I get back we'll see what time it is."

"Whatever." Olivia's deflated voice was almost a whisper as she sulked toward the bathroom.

As the afternoon sun reached its peak, Megan cleaned her paint brushes, pleased with the peach color she had spent hours trying to produce. She stood back from the mural and crossed her arms, thinking not about its beauty, but about the sickness inside of her—the sickness that was taking her away from Olivia. "God damn it," she mumbled to herself. She looked around at the scattered paints, the flecks of color across her tarps, and was struck by how meaningless it all seemed. *What the hell am I doing?* She went through the motions of cleaning her brushes and collecting her supplies—guilt wrapped around her mind like a vice. She should be with Olivia. *To hell with the cancer. To hell with giving her space!* She stacked her paint cans, folded her tarp, and threw her cloths and brushes, along with other miscellaneous supplies, into her car and headed home.

As she drove, her mind was fixated on Olivia. She *needed* to be with her, near her, but she also knew that she might hurt Olivia more by doing so. Her head spun with confusion. She pulled off of the road quickly as a wave of dizziness passed through her. She stepped onto the road, and leaned her shaking body against the car. She wiped her forehead, sighed, and looked to the sky.

"What have I done?" she asked the clouds, which lingered above in halted silence.

She climbed back into the front seat and felt a familiar prickly sensation crawl up her legs. "Shit!" She braced herself for what she knew was coming, Olivia was in distress, and at any second Megan would lose awareness of herself and link to Olivia's senses as if they were her own. Suddenly, flames of agony ripped through her middle. Her breath came in short spurts. Sweat streamed down her brow. She wrapped her arms around her middle and folded into herself just as the edges of her sight began to fade. Images of Olivia rolling on the couch clutching her stomach, thrashing about in pain, hit with such force that Megan fell sideways across the front seat, writhing as if her intestines were tied in knots. The pain from her illness was mild compared to the torture that accompanied her visions. Megan's entire body went rigid, and just as quickly, fell limp.

She blinked several times, trying to make the foggy feeling in her mind disappear. "I empower thee," echoed in her head, words she both loathed and treasured.

The encounter was not new for Megan, having felt each of Olivia's major traumas as if they were her own since Olivia was just two days old. The feeling it left her with, one of a limp rag doll, was one she never seemed to get used to.

Megan sat up, fumbled for her cell phone, and dialed frantically. *Come on! Come on!* Her words tripped over each other as they tumble out of her mouth, "Holly! Olivia. Go to...go to her!"

"Megan? What's wrong, honey?" Holly's voice was filled with concern. She knew of Megan and Olivia's spiritual connection. She had seen it firsthand on several occasions. Though she had never understood it, she trusted it inexplicably. She also knew what it did to Megan, which was what worried her most with each episode.

"Olivia! It's Olivia!" Megan spat, exasperated. "She's in pain. She's at home. Please, go!" Megan's vision was clear, but her mind remained unsteady.

"I'm there! Don't worry," Holly said. "I'll call you. Are you okay?"

The sound of Holly's keys jingling brought relief to Megan. "Okay. Okay. Yes. Just go!" she said, depleted.

"I'm gone."

Megan didn't hang up until the line had gone dead. Her arms and shoulders trembled with fear and fatigue. She rested her head on the steering wheel, moaning with pain and worry, and wondering who would know when Olivia was in trouble after she was gone.

Olivia lay nestled amongst the cushions of the amber couch, her legs covered with a cranberry afghan. A cold compress rested on her forehead and a heating pad on her stomach. Holly sat by her side, stroking her face with one hand and holding her hand in the other.

Holly's words were gentle, "You'll be okay, Olivia. You just need to watch what you eat." She silently thanked God that Olivia was okay and that she had been available to help her. She constantly worried that He might strike her down, or worse, hurt Olivia as repayment for what she had done so long ago. The worst of all her secret thoughts was the anger she harbored toward Megan. She stowed those ugly feelings deep within her, knowing that Megan was just a scapegoat for her own anger.

"I know," Olivia said shyly. "Thanks for coming over." She looked up as she heard her mother's car in the driveway.

Megan drove quickly down the dirt road and pulled into the last driveway on the cul-de-sac. The familiar crunching sound of the seashells beneath her tires calmed her racing pulse. Her cedar-sided cottage sat peacefully before her, and she wondered what dilemma she would find inside. She sighed, gathered her purse into her arms, and started toward the red front door.

She heard Holly's voice before entering the small taupe family room. She took a second to get control of her breathing, and then walked into the room and faced her daughter. A shameful flush ran across Olivia's cheeks. Seeing Holly, the woman who would love and cherish her daughter after she was gone, sent a mixture of comfort and grief swirling through Megan like a hurricane. She grabbed hold of a nearby chaise lounge and lowered herself into it.

"Hi, Mom," Olivia said, apologetically.

"Hi, baby girl. Are you okay?"

"Yeah." Olivia looked down at her hands and fiddled with the edges of the afghan. "I was a little upset, that's all. I'm sorry. I forgot you'd *know*."

"The curse of the mother!" Holly laughed. "It's a wonderful thing, you know. Just think about it. When Olivia first fools around, you'll experience it right along with her."

"Oh, great," Megan laughed, "like that's such a wonderful feeling! She's fourteen. Let's not go there yet!"

"Geez, don't worry, Mom, for God's sake!" Olivia blushed, turned away.

Megan and Holly exchanged a look that held years of shared secrets. Holly saw something more in Megan's eyes, but could not figure out what it was. Her eyes held a silent question. Megan looked away.

"What were you so upset about?" Megan scanned the table where the empty ice cream container and spoon sat guiltily. "A whole quart, Livi? You know you're lactose intolerant. You must have been in awful pain."

"Sorry," Olivia said, sheepishly. "Holly gave me my medicine, and it's settling down now." Sadness swept across Olivia's face. "Why wouldn't you let me go with you today? You always do!" Her voice elevated, "You always say you *want* me with you!"

Memories of Olivia at five years old instantly resurfaced. *Why can't you sleep in my room tonight? I know the boogieman isn't real, but I need you here.* At that time, Megan had been teaching Olivia to deal with her fears. Now, was she hiding from her own? Megan's heart grew weak.

"Oh, honey. I just had a cranky client, that's all. I thought it would be harder if I had distractions." She hated the feeling of lying to her daughter.

"Oh. Then I'm *really* sorry," Olivia said with true remorse.

"Olivia, why don't you come to my house when your mom has to work?" Holly offered. "I mean, if you don't want to hang out with your friends." Holly had cherished and babysat Olivia since the day she was born, as if she were her own daughter. She often kept Olivia overnight on the evenings when Megan had to finish painting to meet a deadline or had to leave at the crack of dawn to get into the city. She had cared for Olivia when Megan had gone through chemotherapy and radiation months earlier, and had lain next to her while she had wept for the health of her mother. The bond they shared created a longing in Holly that bore into her often. She yearned to go back in time and reverse her most-loathed decision.

"That's a great idea!" Megan said. "Livi, I'm sorry I couldn't take you, but you're *fourteen*. You shouldn't need me by your side so much."

"I *know*, Mom. It's just—" her unspoken words hung in the air with the weight of lead.

Olivia didn't have to say the words that followed, Megan had heard them daily after her first round of chemotherapy. Olivia's frail voice had pleaded, *I'm scared! You had cancer, and you could get it again! I'm not sure how long you'll be here, and I don't want to miss even one second!* Megan also knew that Olivia didn't speak those words now because saying them out loud, in Olivia's mind, might make Megan's illness real once again.

Holly and Megan exchanged a knowing look.

"Livi, your mom is taking medications that help her stay healthy. You need to live your life, too. She's fine." Holly looked at Megan, and for the second time in a month noticed how tired and pale she looked.

Megan's guilt wrapped around her like a woolen shawl, weighing her down and making her limbs heavy. She lay back in the chaise lounge.

"Well, I'm home now, Liv," Megan said softly. "I'm just going to rest here for awhile with you." She closed her eyes, hoping to relax, and trying not to think about the gravity of what was happening to her daughter's life—wondering whether it was all her fault. *Am I doing the wrong thing?*

Holly started a fire to take the chill out of the New England evening, and turned on Lifetime television. She picked up Olivia's medication bottle, and the empty ice cream container, and set them on the bar that separated the kitchen from the family room. Then she busied herself in the kitchen, brewing tea, setting mugs on a tray, and giving Megan and Olivia a little privacy. She listened to the silence between the two and wondered why she felt like something was missing. There was a piece of Megan that seemed to be hidden, tucked away. They had been friends for many years, and never before had Megan held any secrets, besides the name of Olivia's father, whom she assumed was Lawrence Childs, but lately, there was an air about Megan that was different, like she was pulling away.

Holly carried the tray back into the cozy room. "You know, ladies, I think we need a little girl time!"

Olivia put her finger across her lips and pointed at Megan, whose eyes were closed. "Holly," she whispered, "do you think Mom is really getting better?"

"I do, Livi. Remember before her surgery, she was bloated and in pain all of the time." Holly glanced at Megan to make sure she was sleeping.

"Yes, but look at her. She's always so tired." Olivia fiddled with the afghan again. Her words were soft, scared, "I just thought she would bounce right back after her chemo, you know?"

"I know, honey. These things take time."

"But she never even lets me go with her to the doctor anymore. It's like things just changed or something, and look at how many more pills she takes now than before." Olivia's words rushed out, as if they'd been trapped within her.

"I'm sure she just doesn't want you to worry, that's all." She wrapped her arms around Olivia and eyed Megan. She couldn't help but wonder why her friend was so thin. Guilt haunted her as she realized that she, too, hadn't been to the doctor with Megan in the past few months. She squeezed her eyes closed, as if by doing so she could lessen the chance of her worst fear coming true.

Megan lay with her eyes closed, awake, thinking about the life she'd created, and how she had been forced to let it go. She tuned out Olivia and Holly's banter and the din of the television, and she thought about college graduation, which had provided one sure thing for her—the realization that her future was uncertain, at least by conventional terms. Holly, Peter, and Jack, her closest friends, had lined up corporate jobs to look forward to. They had known their earnings would climb like ivy and had planned their lives accordingly: smart apartments, chic clothing, and money that could be counted on each week. Megan's career aspirations had been sewn from a different cloth. She had craved an organic lifestyle. She had looked forward to scraping pennies and living minimally while she developed a freelance career in art. She had been content watching her friends' incomes grow while her income remained as level as grass. Megan had taken pride in her belief that her artistry would eventually pay off.

She had set out each weekend to art fairs and flea markets throughout New England. During the week, she had relentlessly approached galleries to sell her work. Her passion to paint had been stronger than her desire to eat. Her trust in her talent had been unyielding, and every declined offer had fed fuel to her intention to continue.

Her favorite weekend event had been vending at the flea market in Wellfleet, Massachusetts. Artisans packed into the parking lot of the drive-in movie theater, creating row after row of vendors. A constant flow of tourists filtered through, purchasing paintings of Eastham Bay and the lighthouses to remind them of their family vacations, their brief escape from reality. The air carried shrieks of delight from the playground at the center of the parking lot, and the smell of popcorn, burgers, and roasted peanuts from the concession stand floated on the gentle breezes. Each morning, locals stopped by Megan's booth armed with muffins and juice, and tales of what the winter had brought: heavy snows, new grandchildren, and tidbits of tasty gossip.

One particularly warm afternoon, after the locals had come to chat, and before the morning rush of tourists arrived, a tall man had entered the grounds. He had walked with purpose, weaving in and out of vendors, but keeping his eyes trained on her booth. His khaki pants and white polo shirt had been neatly pressed, and he had worn a navy blue blazer, which Megan had found odd for a hot summer's day.

Megan had rarely given notice to men, seeing them as beings that occasionally helped her find art supplies, fix her car, or serve some other utilitarian purpose—none of which were lustful. On that particular morning, however, with the sun striking hot on her bare shoulders, and the smell of salt in the air, she had watched the stranger approach, and had felt an unfamiliar frisson.

His pace had slowed as he had neared her booth, and she had quickly turned and busied herself propping up her paintings. Aware of his presence, a heat behind her, she began to hum. Hum!

His voice, soft as a whisper, gave her pause. She envisioned physically touching his words, sure that if they were tangible they would feel as soft as silk and be colored in smooth reds and faded purples. She glanced up as nervous as a teenage girl. Her eyes found his. They were the color of the ocean in the evening; such a deep blue, she felt as though she might fall into them.

He smiled.

Riveted to the ground where she knelt, she awkwardly tried to use the table to pull herself to her feet. Never before had she been breathless over a man. This was new to her—frightening. She nervously cleared her throat, and produced a faint, "Hello." Inside she screamed at herself, *What is wrong with you?*

He asked about her paintings and her inspirations. She gave brief answers, but her mind was not her own. It was as if something were flittering about in her head, taking her concentration and leaving a light, airy feeling behind. She averted her gaze, to keep from falling back into the abyss of his sensual eyes.

He reached out to shake her hand, "Lawrence Childs."

When she took his large hand in hers, a heat rushed to her center. She withdrew her right hand, unsure if she wanted his hand back in her own or if she wanted to flee. Megan had seen women react that way to men, though she had never understood it, or experienced such a reaction firsthand. She'd seen Holly overcome with infatuation many times over the course of their lives. When Holly had cried over her latest breakup, Megan couldn't understand her pain. *He's just a guy, for God's sake. Get over it. Don't be such a loser, there's a million more like him around the corner.*

Lawrence asked if she had ever painted wall murals, and Megan was so lost in his world of touch and sound that his words barely registered. While Megan had painted murals of all sizes, she had never actually been commissioned to do so. Most of her wall work had been done as donations for charity or helping other artists meet their deadlines. Her large canvases were what paid her rent.

Lawrence Childs, with his deep blue eyes and seductive voice, offered Megan fifteen thousand dollars to paint a mural in his home. He squinted and shaded his eyes from the burning sun. A glorious smile spread across his tanned skin, as an overwhelmed Megan nodded her head in acceptance and wondered what on earth she was doing.

Olivia was pouring over her math homework at the kitchen table when Megan walked in.

"Hey." Megan's greeting was met with silence, and she was becoming a little annoyed at her daughter's teenage attitude—she had been putting up with Olivia's silent treatment for three weeks now and was at the breaking point of being a patient, understanding mother. She was fed up with it. "Olivia, you could at least say hello!"

Olivia slammed her pencil on the table and looked at Megan with angry eyes. Megan lifted her eyebrows in response.

"Mom, why are you getting sick again?" Olivia accused.

Megan was taken aback, silent.

"Uh-huh. I heard you in the bathroom before dinner the other night." Olivia's eyes bored into her mother's back, bony and small, as she moved around the kitchen.

"Oh, honey, I just didn't feel well." Megan stared out the

window, unwilling to let Olivia see the sadness in her eyes.

"Mom! You can tell me, you know. I can take it if you're sick again." Olivia stood up as her voice grew louder, harsher. She couldn't stop her lower lip from trembling or the tears from flowing. "It's like all of a sudden you don't tell me anything! You don't even spend time with me! What's going on, Mom?" Her screams landed hard and cutting in Megan's ears.

"Honey," Megan turned to face Olivia, noticing for the first time how, when she was angry, her eyes saw right through her own, just like Olivia's father's. "I've just been busy, honey. You have to live your life and stop worrying about me. I'm fine, just fine." She reached out to put her arms around Olivia, but Olivia shook her off, and stormed out of the room.

"Whatever!" Olivia yelled. "Why are you allowed to lie to me, and I'm not allowed to lie to you?"

Olivia's next sentence exploded in Megan's ears like a bomb, though it was spoken no louder than a whisper, "No wonder I don't have a father!"

Megan slumped down onto the hard kitchen chair and let the tears roll down her cheeks. She jumped when Olivia's bedroom door slammed shut.

As the sun set, Megan hesitated in front of Olivia's room, perched to knock. She heard Olivia typing on her keyboard, thought better of it, and padded softly down the hall to her own room. She marched directly into her bathroom, took the seven dwarfs from their bottles, and squeezed them until her knuckles were white. She held her breath and threw them into her mouth. Tears streaked her cheeks as she filled up a cup of water, and brought it to her lips. She shut her eyes tight, preparing for the awful taste of the medicine as it slid down her throat. She lifted the glass and swirled the seven dwarfs and the water around in her mouth. A tortured wail came from deep within her. She turned and spat the wet, sticky pills into the toilet, and sunk back onto her heels, moaning in desperation. *What the hell am I doing? Am I really saving Olivia months of pain or creating more pain for her? I know I have to let her go, but I feel like I'm killing her along with me!*

"Holly, I'm worried about her. What can I do to make her understand that she needs to *live* her life?" Megan spoke quietly into the phone, though she was sure that Olivia was already asleep. The clock glowed red in the dark room, twelve-forty A.M.

"Meggie, she's a teenager. She'll be fine. Remember how we were? We were always pitching fits at our parents. She's totally normal." Holly's voice was gentle and sweet.

Megan's body relaxed. She sighed, taking comfort in her friend's words. "I know, but she's really mad at me this time. It's like she's giving up on me or something. It can't end like this."

Holly hesitated. "What do you mean, 'end like this'?" she asked, suddenly aware of each word Megan spoke.

Megan recovered quickly and said, "The fight. We never go to bed mad at each other. She stayed in her room all night. She never said goodnight and didn't even come down for dessert, and you know how we are about our desserts." Megan curled her legs under her body and rested her head on her feather pillow. "She's always on that damn computer when she's mad."

"Give it time, Meg. Really, just give it time. She's just using the instant messenger that all the kids use these days. It's like the new telephone." Holly took a deep breath, "More importantly, when's your next doctor's appointment?"

"Oh, I'll have to check," Megan lied.

"I thought you went like every three weeks or something. Did that change?"

"No, I still go, but it's been so crazy with the mural deadline and all that, I just can't remember the exact date." Megan took a deep breath and feigned a yawn, "Hol, I need to get some sleep. I'll call you tomorrow. Thank you for listening to me vent," she smiled, "and for making me feel better."

"No problem. Olivia will be fine, mark my word. Love you," Holly said.

"Love you too, Hol." Megan hung up the phone and lay on her thick down comforter. She stared at the ceiling and thought of all the things in her life that she needed to get in order. Lists ran through her head of legal, household, and other items that would need closure. She was surprised at how calm she felt. She didn't feel as though she were in a frenzy of fear. Instead, she felt like she was doing a job, organizing someone else's life.

Olivia grew angrier as the week progressed. Days passed, silent and uncomfortable. Megan was too upset to paint. She was reading on the couch when Olivia arrived home from school.

"Hi," Megan said cheerfully.

Olivia strutted past her mother and ignored her greeting.

The space between them was thick with tension.

Olivia walked past the fireplace in the family room, out the back door, and sat on the porch, stewing. Anger coursed through her veins, but sadness lingered just below. If her mother was sick again, then she was wasting precious time being mad, but that didn't matter right then. What mattered was making her mother see that she needed to be honest, that she needed to treat Olivia the way she demanded Olivia treat her. After all, wasn't that what she always preached? *Be honest so you don't have to keep up with your own lies.*

Olivia took a deep breath of the salty sea air. Her body grew rigid when she heard the French doors open. Megan sat in the pastel-colored Adirondack chair beside her.

"It's nice out here, huh?" Megan was again met with Olivia's silence. "Maybe we should eat dinner outside tonight." Megan ran her eyes along the perimeter of tall pines that surrounded the small yard and created a tranquil, private sanctuary for her and Olivia. She took in the gardens that they had spent years digging and planting together, until the tiger lilies, lady slippers, and Morning Glories were placed just so. She loved how the wild roses grew in misbehaving clumps at the edges, where the mixture of sand and dirt met the few bits of grass that grew sparsely throughout the Cape.

Olivia turned her face away from her mother and gritted her teeth.

"Honey, I know you are mad at me, but can't we just be friends again?" Megan asked.

Olivia remained silent.

"Okay. Well, if you want to be mad, that's fine, but I'm not going to play this game." Megan rose, and turned toward the doors.

Olivia turned to say something, and noticed again how skinny her mother was, which further angered and scared her. "Whatever," slipped from her lips like a secret as tears welled in her eyes.

"I'm going out tonight," anger seethed in Olivia's voice.

"Where are you going?" Megan asked as she picked at her dinner.

"Out."

"With who?" Megan skipped over Olivia's attitude, happy that her daughter was finally going to do something other than skulk around the house or hide out in her bedroom.

"Kids from school," Olivia said, "they're picking me

up." She sat, stiff and rebellious, at the table in the kitchen.

"Who?" Megan asked a little more sternly, uneasy with Olivia's terse answers.

"People!" Olivia yelled, standing abruptly, her rigid arms at her side, fists clenched . "Why does it matter? You're always telling me to go out, and now I'm going! Geez!" Olivia picked up her dishes, clanked them into the sink, then stomped upstairs.

"Holly, it's ten at night, on a school night!" Megan complained into the telephone receiver.

"Meg, she's only doing what you asked her to do. You should be happy."

"I know, but she never goes anywhere, and suddenly she's out until all hours."

"I wouldn't call ten o'clock all hours," Holly said. "Remember us? Now that was all hours!" she laughed.

"Yeah, well God forbid she does what we did. Thanks, by the way, for the visual." Megan's voice was rushed, strained. Her stomach hurt, and she was worried sick about Olivia, who had been so angry at her for the past week that God only knew what she'd do.

Megan awoke with a feeling of dread. She couldn't place it, but it loomed in the air like a bad dream. Her stomach was on fire. The clock next to the couch chimed. *Midnight*, she vaguely acknowledged. Then with a start, *Midnight! For Christ's sake! Where's Olivia?* She ran upstairs. Her joints were achy and stiff. Olivia's bed was empty. Her covers were still drawn up over her pillow, her cell phone lay on her nightstand. She rushed back downstairs to the answering machine. The message light blinked a digital zero. Megan's heart raced as panic spread through her body. Unsure if it was her own panic or her daughter's, she picked up the phone to call Olivia's friends. She checked with the few girlfriends that Olivia had—each one sound asleep in her own home, their parents' groggy, concerned voices spewed empty offers of help.

Megan rushed upstairs and turned on Olivia's computer, unable to remember who she was going out with. The website myroom.com was minimized, hovering at the bottom of the screen like a scandalous criminal. Each heartbeat pounded in Megan's head like a bass drum. She remembered the many conversations she and Olivia had had regarding myroom.com. Olivia knew that the website was off limits because of recent articles stating that those types of sites made kids easy prey for child molesters.

Megan clicked on the myroom.com tab, and the page came to life. Photos of Olivia spread across the screen: Olivia laughing with two girls Megan did not recognize; Olivia alone, looking serious sitting in a chair; Olivia standing with her back to the camera as she looked over her shoulder, her finger in her mouth.

"What the hell?" Tears sprang to Megan's eyes as she realized that Olivia had a life that she hadn't been privy to, and she wondered how long it had been going on. Anger grew in her chest. Her hands began to shake, and a flush spread up her neck and face. She looked through the other five photos and realized that in each one, Olivia wore a bracelet that she had just given her in April. *Maybe this hasn't gone on too long.* When she neared the bottom of the page, there was a chat box. She quickly glanced at posts from surferdude97 and hotrox42 and began to sweat. Olivia's screen name, Mommasgurl92, scrolled across the top of the box. Megan's tingling hand flew to her mouth, "Oh my God!" She shuddered as her vision faded to black and she crumpled to the ground.

She fought to stay conscious as the visions of Olivia struck her with tremendous force, and once again Olivia's terror became her own. She could feel that large hands were gripping Olivia's shoulders, cold and strong. She kicked and struggled to break free. Thrown to the ground, two people hovered above her. She thrashed about on the grass. A water tower loomed behind them. A lime green truck stood sentinel in the distance.

When the focus came back to Megan's eyes, she was still rolling around on the floor, feeling Olivia's fear, the remnants of the cold, strong hands on her shoulders. She willed herself to stand, though the energy had been sucked out of her. She snagged the phone and dialed Holly's number. Busy. "Shit!" She made her way downstairs, her vision still fuzzy, and dialed Peter's number. Busy. "God damn it!" She threw the phone to the floor, grabbed her keys, and flew out the front door into the brisk night air.

Fumbling frantically, she started the car and thrust it into Drive, heading for the only water tower she knew of—the one just outside of town by Dave's Drive In. *What have I done?* Tears streamed down her cheeks, her legs shook as she pushed the gas pedal and sped down the highway. *Oh Olivia, hang on! I'm coming, Baby!* She reached for her cell phone to alert the police and realized that she had left it back home on the counter. *Damn it!* She pushed her car to eighty, then eighty-two miles per hour, and sped off the ramp of Exit 49, heading toward the tower. As she passed the drive in, she saw the water tower in the distance, shrouded by a mass of trees. When she reached the dirt path that led to the tower, she turned off her lights and slowed her speed, maneuvering around dips and ruts in the overgrown path. A large pine tree had fallen across the road and blocked the way. Seeing no way around it, she slammed the car into Park and got out. Pain, like knives, worked its way from her stomach to her arms. She was unsure if the pain was Olivia's or her own. She pushed ahead, keys in hand.

Her eyes quickly adjusted to the darkness. She followed the dirt path that soon became thick, tall grass interspersed with lofty pitch pine trees. She weaved her way around masses of prickly shrubs and over fallen leaves from giant scrub oaks. The tower perched atop a mild hill which at that moment appeared to Megan as ominous as a mountain. She strained forward, driven by Olivia's plight. As Megan approached the tower the wind amplified in her ears. She felt exposed, vulnerable. She looked around for a weapon, and grabbed a substantial fallen tree limb. She turned toward the sound of a vehicle engine, and spotted a bright green truck speeding off through an overgrown field about fifty yards away. Her mind reeled. *Oh God! Don't let Olivia be in that truck!* She stopped dead in her tracks as she felt a large, rough hand grab her wrist. She looked down, and in her panicked state was surprised to realize that it was not her trembling arm that the hand was grasping, but Olivia's. She closed her eyes, willing Olivia to stay strong. Megan knew Olivia was being pushed deeper into the woods. She could taste her daughter's fear, bitter and pungent. She quickened her pace, trying to remain silent, unnoticed. She saw a glimmer of light up ahead, smaller than a flashlight. It moved along slowly, illuminating a spot just large enough to see her daughter's shaking shoulders. *A lighter maybe?* She forged forward and the incline lessened.

Olivia's pleas and promises shot out of the dark and pierced her mother's heart. Megan swallowed a yell. The light ahead stopped, hovering in the cool night air. Megan stopped, listened, then silently moved deeper into the woods.

Twenty feet away, she could make out a large, ungainly man with a flannel shirt and torn jeans looming over her daughter. Olivia's face, a palette of panic, her arms crossed over her chest, were enough to make Megan's heart explode, her anger rose to an insurmountable level.

The man spoke in rough, harsh murmurs. Megan moved closer, desperately hoping Olivia would not see her and give her away. She had not one thought of caution. Adrenaline and fear for Olivia had repressed any suggestions of delay or defeat. She rounded a thick bush, ducked behind it, and closed her eyes long enough to think, *One chance, that's all I have—one chance to get her out of this alive*.

With white knuckles, she gripped her keys, the largest jutting out between her index and middle fingers like a knife. She placed the stick on the ground, deciding it was too cumbersome. She did not see a weapon, no gun in the man's hand. He hulked over Olivia, and violently rammed her back into a tree. Megan could hear her daughter cry out in pain as Olivia pushed him away with all her might, "No! No!" Olivia screamed.

Megan crept quickly behind him, hoping to remain undetected. Too late, the crumbling leaves beneath her feet gave her away. The captor spun around just as Megan lunged at him. Her five foot frame was no match for his height and bulk. She dropped her keys and clung to his body, her legs wrapped around his middle, her left hand clenched his hair and her right thumb dug into his eye, pushing past his eyeball and into the socket.

Somewhere to the side, Olivia screamed, "Mom! No, Mom!" her terror evident in her shrill voice.

Megan pushed and thrust with all her might, while screaming at the top of her lungs, "Run, Livi! Run!"

Olivia was paralyzed with shock, her mind too consumed with fear to function. She watched her mother attached to her assailant and cried uncontrollably.

Megan continued screaming for Olivia to run. She gauged her thumb deeper into the man's eye socket. Blood spurted and oozed across her hand and arm. The man flailed between pushing her off his body and grabbing at his eye.

Olivia broke free of her fear, scanned the ground for a weapon. She picked up a heavy rock and smashed it into the back of the man's head. He rocked forward, and she drove it into his head again, harder. Megan fell to the ground. The man stumbled. His head spewed blood onto his shirt, and his eye was no longer visible.

Megan lay on the ground. Her body ached. She screamed, "Run, Livi! Run! Run!"

Olivia grabbed her mother's frail arm and yanked her to her feet. Together they ran back through the woods and down the path, tripping and holding onto each other. Megan shot a backward glance and found the abductor's hands over his face, blood covering his head like a gruesome mask. His screams of torment filled the night.

When they reached the car, Megan's relief was overshadowed by her panic, as she realized she didn't have her car keys. With much struggling, she forced Olivia into the car, and demanded her to lock the doors. Olivia's body wracked with sobs and trembled with such force that her teeth chattered.

Olivia screamed, "No!" several times, but her mother ran back up the path to find her keys.

When she neared the water tower, the man was nowhere in sight. She dropped to the ground by the bush and felt around the rocks and dirt. She saw a twinkle of light about ten feet in front of her and dashed for the keys, which were splattered with fresh blood. Without hesitation, she spun around, pushed past the pain of what felt like a broken rib, blocked out the stinging of the cold air in her lungs, and rushed toward the car, praying Olivia was safe. She looked behind her several times but didn't see the man.

She reached the car, out of breath, and trembling so badly she feared not being able to remain erect. Olivia was nowhere in sight.

"Olivia!" she screamed, running from door to door, all of them locked. She screamed again, "Olivia!"

Olivia peered out from under the dashboard, saw her mother, and reached up to unlock the door. Megan scrambled into the car and locked the doors, shoving the keys in the ignition and pitching the car into reverse. She spun out and fishtailed onto the dirt road, nearly hitting the side of a van as she raced onto the highway. She could not find her voice. Her hands felt glued to the steering wheel, her foot to the pedal.

Olivia remained on the floor, huddled in a ball and sobbing.

Twelve minutes later, Megan pulled into the police station and eyed the brick building, illuminated like a Christmas tree. A sense of safety blanketed her. She turned to Olivia, her arms outstretched.

"I'm sorry, Mom!" Olivia cried. Her body trembled. Her words rushed out like a waterfall, fast and hard. "I'm sorry! I'm sorry!"

Megan's tears fell, salty and warm, onto her own lips, "Livi, it's okay. It's okay. I'm here. Are you okay?" She held her tight.

Olivia nodded. Her face was swollen and red. "I'm so sorry, Mom. I thought he was someone else."

"I know, honey. I know." Megan said. "Whatever happened out there, whatever brought you there, Olivia, it's not your fault." *It's mine*, Megan thought. She scanned her daughter's young body. Seeing no gashes or obvious injuries, she breathed a little easier. "Did he...hurt you?" Megan braced herself for the answer.

Olivia looked down at her lap, tears fell unabashedly. "My back against the tree...my arms," the words emerged with difficulty as shock began to take over. She wrapped her arms around herself and sobbed, shivering.

Megan held her, willing away the tears and thanking God she was there. When Olivia's sobs lessened, Megan whispered, "We have to tell the police."

"But they'll think I'm awful! They'll think I'm a slut!" Olivia buried her face in her mother's shirt.

Megan stroked Olivia's hair and held her close. She felt each sob deep within the pit of her own stomach. "Livi, do you want to tell me first? Would that help?"

Olivia tightened her grip around Megan. "That's worse! You'll hate me!"

"I could never hate you! I love you!" She lifted Olivia's dirt streaked face in her hands, and was met with dark circles around her daughter's haunted eyes. *What on earth have I done to my baby?* Each beat of Megan's heart hurt with the answer. "Olivia, you did nothing wrong. I could never think badly of you."

Olivia yelled, "But I did! I went to myroom.com! You told me not to! You said something bad could happen!" Olivia threw herself against the passenger door, arms crossed over her chest. She stared out the window. "You told me, Mom! You warned me! God! I'm such a mess!" She buried her face in her hands and brought her knees up to her chest. "You must hate me!"

Megan slid over to Olivia's side of the car, wrapped her arms around her daughter's shaking body, and let her tears fall onto Olivia's shiny hair. "Baby girl," she crooned, "you made a mistake. God knows I've made a ton!"

Olivia laughed, "Yeah, right. You? You are like Miss Perfect. You never fuck up."

Megan flinched at the word. "Yes I do...fuck up," she said, and they both laughed through their tears. "I fuck up all the time, Olivia! I just hide it well!"

"Oh, Mom!" Olivia threw her arms around Megan's neck. They remained there, safe in each other's arms, until their sobbing stopped and their hearts calmed. "What am I going to do? Do I have to tell the police?"

"Yes. Otherwise that maniac can hurt someone else."

"But, Mom, he isn't the one I met. I met a younger guy.

Someone...like...my age. No! He must have been sixteen because he drove. He drove me to this guy and then took off."

"The green truck!" Megan looked out the window, remembering the vehicle speeding away through the field, the bright color of it, almost fluorescent.

"Yes! He drove a green truck!" Olivia said.

"We have to report it, Livi. Besides, I might have killed that guy. What I did to him was so..." Megan felt sick remembering the awful sensation of her thumb digging under the man's eye socket and rifling through the remains.

"Brave. It was so brave, Mom. You saved my life."

"Well, someone had to do it!" Megan swallowed her impulse to cry, trying to remain strong for Olivia.

Just before Olivia fell asleep, she said to Megan, "If my father was around, he would be so ashamed of me. I'm glad I don't know who he is. It hurts less this way."

Megan tried to console her while wrestling her own private demons. How had she let this happen? Why hadn't she forbade Olivia from going out earlier that evening? *How can I leave her?* Thankfully, the Valium that the physician had given Olivia kicked in, and she faded off to sleep with her worries written all over her young face.

Megan couldn't leave her bedside. The guilt she felt swirled through her like a whirlwind, dusting up all of her confusion and pain.

Jack and Peter had come and gone, staying much longer than Megan had the energy for, though she was thankful for the comfort from them. They had both offered to go look for the man that Megan fought and the green truck, but the police said they were already doing that, and Megan didn't want her friends to be bothered anymore than they already had been. Their guilt for not having been available when Megan had been in a crisis was evident in their eyes, their actions. What they didn't realize, however, was that the time was yet to come when she would truly need them like she never had before.

While Holly waited downstairs, Megan reflected on the scene at the police station. It had been heart-wrenching to watch Olivia describe how depressed she had been, and how that was the first time she had "chatted" with anyone online besides her two best friends. She said she had heard about myroom.com and had wanted to check it out. Normally, she had said, she would never go against her mother's rules, but things had been so weird lately, and she was so angry and sad that she didn't know what she was doing. She said she had felt driven, recklessly she admitted, but as if it were the right thing to do—to do something that she knew was wrong.

Tears streaked Megan's cheeks. She left Olivia's bedroom so as not to wake her and paced the hallway. She pulled her sweater tight around her body and crossed her arms, only to drop them again and worry her hands. She shook her head, trying to make peace with the confusion that rumbled inside it.

The police station had felt safe, yet sterile. Linoleum gray floors met equally dull walls. The faint ticking of keyboards panged beyond the glass of the office where they had sat, shocked and trembling, as the police officers had peppered Olivia with questions. They had asked about the photos, which, Olivia said, she had her friends take of her so she could post them online. It had been relatively easy with her digital camera. She didn't believe that anything bad would happen, and she had gotten so caught up in the attention and flattery from those guys, hotrox42 and the surferdude97, that even the thought that it might be wrong had gone out of her head.

The officers nodded as if they had seen many young girls go through the exact same scenario. Megan wasn't certain if it was compassion or annoyance she read in their eyes. That upset Megan even more. This wasn't any girl. This was Olivia—her daughter. She let it pass with a heavy heart, and they had continued to ask pointed questions. They wanted details about their online chats. Olivia promised that she didn't give out any personal data, but the police were going to come by later and check it out for themselves.

The friend that Olivia had pick her up and take her to the library, where she was to meet hotrox42, knew nothing of the clandestine meeting. She thought Olivia was meeting another girlfriend there. The police said it wasn't abnormal for teens to keep details of this type of tryst to themselves, especially given the fact that this was the first time that Olivia had strayed. *Olivia strayed.* The mere thought of her daughter doing something so dangerous, so rebellious, made Megan's body shiver.

Apparently hotrox42 was the frontrunner for the older guy, surferdude97, and the police had been trying to track them down for the last few weeks. They'd had a few sketchy leads, but Olivia and Megan provided them with a description of the green truck, which the officers indicated should be fairly easy to trace given the color.

They seemed excited that Megan had been able to physically harm the older man and were going to contact the local hospitals, shelters, and walk-in clinics in case he went for medical assistance. They concurred that such an injury could kill the man, if she had reached his brain, and that he certainly couldn't go on walking around without getting medical attention for such a wound.

They had called a physician into the station, since Olivia had not been raped, and took DNA samples from her and Megan's fingernails and hands. Hair and other fibers were going to be removed from their clothing, and they were given sweatpants and t-shirts to wear home. The sketch artist had been able to draw a pretty true-to-life image of the older man. The police were fairly certain that they could nail the predators.

Megan had sustained bruised ribs and Olivia had a few bumps and bruises and a sore back, but thankfully there were no further physical injuries. Emotional injuries, however, were not as neatly observable for either Olivia or Megan.

Megan had been petrified that they would have to go to the hospital for blood tests and her secret would be revealed, but she was spared that scene. Megan's tears continued to fall; not from the encounter they had had with the awful man, but for the shame that she knew Olivia had felt in front of the officers. She wept for her love of Olivia, a love that could never be tainted by bad decisions. She wept because all of that mess was her fault and her daughter was paying the price. She wept because she wasn't sure, at this juncture, that she was following the right course with her own life.

Relief over Olivia's safe return swept through Megan. Her eyes grew heavy, she fingered the business card of a therapist that the physician had recommended for her and Olivia. She was lost in thought when Holly appeared in the hallway at the top of the stairs.

"How's our girl?" Holly asked in a sleepy voice, leaning her body against the wall.

Megan glanced up and smiled. She put her finger to her lips and walked down the hall, motioning for Holly to follow her to her own bedroom.

They sat on her bed. "My God, Hol, how did all this happen?" she asked.

"Remember us, Megan? She's a typical kid." Holly lay back on the bed, staring at the ceiling. "No, she's not even a typical kid. She's better than a typical kid. She never gives you a hard time. She was just...exploring, that's all."

"Yeah, well..." Megan's sarcasm trailed off as she thought about the crazy night.

"Thank God you were there, Meg. I mean, whatever it is that you and she share, well, it's really remarkable." Holly propped herself up on her elbow and looked at Megan, who was splayed out beside her. Jealousy tiptoed through Holly, and guilt shadowed right behind it.

"I know. I worry, you know. What if something happens to me? Who will take care of Olivia?" she asked.

Hurt and disappointment floated into Holly's eyes. "I thought we had all of that worked out. Remember? When she was five we drew up the documents, just in case something ever happened." Holly played with a string on the comforter. "Or have you changed your mind?" she asked, tentatively.

Megan sat up, "Oh no! No, I didn't change my mind at all. Gosh! I just meant, who would know when she was in trouble like I do, that's all. Goodness, there is no one else who I would rather have take care of Olivia than you and Jack. You know that."

Holly breathed a sigh of relief. "Thank God! I was worried there for a minute." Holly lay back on the bed again.

"Meg?" Holly whispered.

"Yeah?" Megan looked at her friend, curious.

"I, um," she looked up again, away from Megan, "I got some news today."

"Yeah? From who?" Megan asked lightly.

"From the doctor," Holly answered.

Both women looked toward one and other, Holly uncertainly, and Megan with burning curiosity. *Does she know?*

"Holly, what is it?" Megan asked in a serious voice. A rush of adrenaline pushed its way through Megan. Her eyes opened wide as she waited for Holly's reply.

Holly reached her hand out and took Megan's hand off of her concave stomach and rested it in her own, between them. A tear escaped from her eye as she stared at the ceiling, the lump in her throat made it difficult for words to slip by.

"What, Hol?" Megan whispered.

"I can't," Holly said, the hot tears now streaked her face, landing in her hair.

"Can't what?" Megan turned toward Holly. "It's okay, Holly. What is it?"

"I...I can't have children," she said.

Her words landed empty and hollow in Megan's ears. "Oh Hol, I'm so sorry!" Megan sat up and took Holly into her arms. "I'm so sorry. I knew you were having tests, but I never thought..." Her sentence hung in the air as her tears fell onto Holly's shoulder.

"I know. We didn't either. We waited, you knew that. After Alissa Mae...well, you know. For the longest time I wasn't sure that I wanted a child. I wasn't sure that I could be a good wife and a good mother. And when she...well... anyway...let's just say that it was probably for the best." Holly took a deep breath. "There just didn't seem to be a rush to have children, you know?

"We always thought that eventually we would, and we were really happy, so it didn't feel like anything was really missing, but then," Holly let go of Megan and sat on the end of the bed. "When you first got sick, it made me think about things." She looked at her friend's tired face and smiled, "I'm sorry. It just made me realize that time was so precious—and so we tried, I mean, we *really* tried." She gave a little laugh, walked to the window, and ran her finger along the windowsill.

"Why didn't you tell me?" Megan asked, hurt to be excluded from this part of Holly's life.

"Because, Meg, you were sick. You were taking care of yourself and Olivia."

"No, you were taking care of me and Olivia, remember?" Megan said.

"Well, you were otherwise pretty busy trying to get healthy. Anyway, I figured you didn't need to be burdened with my foolishness." Holly returned to the bed and sat next to Megan again.

"Oh, Holly, your getting pregnant is certainly not foolishness. It's one of the most important things in our lives—yours and mine. You should know that. Maybe I've been selfish. I'm so sorry." Megan put her hand on Holly's hand, and they sat in silence for a moment. "I really am sorry, Holly. I was busy being sick and taking for granted that you were always there. I should have seen your stress. I should have noticed *something*."

"It's not your fault, Megan. My God, you weren't selfish, you were sick. There's a huge difference. You are always there for me and Jack. I think we both would have crumbled under the weight of Alissa Mae's funeral, but you were there, handling *everything*. And when I had that awful flu," she looked up, as if remembering a specific scene, "you made Jack dinners, and went grocery shopping for like two whole weeks for us. You even cleaned up my puke!" They both laughed a quiet, gentle laugh. "Besides, what good would it have done for you to ride that emotional roller coaster with me? It was awful; every few weeks wondering if that would be the month. It was so painful."

"I should have been there to go through it with you. You shouldn't have had to do it alone."

"But I didn't do it alone. I had Jack. He's been wonderful. He rode the highs and lows with me. The man is a saint. Without him I would have strangled myself by now!"

"Consider yourself lucky," Megan said softly.

The room became quiet. As Megan and Holly lay easily next to each other, years of friendship provided safety and a sense of comfort. Megan's thoughts turned inward. A wave of sadness passed through her when she realized that she did not have her own saint. Then she realized that she'd given him up. Megan recalled the ferry ride so long ago. The memory of sitting on the ferry bench was so vivid, it was as if Megan were twenty-four years old again, carefree and contented, feeling the cool rush of the sea breeze against her warm body. She had sat on a bench facing the water, but her eyes were riveted to the pages of the book she was holding in front of her body, as if reading to a crowd. The sandy shore faded as the ferry left the dock, unnoticed by Megan. Her body rocked gently with the movement of the ferry, and her hair blew in the wind behind her. She kept her face tilted up, just slightly, to keep the wayward strands from slapping her face like a whip. The ferry ride was forty-five minutes from the Cape to the Vineyard, and Megan looked forward to the serenity of the familiar trip. She had been traveling to the Vineyard to paint murals for months.

A voice had suddenly pulled her out of her world of mystery in her novel and reeled her mind into a frenzy of desire that she had been trying to forget. It was the last voice she had expected to hear. *Lawrence*.

"Megan?" he'd said softly.

Just one word—her name—a name she had heard thousands of times in her life. A word that suddenly made her heart feel as though it might pound right through her chest, and her breathing become rapid and hindered. She looked up into his eyes, and something ignited between them. All of the old uneasy feelings of desire, laden with unworthiness, rushed back to Megan as she recalled painting the mural at Lawrence's home so many months ago—the way Lawrence's presence had made her heart speed up, how just the sound of his voice had sent the pit of her stomach into a fury, and how neither one had been able to look the other in the eye. Lawrence had been able to manage a moment or two before looking away. Megan had simply been unable.

Megan's grassroots utilitarian persona had chafed against his extravagant wealth and class, causing her to repress the ache she'd felt for him. Though not once, to Megan's dismay or her delight, she wasn't sure which, had Lawrence insinuated that he was interested in anything other than her work nor had he ever looked down on her. The growing electricity between them, however, had been palpable.

The time she'd spent on the project had been well worth the two months of heart-racing discomfort. Mr. Childs was very well connected amongst New England's aristocracy. Word traveled fast around the small New England towns, and Megan soon found her every hour booked with painting murals for the wealthy residents of the Cape, Martha's Vineyard, and Nantucket.

Lawrence sat down next to her on the bench, and kissed her cheek. She smiled, trying to hide her excitement, and secretly delighted at the casual tied cotton pants and sandals he wore, which were in stark contrast to his normal preppy appearance. He reached out and touched the back of her hand. His touch sent an unfamiliar warmth and yearning through Megan's center.

He smiled, sensing her heat, welcoming it, yet giving her the space she needed, not moving forward with his own desires. He inquired about her visit to the Vineyard, knowing full well why she was going. He was, after all, the reason Mr. Clark had hired Megan. His referrals had opened a door for her success, as he had wished for her since he had first set eyes on her.

As the harbor came into view, Megan's heart still raced, her forgotten book lay on her lap. She described the Martha's Vineyard home which she had been hired to paint, the turrets that stood like steeples peaking high up in the air, and the wraparound porch overlooking the magnificent gardens. She had no way of knowing that Lawrence already knew these things, as he appeared to marvel at her descriptions with genuine interest. She felt a little silly, wrapped up in the mindless chatter which kept her from saying something she might regret. *I just want to kiss you*, she thought. She was relieved as the ferry pulled into port, and the patrons began their slow descent down the metal ramp.

Megan had paced the hotel room, checking her watch every thirty seconds. She had just thirty minutes to settle her nerves before meeting Lawrence for drinks and dinner. *Why did I agree to this? I won't even be able to speak.* She went to the mirror again. Her curly hair behaved perfectly. *Thank goodness.* She stood up straight and ran her hands down her sleek black dress. She sucked in her stomach, turned sideways, and then decided she couldn't do *that* all evening. He'd have to accept her for her five-foot-two, one-hundred-twenty-pound frame that she tried hard to keep in relatively firm shape.

The din of the quaint waterside restaurant brought a feeling of relief to Megan. If nothing else, she and Lawrence could talk about the seagulls that hovered, awaiting a piece of a roll to drop below them.

She nervously pushed her food around on her plate, blushing as she became aware of Lawrence watching her, his eyes silently telling of his growing desire, heightening the sexual tension between them. She desperately tried to lessen her own lust, but was unable. She was drawn to him, like metal to magnet, and experienced a confusing moment of relief and excitement as they left the restaurant.

Megan unlocked the wooden door to her hotel room, and turned to find Lawrence standing very close—so close she could smell the wine on his breath. "Thank you for a wonderful evening, Lawrence." She looked up at him through her thick curls, hanging seductively in her eyes. Her fingers nervously played with her room key.

Lawrence leaned toward her, placed his hands on the wall behind her, and looked deep into her eyes. "I'm sorry—for this," he whispered, and he leaned in to kiss her. His tongue found its way around her mouth, circling inside her upper lip and then licking her lower lip ever so gently.

He closed his eyes and slowly backed away from her.

Megan's eyes remained closed. She was afraid to open them, afraid if she lifted her lids he would see her lust-filled heart beating fast and hard within them.

Lawrence ran his hand slowly down his face, fearing he'd made a horrible mistake. He whispered again, "I'm sorry," and began to turn to walk away.

Megan's body moved as if it belonged to someone else. In the space of a single breath, she opened her eyes, arched her chest hard against his, and brought her shaking hand softly around his neck. She pulled him into her and disappeared into his kiss. He backed her against the wall, his eagerness hard against her belly, aching to be set free. His mouth moved to her neck, further igniting her desire.

Lawrence pulled her into her dark room. His mouth never left her body as they moved to the bed. Megan's hands trembled as she unbuttoned his trousers and he removed his shirt. He moved quickly back to Megan, kissing her neck, his heart beat hard against his chest, and he fumbled with her dress as he lifted it over her head, exposing her supple breasts and silk panties. He breathed heavily, taking in her beauty. His desire was almost too much to bear. A moan escaped his lips as he lowered her to the bed and his mouth found her heaving breast.

When the sensation became too much, she rolled him over, straddled him, and took him inside her. She gasped with pleasure as they joined together. His throbbing organ and their insatiable hunger burned deep within her loins.

Chapter Two

Megan awoke to an empty room, warm with her memories of Lawrence, even after all those years. She got up, the memories of the evening before slowly moving through her mind. She closed her eyes against them, wondering when Holly had left, and as much as she loved Holly, she was glad to be alone. Megan sighed, slid off the bed and crept into her daughter's room, noticing that it was three A.M. as she walked by the antique clock that hung in the hallway. Her calm focus had only lasted an hour, and then fear and confusion had set in, making it impossible for her to sleep. Emotions of guilt and frustration swirled in her head, clouded by love in her heart. She needed to be near her daughter—needed to feel her energy.

She hesitated in front of Olivia's computer, and then settled into the chair. She sat with a blanket pulled close around her shoulders and her journal in her lap. As she watched her daughter sleep, she began to write.

Her heart poured onto the paper, the apologies for all she'd done wrong as a mother, for her need to slip away.

She uncovered her darkest secret and the reasons why it had been held for so long. She wrote until her fingers hurt and her tears ran dry. Then she carefully tore the sheets, dappled with tears, from the journal and folded them carefully.

Megan had spent years dodging Olivia's questions about the identity of her father. When Olivia was little, she had told her, "Some children have a mommy and a daddy. Some children have two mommies or two daddies, and you have just one mommy." That had stopped the questions for a while. As she had entered puberty, she had asked about her biological father more often. Megan's typical response, "He was a wonderful man, but we weren't in love with each other," had bought Megan time, but had never stopped the inevitable, "I want to meet him!" from Olivia. Megan's standard answer seemed to have worked thus far, "You will, honey, when you're older."

Now, Megan realized, she would not be the one to hold Olivia tight when she was exposed to the truth about her father. She would not be there to field her questions, or make her understand the validity of why her father's identity had been kept from her, from everyone. Still, Megan remained unable to hand Olivia the information that she herself, fourteen years later, could not figure out the right way to expose. She knew how many lives it would affect, and she wasn't willing to risk losing those closest to her when she was so close to the end of her own life.

Megan thought of Olivia growing into her twenties, and of all of the mother-daughter conversations she would miss.

She thought of writing more—all of the maternal advice that Olivia may need throughout those chaotic, finding-yourself years, but the thought overwhelmed her. How could she possibly think of every situation? Without knowing what Olivia's personality would be like at the time, how could she give her any insight into hypothetical situations? No, she decided, those conversations would be between Olivia and Holly, or whomever Olivia trusted at the time. *Trust*—the word stung. Megan knew she was breaking the biggest trust of all—to Olivia, to her dearest friends, and to her mother. She could not bring herself to call her mother. The last time she had visited, her mother had barely been able to move and had been on so many medications that her cognition had wavered. No, she'd rather remember her mother as she used to be, and she could not bring herself to confuse her mother any further than she already was.

She held the letter against her heart and rested for another moment as she remembered the doctor's words, *This medication will only buy you time*. She once again felt the piercing pain that shot through her heart when she had been told that the cancer was not only back, but had spread. There was no beating the beast that gnawed away inside of her, silently stealing her life.

She knew that she could not put Olivia through any more turmoil than she'd already endured. The weeks of chemo and radiation, the surgery and recovery—they were all too much for Olivia, and she had clung to Megan and still had not let go. Thank goodness for Holly. Holly had been there to nurture and love Olivia when she, Olivia's own mother, had been unable to open her eyes, when all she had been able to do was throw up and sleep. Holly had made sure Olivia had been well cared for, had taken her to school, had checked her homework, had cooked her dinner, and had even kept their home clean. She had been there for Olivia when she had needed to be held, or needed a diversion from her mother's illness. Holly had, in Megan's eyes, already started to become Olivia's mother.

Megan watched Olivia sleep, the note still held tightly in her grasp. *I don't want you to remember me dying*, she thought. *I want you to remember my love for life*. She sighed, disgusted at her frail limbs. *Don't remember me like this, my mind and body withering away. Don't remember me sick. And please, Baby, forgive me. Forgive me for taking myself away sooner than I had hoped. Forgive me for making this decision for the both of us. Forgive me for not telling you the truth about your father while I am still here to explain.* Despite her best efforts to withhold her emotions, she sobbed, overwhelmed with the magnitude of the truth—she was dying.

Megan sat on her bed with the small mahogany chest in her lap, her letter to Olivia safely locked inside. Her fingers lingered over the smooth surface, the dips and angles of its elegant design comfortably familiar. She closed her eyes as a single tear slid down her cheek, landing on her sleeve and spreading like a snowflake, deep in the center and soft on the fringes. She thought of the next time the box would be opened and the contents set free, and she was overwhelmed by sadness.

She set the box next to her and stared at it, stood, and took a few steps away. Her cotton dress swayed as she turned back to look at the box. She furrowed her brow, wrapped her arms tightly around her body, and continued staring, as if the box would give her the answers she so desperately sought. After a moment, she stood up straight, smoothed her dress with her hands, and took another deep breath. She let the air out of her lungs slowly. She pursed her lips and moved forward, taking the chest into her small hands. She carried the box carefully, coddling it as if it were a newborn, fragile and trusting. She placed it gently back on the top shelf of her closet, tucked between her thick sweaters and old pocketbooks. She sighed, steepled her hands together at her chin, and silently said another prayer, this one for Olivia—that the letter would offer answers and bring with it relief, without inflicting torment and anguish to those she loved.

Megan lit candles around her room, turned on her meditation CD, and allowed her body to relax. She sat with her palms facing up to release the bad energy and accept the good, her legs crossed. She welcomed the emptying of her mind and replenishing of her soul. She fought the thoughts of her earlier spat with Olivia, bidding them to be gone as if they had never existed, and willed away the pains in her stomach—pains that she knew she was experiencing as they lingered in Olivia's body and not her own, angst from earlier in the day. She smiled as they gently subsided. The music weaved its way through the air and she took it in with each breath, consoled by its life-affirming comfort. At last, her mind settled peacefully into acceptance.

Music vibrated off the walls of Megan's client's office. Her body swayed to the rhythm, enjoying the freedom and release it provided. She was mid-spin with a paintbrush held high in the air when she saw Peter in the doorway.

She laughed, "Hey!" She smiled, turned the volume down, and hugged Peter's slim waist.

"How's my girl?" Peter kissed her cheek.

"Awesome! How are you?" Megan realized, suddenly, that today she *did* feel awesome. Her body didn't hurt quite so much. She hadn't thrown up or had diarrhea yet, as she had most days since discontinuing her medication, and Olivia had actually said *good morning* with a slight smile instead of a grunt.

"Great. I had to come by and see how the Bourbon Street scene was turning out." He was visibly pleased with what he saw, smiling with little nods as he took in the mural. "You are an amazing painter."

"Yeah, well, I had good direction." Megan watched Peter's eyes dance over her artwork. She'd known Peter since their second week at college. His boyish good looks had been the first thing that had caught her attention. It had only taken one conversation for her to learn that he was gay, which had suited her just fine.

It had been Peter who had wheedled his way into her and Holly's tight friendship. He had bumped into Holly in the hallway outside her English class. They had both dropped their books and laughed. Peter, always the gentleman, had walked Holly to her class, and it seemed he had tagged along with her and Megan everywhere after that fateful day. They didn't mind. They loved his insight on clothing and art, his quick wit, and the convenience of his willingness to act as if he was their boyfriend when undesirable men approached them.

He had complemented their friendship with his ability to add calm to Megan's far-beyond-the-norm views, and quell Holly's obsessive need for perfection, which eventually subsided. Holly's calm demeanor fit well with Peter's rightfully-owned chip on his shoulder. When Peter spouted off about women's inability to get men and their constant wrongdoings, Holly would soothe his hurt soul, knowing that Peter's own mother had left him and his father when Peter was only five years old. Her loving touch had a way of soothing even the angriest of souls.

Megan and Holly's schedules had often conflicted, leaving little time for each other. Even as roommates they had felt as though they bumped in the night rather than spent any quality time together, which was why they had begun their weekly roommate dates.

They had met faithfully every Tuesday and Thursday at the local coffee shop that doubled as a literary nook, the Women's Nest. Originally opened as a gathering place for women in the 1970s, the Women's Nest was quickly infiltrated by the opposite sex, who, rightly so, knew it was an ideal place to meet women.

Peter had slipped his way into those private meetings and seamlessly become an intimate part of their weekly get-togethers, and therefore, their lives. The Women's Nest offered coffee and baked goods. The walls were lined with shelf after shelf of donated books that the patrons could read while relaxing in the oversized armchairs and fluffy sofas. Music played in the background, as warm and soothing as the soft hues of the walls.

It had been during those weekly gatherings that their friendship had blossomed and wrapped its roots around them until they could practically read each other's thoughts. They helped each other pick up the pieces of many fallen relationships and failed exams. The three of them were each other's lifelines. Why, Megan wondered, wasn't she confiding in them now, at her most fearful moment?

Megan was lost in thought when she felt Peter's hand on her arm. "Meg? Hello?"

She shook her head, "Sorry." She smiled. A funny feeling came over her—not one of sickness, but a feeling of being lost, confused, as if she were standing amidst smoke and clouds, and not sure where she was. She grabbed Peter's arm, unsure if she was going to lose her footing.

"Meg? What is it?" he asked. Fear stretched across his face as Megan lowered herself to the floor. He wrapped his arm protectively around her. "Meg, what is it? Are you okay?"

Megan's eyes stared straight ahead. She struggled for the right words. "It's...it's not me. It's Olivia." Her limbs tingled, her chest ached.

"Livi? What? What is it?" Peter's words rush out.

"I don't know. There's no pain. It's like she's...lost or something." She shook her head as the feeling faded. "It's probably nothing. She's at school. We had a fight the other night. I'm probably just worrying too much."

"You guys have such a strange connection, Meg. Are you sure she's okay? Do you want me to run over to the school and make sure?" Peter took Megan's hand.

"No. She's fine." Megan smiled as the feeling dissipated, lingering just enough to make the hair on the back of her neck stand up. Megan laughed, "How on earth did she and I become so connected?"

"She was *inside* of you! Of course you are connected!" Peter said.

"Yeah, but you were inside your mother, and..." her words hung in the air like dirty laundry.

Peter's face strained.

"I'm so sorry," Megan said quickly. "That wasn't meant to hurt you, just to make a point. I mean, really, mothers and their children usually don't *feel* things for each other!"

Peter's face softened. "I know, Meg, no hard feelings."

He took a deep breath, and said, cheerily, "It is weird. You're just a freak, I guess, and I'm just used to it. I'm surprised you aren't."

"I didn't even feel anything weird until two days after she was born, until after Holly's baby—" she turned away, unable to finish the sentence.

The silence between them was filled with grief from long ago. Megan busied her hands organizing her brushes, and Peter gazed out the window. When he felt the sorrow subside, he carefully eased into the subject he was there to discuss, "By the way, are you doing alright these days?"

"Uh-oh, Holly got to you, right?" Megan asked. She stood up and admired her painting.

"No." Peter walked to the window and looked out at the busy street. "Okay, yes, she's worried about you."

"Yeah, I know. I'm fine, really." Megan felt a pull to tell Peter the truth, but squelched it, knowing he would try to change her mind. She feared that if he told Holly, she would not be able to remain true to her decision. "Peter, if you knew you could save someone you loved heartache, would you do it?"

"Of course I would." Peter paced along the hardwood floor.

"No question in your mind?" Megan asked.

"No question."

"Tell Holly not to worry—and not to send a messenger next time!" Megan snapped, annoyed. She turned her back to Peter and picked up her paintbrush.

Peter watched her resume her work on the painting from behind. He knew she was not telling the truth, but wanted to believe her just the same.

Megan walked into the Chatham Village Café looking forward to telling Holly the news about Olivia's kidnapper. She spotted her in the rear of the dining area and hurried toward her. Megan threw the newspaper down on the table, and smiled victoriously. "Did you see it?" she raised her eyebrows, excited. "They got him! The fool was stupid enough to go to the hospital!"

"I know, I saw!" Holly stood up and hugged Megan. "What about the younger guy?"

"They said they have a line on him. They tracked down his truck and apparently he and this guy are related somehow. He skipped town, or that's what they think, but I know they'll get him!" Megan sat, cringing as the wooden seat hurt her bottom. "Life is getting better!" she said with a smile.

"How's Olivia taking it all?" Holly asked.

"Olivia's been acting just like her old self again. It's like it all never happened, but I'm still worried about her."

"That's so weird. I would think it would have been more traumatic for her, that there would be some lingering effects." Holly noticed the dark bags under Megan's eyes. "How about you, Meg, are you doing alright?"

"Yeah, I'm not so sore anymore, and since the police came and went over Livi's online conversations with those men, I'm not as concerned. They said she didn't give out any personal data, thank God!" She shifted in her seat.

"You know, Meg, you were quite the hero," Holly swallowed the wish that she had been the one who had helped Olivia.

"No way! I was just a mom. You would have done the same thing."

Holly looked down at her food, wishing she had a daughter to worry about. Megan laid her frail hand on top of Holly's strong one. "I'm sorry, Hol, I didn't mean to make you sad."

"I'm not sad," she said, smiling. "Okay, well, sometimes I'm sad," she admitted. Tears welled in her eyes.

Megan took a deep breath and began to tell Holly about her decision. "Holly, you know, sometimes God does things for bigger reasons. Maybe you were put here to take care of me and Olivia. Maybe we are your surrogate children. I mean, you spent night after night at my house while I went through treatment, and you are *always* here for us."

A tear slid down Holly's cheek. "Maybe," she said, softly. "I just always thought I'd have a child of my own—and poor Jack, he didn't sign up for a life without children."

Megan swallowed her confession, knowing that at that moment, it would only hurt more. "He signed on with you, Holly, with or without children. Jack is happy with you, he doesn't need more."

"You think?" Holly wiped her face, and silently wondered if she were selfish to keep Jack to herself, or if she should let him go make a real family with someone else.

"Oh, Holly," Megan slid into Holly's side of the booth and wrapped her in her arms, "Jack loves you. You are his family!"

"Look at me. What a mess I am. This is the time we have to talk about you and Livi and what you guys went through, and here I am, taking center stage and being selfish."

Megan laughed, "Nonsense. There is no *my* time or *your* time. There is only *our* time!"

"Thanks, Meg."

"Listen, Olivia and I started seeing the therapist that the doctor recommended. It's weird, you know, that one day can change your entire life so dramatically. Anyway, she's really good and is helping me and Livi communicate better. Things have been...weird lately. Maybe you should talk to her about...all this."

Holly jumped at the chance to steer their conversation away from her pain. "You two have never had trouble communicating. What's up with that?"

"I don't know. I guess I've been busy and she misses me, or misses my attention."

"You've been more than busy. It's almost like you want to be away from her. It's so unlike you, Meggie. You have always spent your time with Olivia. What's going on?"

"Nothing!" Megan snapped, and then looked down at her lap. "I'm sorry, I've just been a little stressed." Hearing her friend's concern only magnified the torturous feelings of guilt that were eating away at her.

"I shouldn't have said anything," Holly said.

Megan wrote down the therapist's number and told Holly that her next doctor's appointment was on June 30 and that she was welcome to go along with her.

In an effort to lighten the conversation, Holly brought up Megan's birthday, May 1st, and the annual ritual that she, Megan, Jack, and Peter held around a campfire, as they had been doing together since their college years to celebrate her birthday.

A chill ran down Megan's spine as she realized that the night of the ritual was perfect to carry out her plan.

Olivia had been swimming in her own thoughts for weeks. Concerned about why her mother was lying to her and disgusted with herself about the myroom.com incident, she felt like her whole world was spiraling out of control—if only she had something solid to hold on to.

She looked around the hallway, watched the girls huddled together and the boys slapping the lockers as they walked by. She felt as though she no longer belonged in school. The other kids' lives were so *normal*, and hers felt anything but normal lately. She didn't even feel as though she could relate to the few girls she normally strolled the halls with. She flipped open her cell phone and quickly dialed.

"Peter?" Olivia pleaded.

Olivia sat silently in Peter's car. She looked out the window and fidgeted with her seat belt. Peter watched her out of the corner of his eye. She had seemed on the verge of tears when she called. She spoke quickly about having to get out of school fast and not feeling very well. He had tried to reach Megan, and when he had been unable to, went to pick her up. With what she had recently been through, he could understand her feeling overwhelmed and out of place. Now she simply seemed uncomfortable in her own skin.

Her hair was swept off her neck in a loose pony tail, and her green tank top set off her eyes. Although her coloring was the opposite of Megan's, she reminded him of how beautiful Megan had been before her illness.

He couldn't help but be angry with God that Olivia had had to endure her mother's fight with cancer.

"Thanks for coming to get me," Olivia said as she stared out the open window, wisps of her hair blowing in the wind.

"No problem. Are you alright?" Peter asked, trying to sound very non-parental.

"Do you know who my father is?" she asked. Just like that, simple and plain, she laid it out before him with no warning.

Peter's heart beat faster. He was caught off guard, and took a minute to gather his thoughts, then decided that honesty was best. "Well, no, not really."

She turned to him, pulled her legs up onto the seat. "Come on, Peter. You know everything about Mom! I can't ask Holly, she'll tell Mom I asked. Please?" she pleaded, her hands clasped together under her chin.

Peter shifted his position and spoke gently, "Olivia, I think you should ask your mother."

"Come on, Peter. I know you know, and I know my mother. She couldn't keep that big of a secret, not for this long—and she tells you *everything*!" Olivia was testy. Her voice grew louder. "I'm fourteen years old! *Fourteen*, Peter! Don't you think I'm old enough to know?"

"That's a question only your mom can answer. Olivia, I really truly do not know. I promise you that, and you know I've never lied to you!"

"Whatever," she said, and set her eyes on the passing trees beyond the passenger's window.

Peter pulled the car over. He reached out, and with his index finger, lifted Olivia's chin toward him. "Olivia," he said sweetly, "I promise you that I don't know. What is all this about? Why are you wondering now?"

Tears, fresh and warm, streamed down her cheeks and over Peter's hand. "She's gonna die, Peter, and I'll have no one," she whispered, then, completely overwhelmed by the thought of losing her mother, she collapsed into his arms.

Peter held her tight, his own eyes brimmed with tears. "She's not going to die, Olivia. She beat it, remember?"

"But she's throwing up every day, and she never eats!" Olivia burrowed into his chest. "I know she's lying to me. I know she's really sick! I can just...feel it."

"Olivia, your mother doesn't lie to you. It's probably the stress that you see her going through. You know how her body reacts to stress."

"Maybe," she said, sniffling. "What will I do, Peter? If she dies, what will I do? Grandma can't take me, she's too sick, and I don't want to be alone! And I have no idea who my father is, and—" she sobbed into her hands.

At the height of Megan's illness, Peter had thought of this scenario often. He had asked, many times in fact, who Olivia's father was. Megan had insisted it was someone from overseas, someone she had met on her three-month painting excursion a few years after college, but Peter had never believed it. He had tried pushing, but she had always maintained the same story: *It was a fling with a handsome foreigner*. The story was too cliché for Peter to believe. Megan didn't *do* flings. She hadn't dated many guys in college, always too busy with painting, classes, or Holly. There was no one *who turned her head and set butterflies loose in her stomach*, or so she had said. She had been content to hang out with Peter and Holly. Peter had always believed that some day she'd come around and tell them the truth, or at least tell Olivia.

"You can't think this way, honey. Your mom isn't going anywhere, and if she were, well, she'd make sure you were well taken care of." Peter felt his heart crumble with sadness, and tried his hardest not to give in to the tears that were threatening. He knew Olivia was right. He could feel it in his soul, but he held that secret deep within.

Peter remembered the night, several years before, when Megan had asked Holly and Jack if they would adopt Olivia if something were to happen to her. At first, Holly and Jack didn't even want to think about it, but Megan had insisted.

Since she was a single mother, she had explained, she had to think about those types of things. Holly had cried, Jack had been strong for Megan, and Peter had felt left out.

Though now he understood that raising a small child would have been an all-consuming responsibility that he had been nowhere near ready for, back then he had simply wanted to be included.

Peter looked at Olivia's fourteen-year-old, confused face, and realized for the first time the true depth of her turmoil and pain. Unsure of exactly what to do, he did what he knew best. He was kind and loving. He smiled comfortingly and said, "Come on, sweetie, what do you say we go find some chocolate?"

Olivia smiled up at him, "You won't tell Mom I asked?"

"Of course not," Peter said, and hugged her again, silently hoping that Megan was not ill once again.

"Thanks, Peter. I'm sorry. I just get so sad sometimes, and I don't want to do something stupid again."

"What was *that* about, Olivia? That was so unlike you," he said, immediately regretting his parental tone. "I mean, it's a pretty typical teenager thing to do, but you usually err on the side of caution, not the typical."

She gazed out the window again. "I was so mad at Mom for not spending time with me, you know?" She turned her green eyes toward Peter, solemn and serious.

"I understand, I guess. You were pissed, so you did something that would make her pissed?" Peter asked.

"Yes, exactly! I did something that was wrong, for once!"

She laughed a quiet, ashamed laugh. "Only it wasn't fun. I was scared the whole time. Even when I met the guy who was my age, I knew it was wrong." A tear slid down her cheek. "I'm such a mess, Peter."

"No, you're not a mess, Olivia. If you only knew all of the stupid things I've done. You are just a fourteen-year-old girl, doing what fourteen-year-old girls do!" He smiled. "Hopefully not everything that fourteen-year-olds do!" he laughed.

Olivia blushed.

"You're just a normal teenager. Everyone is confused about everything when they're a teenager."

"Then I can't wait to grow up."

Peter swallowed hard, *Don't rush it, kid. It doesn't get any easier*.

Chapter Three

Megan's entire body was on fire. She couldn't get out of bed, yet lying there hurt right through to her bones. She reached into her nightstand and took another Percocet, left over from her surgery. It sat in her throat like a Gobstopper, hard and wrong, taking far too long to make its way down her thin throat and leaving a dull ache in its path. She had felt like that for days, the aching through her bones. She'd been able to maneuver through each day on pain medication and made a habit of staying away from Olivia and Holly so they wouldn't question her. While Olivia was at school, Megan rested, and just before she arrived home, Megan would take her car to the beach, and sleep in the backseat while parked below three tall pine trees at the edge of the parking lot—they provided just enough shade to keep her cool, though she kept a blanket in the car for the moments when she found herself shivering. The few pounds she had dropped over recent weeks had left her chilly.

At night, Megan brought dinner home for Olivia and

they ate quietly in front of the television. Olivia chatted about school, and Megan listened as best as she was able. Megan continued to use the mural as her excuse for her exhaustion, fabricating tales of spilled paint and bright hues that delighted Olivia.

It had become a daily struggle for Megan to hold on as the urge to end the pain was often so great it was all encompassing, but she had promised herself that she would end her life encircled by her friends, the people she loved.

As she looked around her bedroom, she realized that putting things in order was out of the question and felt badly for having to leave things undone. In her mind, she rattled off the things she would do if she could: put clothes in bags and mark them for whom they were intended, clean out the entire house from unwanted or unnecessary junk, show Olivia each special item she owned and tell her the story behind it (though that she had already done many times before, and she knew Holly could repeat every story, except the history of her Yin necklace).

Megan was thankful that she had already completed the necessary paperwork for Holly and Jack to adopt Olivia, and that she had taken care of her will and life insurance documents, which were both safely tucked away in her mahogany chest.

The phone rang, startling Megan. She didn't answer it, choosing instead to roll over and rest. As she faded toward sleep, she was overwhelmed with sadness. It was hard for her to decipher what caused her the harshest grief: her impending death or the pills. The Percocet won out and she fell quickly into oblivion.

"Mom!" Olivia yelled as she walked in the door. "Mom?"

Holly, whom Olivia had called after school because she wanted to talk and couldn't reach her mother, put her hand on Olivia's shoulder from behind, "Shh. She's probably asleep. She's been working really hard."

Olivia nodded and walked upstairs, dropping her school books in her bedroom and walking quietly to her mother's room. Olivia was standing in her mother's doorway with her hand over her mouth when she again felt Holly's hand on her shoulder. She turned and buried her head in Holly's chest, "Is she...dead?"

"No, baby, no!" Holly said, holding Olivia. "She's sleeping, honey." Holly took in Megan's rail-thin arms spread across her covers, her gaunt face and body appeared as tiny as a child's surrounded by fluffy white pillows. She watched the slight movement of the comforter, up and down, with each of Megan's shallow breaths. "Shh," she whispered, "honey, she's exhausted. She's sleeping."

Olivia pulled away from Holly slowly, looking at her mother. Her eyes wallowed in fear and relief. "Are you sure?" she barely whispered.

"I'm sure." Holly kept her arm around Olivia, and felt the truth of the situation sink into her soul. She was losing her best friend. Olivia was losing her mother. The last few weeks had gone by so quickly that she hadn't even noticed how quickly Megan had emaciated, which was very apparent now as she looked like a shrunken doll in her bed, the life sucked out of her.

Olivia walked slowly into her mother's room and knelt by her bedside. She watched the minute movements of the blanket on her mother's chest. She smiled at her Winnie-the-Pooh doll, matted and loved, tucked under her mother's shoulder. As her tears fell, trembling began just below her knees and worked its way up her body, spreading down her arms and up her neck. A strange understanding washed over her as she realized just how sick her mother was. The frantic feeling of dejection over what she was losing left her as she exhaled and was replaced by one of compassion, filling her lungs and her heart when she took a breath. She reached up and pushed her mother's curly hair away from her face, her fingers gently outlined her mother's cheekbones and ran along the fine edge of her jaw. A tear slipped down her cheek, landing on her mother's pillow. Olivia moved slowly onto the bed and snuggled into her, as close to Megan as she could without waking her. She let out her breath, long and slow, and closed her eyes.

Holly hovered in the doorway, crying, feeling as though she were witnessing something far too intimate, too private, and that she should walk away. She could not. She was riveted by what was before her—the love that transcended their bodies and enveloped them. Her heart ached for

Megan and what she would lose when she left this Earth, and for Olivia, and the things she would never experience with her own mother. Her legs felt heavy, and as she tried to walk away, she found herself walking slowly toward the bed, unable to turn away. She was driven, it seemed, toward her lifelong best friend, her confidant, her soul mate. She hesitated next to the bed for only a moment, and then eased next to Megan's other side, and draped her arm across her friend, taking Olivia's hand into her own. In the silence, their breathing fell into an easy rhythm. It took only a few minutes for Holly to realize that Olivia had fallen asleep. *Poor child, this is too much.* She allowed herself to disappear into the comfort of darkness, escaping the despair in her heart.

The dark night peeked through the curtains which swayed in the breeze. Megan's mind was confused, not sure where she was or how long she had been asleep. The clock on the nightstand read seven twenty-two. *Morning or night?* After another moment of thought, she realized that it must be evening because it was dark out. As the fog cleared from her head, she sat up in bed and realized with a start that she must have slept all day. Olivia! She placed her feet on the floor and tried to stand up, but her legs were too weak. She heard footsteps padding down the hall.

"Livi?" she said, just above a whisper. There was no answer. Louder, she said, "Olivia?"

Holly peered into the bedroom. She hesitated, smiled,

and walked toward Megan doing all she could to keep from crying. "Hi, honey. You were sleeping, so we didn't wake you."

Megan rubbed her eyes. "How long have you been here? Is Livi okay?" As she said the words, she placed her hand on her stomach, feeling no odd pains, just overwhelming calm, and she realized that Olivia was just fine, which Holly confirmed.

"She's watching television downstairs. I made her dinner." Holly sat close to Megan.

"Thanks, Hol. I'm so sorry. I must have been really tired," Megan looked away.

"We know, Meggie," Holly whispered.

Megan sat silently, understanding the words, but uncertain about what to say. Her eyes stared vacantly at the wall in front of her.

"Meggie, we *know*. It's okay," Holly said gently.

Megan looked down at her lap, examining her palms as if it were the first time she had seen them. She ran her index finger over the deep lines, *Lifelines*, she thought, and let out a little sigh of skepticism.

"I'm sorry, Holly," she said, and turned to face her friend, whose eyes welled with tears. "I'm so sorry. I just couldn't let Olivia...let you guys, all of you, watch me fade away, piece by piece, losing my mind, my hair, my..." Her words hung in the air, not needing to be heard.

Tears rushed down Holly's cheeks as she pulled Megan into her arms, "Oh Meggie, shh," she said, comforting herself as much as Megan. "Meggie, I love you."

"I love you, too." Megan's tears soaked Holly's shoulder. She held on tighter, craving the embrace, letting relief wash over her, and her lies of the last few weeks be whisked away with her tears.

"I've been so afraid. I just didn't know what to do. The doctor said..." she sobbed, unable to continue.

"I know, honey. I called in a favor, and, well, it wasn't what the doctor told me, but what he didn't."

"I'm so sorry. I should have said something but somehow I kept believing that this whole mess would go away, that it wasn't happening to me, that if I didn't talk about it, by some miracle, I would get better." She turned away from Holly. "Now look at me! My God, what have I done. To Olivia? To you? To myself?"

"Megan, can we try something else? There are all sorts of new treatments."

"New treatments? Didn't the great doctor tell you? It's in my bones, Holly—my bones for God's sake! What are they going to do, give me new bones? This God damn disease is stealing me away piece by piece. I thought if I could just fade away quietly that it would be easier!" Megan's voice caught in her throat. She threw her arms up toward the ceiling and cried, "Treatments—treatments give hope. There is no hope. I don't want Olivia to watch me going through treatments again, hoping, praying that I'll get better when I won't." She paced the room, stopped, turned toward Holly.

Holly tried not to lose control, though tears flowed like a river down her cheeks. Her voice was soft, "Meg." She reached for her, hugged her close. "Shh, it's okay. We'll figure this out."

"There's nothing to figure out," Megan said quietly. "It's already been decided."

They remained holding each other for what seemed like hours, until the effort was too much for Megan's weak arms, and she let them fall to her side, allowing herself to look into Holly's eyes. "How is Olivia?" Panic rushed through Megan's body at the realization that Olivia knew what was happening to her. Her body began to shake.

"She's—" There were no words that would take away Megan's pain. Holly missed her already although she was right there beside her. She had spent the last few hours talking with Olivia about Megan and why she thought her mother had hidden her illness. She cried with her, held her, and even absorbed much of Olivia's anger, which surprisingly, was less than Holly had anticipated. "She's just how you think she is, Meg," Holly said.

"I should have told her," Megan said, slumping over into herself. "I just couldn't. I didn't want her to try and change my mind. I didn't want her to hurt longer than she had to." Megan sighed, looked out the window, and whispered, "I didn't want to see her pain any longer than I needed to." Hot tears left glistening streaks on her face.

"What do you mean, *change your mind*?" Holly sat up straighter, waiting to understand.

Megan pushed herself away, ashamed of the selfishness of her decision. *Did I do this for me, or for Olivia?* She summoned the will to stand, rising slowly, determinedly, but unable to pull herself fully erect. Gimping past Holly to the window with her right arm holding her abdomen, she looked outside and leaned her face against the screen in front of the breeze, relishing in the coolness of it, the *life* in it.

"It was my decision to stop taking the medications," Megan admitted, turning toward Holly, ready to take her due. "The cancer came back *everywhere*, and there was nothing they could do. It hit me fast and hard, I guess. The lucky one, right?"

"Oh, Meg," Holly said empathetically.

"The doctor said I could buy some time with meds, but Holly, it would be a slow death. It would really be just *buying time*, not getting better. I just...I just couldn't do it. It was too much. I couldn't live each day knowing I was giving everyone hope when I really just had a few months left. It was—" She couldn't go on. The words stuck in her throat and formed an unforgiving lump.

Holly went to her, held her again. "I know. It's okay." She purred, "It's okay, Meggie."

"But it's not okay!" Megan blurted out, loud and strong. Her body was driven by anger. "It's not okay! I shouldn't die before Olivia is even out of high school! I shouldn't die before she is an adult! She shouldn't have to watch me die at all! It's not okay, Holly! It's not!" Megan yelled. Adrenaline pumped through her body as she paced around the bedroom on her frail legs. She came to the edge of the bed, sat, and wept into her hands, spitting her words out between the tears, "It's not okay!"

Megan jumped when she heard Olivia's voice, "Mom?"

"Livi." The word sounded unexpected as it left Megan's lips.

Olivia hurried to her mother's side, wishing she could burrow a hole into her mother's skin and crawl inside her. She held her tight, their grief commingled and came out as large salty tears. Olivia clung to Megan as she had the night at the police station. "Mama, I love you," she said.

"I know, baby. I love you, too," Megan said, understanding the growing pain in the pit of her stomach as Olivia's. "Olivia, I love you so much, baby, so much."

"Mom," Olivia said again, barely able to speak, unable to form other words through her sadness.

Holly snuck out of the room and downstairs to phone Jack.

When the air around them settled, they released their grips and eased their hands into one another's. Megan felt consumed by Olivia's emotions: confusion, love, hurt.

"Mama, why didn't you tell me?" Olivia asked, her tears morphing into sniffles.

Megan regained her composure, "Oh, Livi," she looked sadly into her eyes, "how could I tell you that you weren't going to have a mom anymore? I just couldn't." She shook her head, brought her hand up to cup Olivia's cheek. "My baby girl—I love you so much. I didn't want you to suffer longer than you had to."

"But what about you, Mom? Aren't you...suffering?" she asked quietly.

"Only in my heart, baby," Megan said.

"What happened?" Olivia asked.

Megan explained about the cancer and the speed with which it had taken over her body. She told Olivia about her prognosis and the great pain that she took in making her decision to stop taking the medication and to forgo further treatment. While she relayed her battle to her daughter, she couldn't help but second guess every decision she had ever made throughout her life. Should she have told Olivia who her father was? Should she have taken the medication? Should she have ended things with Lawrence?

Olivia listened intently, trying to imagine her mother actually making the final decision to let herself die. She couldn't put the picture together in her mind. She knew her mother had been sick, and it was obvious by her size and demeanor that she was not going to get better, but the thought that her mother had *made that choice* was too much for her to bear. She tried not to hear the rest of what Megan had to say, staring out the window and filling her head with thoughts of the previous summer instead.

Megan continued, noticing Olivia's vacant stare. She explained to Olivia that if she were to continue medications and try surgery, it would be weeks of hospitalizations and months of chemo and radiation, and in the end, she still wouldn't live. As she spoke, Olivia's facial expression didn't waiver. Her eyes didn't shift, her breathing didn't hitch. She was no longer there. *She's found a safe place to hide.*

A single lonely tear slipped silently down Olivia's cheek.

"I'm so sorry, Olivia," Megan said, her own eyes turning to liquid. Her voice became a whisper, "The idea of you watching me deteriorate, all the while hoping that I would live longer, it just—"

Olivia leaned into her mother, resting her forehead on her chest, or what was left of it. She whispered, "Stop, Mom. I get it. I know. I can't hear anymore."

Megan stroked her daughter's head.

"What will I do without you?" Olivia asked, the words, muffled by Megan's chest and shirt, filled with fear.

"You will go on, baby. You will live your life, and love your life. You will live as if I am still here." She leaned back and put her hands on Olivia's wet cheeks, wiping her tears with her thumbs. "Baby, I'll still be here." She placed her hand on Olivia's heart. "I'll always be here. You just won't be able to see me."

"Or maybe I will," Olivia said, and tried to force a smile. "I mean, how many other mothers feel their children's pain, right? Maybe I *will* be able to see you." Olivia had hope in her eyes.

"Maybe, I hope so, and if there is a way, I will try, but Olivia, you must know that I want you to continue on with your life. Have a wonderful life! Do it for me."

"Where will I go, Mom? I mean, who will want me to live with them?" Olivia asked, letting her sad gaze drop toward the bedspread.

They both turned at the sound of Holly's voice. "Why, Olivia, how could you not think I would want you? I adore you. Jack adores you."

Olivia looked at her mother with a question in her eyes, but remained silent.

Megan nodded her head. "Holly has always been like your mom, right? She's been here for us always."

"Yeah, but—" Olivia said.

"But what, honey?" Megan asked.

"But they don't have kids. I'll be a pain to them, a burden," Olivia said.

Holly walked to the bed and knelt in front of Olivia. "Livi, how could you ever be a burden to me? I cherish you. I love you. We both do."

"Livi, we decided this long ago when you were just a little girl. Holly has always wanted you. She's your godmother. She and Jack love you."

"Yeah, but—" Olivia said again.

"What is it, honey?" Megan asked.

"Do I have a dad, Mom? What if after you—you know—what if he comes and wants me?" Olivia asked.

"Livi, I know that I haven't told you much about your father—" Megan started.

"Much? How about *anything*," Olivia interrupted.

"Okay, that's fair. I promise you, your father will not...

interrupt your life. That's a guarantee," Megan said.

"But how can you know? What if I want to meet him, and I can't because I don't know who he is?" she asked.

Megan eyed Holly, hoping she would catch on to the look, "When you are eighteen, Holly will tell you everything. Until then, I just think this is better. Even though you think you should know, there's a lot of confusion that goes with things like this, a lot of responsibility. You may not be ready for it. On this, Olivia, you have to trust me."

Olivia relented with a sigh, not wanting to upset her mother any more than she already had.

Holly gave Megan a look that said, *What? I don't even know who he is.*

Chapter Four

Megan's heart filled with pride as she watched Olivia set out candles and put up decorations, bringing their little cottage to life for her birthday ritual. Olivia's actions were soft, her arms and legs flowed like the delicate branches of a willow tree, and her fine hair brushed her shoulders in soft, swift movements. Real life hadn't yet marred her skin; innocence and tenderness remained on the surface. From her perch on the couch, Megan could feel the angst that Olivia was swallowing and watched as she tucked it behind the lump in her narrow throat. Megan's pride was replaced with guilt which simmered just below the surface of her skin.

"Livi," she said gently. "I know you want to be there tonight, but you understand, don't you? This is something that I do with them every year. It's..." she gazed out the window and watched the trees blow in the gentle breeze, "it's *our* thing."

Olivia rolled her eyes, turned to her mother, and sighed. She planted her hands on her hips. "I know! Okay? I hear it every year," her voice rose. "*Your* friends, *your* thing. When do *I* get to be part of it, Mom? When is it *my* turn to be part of *your* world?"

Megan cocked her head and raised an eyebrow, pursing her lips as if taking a stance. When her mother's silence grew too thick to bear, Olivia turned her back and stormed upstairs. Her words, "That's what I thought," wound their way through the air and stung as they settled roughly in Megan's ears.

Megan hunkered down beneath her chenille afghan and waited for her daughter's storm to pass.

The chime of the doorbell woke Megan from her light nap. She climbed off of the couch, adjusted her long cotton patchwork skirt of pale and muted pastels, and straightened her watery green crushed cotton top. Just as she reached the door, Olivia bounded down the stairs, "I've got it!" she yelled, barely missing barreling into her mother, who simply smiled and stepped aside.

The heavy oak door swung open. Standing on the front porch in her comfortable black wispy skirt, matching vest, buttoned only halfway up, her white cotton shirt open to reveal a hint of cleavage, was Holly. She thrust a large red box beautifully adorned with a fat gold ribbon toward Megan with a smile.

Megan reached for the box. "Thank you!"

"Olivia!" Holly exclaimed as she pulled the young girl into her arms and shot Megan a look that said, *Another teen-*

age mood? "Ready for the big night?"

"Hi, Holly!" Olivia replied, as she embraced the woman who one day would be her *new* mother. "Holly," she said as she eyed her mother, "can you please talk to Mom about me coming to the bonfire tonight? *Please?*"

Holly patted Olivia's shoulder as she brushed past her and reached out to Megan. "Oh Meg," she said. Her breath left her with a whoosh as she took in her best friend's frail frame and dark circles under her eyes. Hugging her tightly, she said, "You look wonderful, honey." She stepped back and rubbed her hands together, the unsettling feel of Megan's fine back bones lingered on their surface.

Megan smiled, "Thanks, Hol." She glanced down at her outfit which hung loosely around her body and felt a wave of shame. She remembered how she used to torture herself, wishing that someday she would be thin enough to look beautiful in any clothes she put on, like the young models in fashion magazines, tall and lanky with smoky eyes and tiny little waists. Now, though, she didn't find the look so appealing, and she would have gladly welcomed back the extra ten pounds she used to wear around her middle.

Olivia bounced on her toes as she took the package from her mother and placed it on the table in the foyer. "Holly?" Motioning with her hands for Holly to hurry up, she put forth her saddest look, pleading her case.

Holly looked from Olivia to Megan, "Oh, Livi, that's a decision of your mom's. I'm not sure I want to be in the middle of that battle."

"Whatever!" Olivia stormed out of the room.

Megan and Holly shared a laugh as they followed Olivia. Candles illuminated the rich textures and warm dark hues of the cozy living room. The stone fireplace threw just enough heat to take the chill out of the evening—and an occasional spark. Holly poured herself a glass of wine. "Meg, would you like a glass?"

Megan took the glass slowly and sipped the White Zinfandel, reveling in the sweet floral taste as it wound its way down her throat. She closed her eyes, and tried to memorize the feel of the soft liquid, the swell of the cool glass in her hand.

"So, Holly, what's new in the life of the world's best editor?" she asked, lifting her glass to her lips again.

Just as Holly started to answer, the doorbell chimed through the hall. Olivia rushed toward it. "I've got it!" she hollered.

Holly turned to Megan and spoke quietly, "What's up with her, Meg?"

"Oh, she hates that she isn't included in our little ritual."

"Well," Holly said as she placed her hand on Megan's shoulder, and took it back quickly as the feel of her bones made her too sad to let it remain, "maybe it is time. I mean, she's fourteen, that's old enough to join us."

"I know, Holly. It's just that…well…" Threatened by a veil of tears, she closed her eyes tightly and walked away. She hesitated by the French doors and looked out at the dune grass in the distance. "I need one more time. For me, you know? I know that sounds selfish, but I do. I need it." Megan placed her hand flat against the cool glass. As she committed the feeling to memory, she realized there were many little details of life that she wanted to hold on to; the smell of the fireplace after the fire had died down; and the sound of Olivia in the bathroom after her shower, humming and dancing around as Megan knew that she did; the angelic look of Olivia's face when she was fast asleep, and the smell of her breath in the morning; the soothing sound of the dishwasher at night, and the wintry gust of the winds across the beach; the sound of that crazy cardinal running beak first into her window. Her heart skipped a beat when she realized that the bird had not appeared that morning.

"I just always thought," Megan said as she turned to face Holly, "that I would have more time, that she would grow up doing the ritual with us, with me. Now I just feel…rushed, like I have to make a choice, like it's either my time or hers."

Olivia popped back into the living room, "One of your men has arrived, Madam," she smirked, smiling at her mother.

"Livi, come here," Megan said, motioning to Olivia with open arms.

Sighing, Olivia fell into the familiar safety of her mother's thin arms, taking in the smell of her body lotion, lavender and coconut, and whispered in her ear, "I love you, Mom."

"I love you, too, muffin," Megan whispered in return, holding back the wave of tears that vied to be set free. She moved Olivia's hair to the side and kissed her daughter's cheek.

"Then can I join you?" Olivia asked excitedly. "For the ritual?" She held her mother tighter, hoping for a positive answer.

"Let me think about it," Megan said, happily.

"Really! Oh, Mom, thank you!" Olivia's voice danced with excitement and hope.

"I said, *think about it*."

"I know, I know, but usually when you say that, it means there's a good chance!" She gave her mother a quick kiss on the cheek. "Oh, thank you, Mom! Think about it!"

"What was all that about?" Peter asked, his lean body came forth to embrace Megan, tensed, and took extra caution not to squeeze Megan too tightly.

"Hey Peter! I assumed Jack was coming with you," Megan said, as she hugged him and moved slowly across the shining hardwood floor towards the couch. "Where is he?" she looked toward Holly. "And Peter, I thought you were bringing Cruz."

Holly said, "Oh, you know Jack. He has so much to do—always has a list—but he promised to try and come later. Besides, it's more fun without the men!" She smiled and sat down next to Megan, propping the oversized cranberry pillows comfortably against her friend's sides and leaning back against the corner of the couch.

Peter cleared his throat with a loud, "Ahem!"

Holly looked at him and laughed, "Well, you know what I mean. You're like one of us!"

They all laughed.

"Cruz couldn't make it. Besides, it seems like he'd be invading our time together, and I'm not really there yet."

A knowing glance passed between the friends, as, in unison, they said, "Uh-huh."

"Peter, after three years, don't you think you could let him into your life a little?" Holly asked.

"Only if he wants to keep him," Megan interjected, "and therein lies the problem."

Peter plopped down on the chaise lounge, sinking in as if it were memory foam. "Whatever, you guys. I let him in. He's with me two, three nights a week." He sipped his wine.

"Commitment-phobe," Holly said.

Olivia brought in appetizers from the kitchen. Hearing the tail end of the conversation, she asked, "Are we discussing the trials and tribulations of Mr. Peter Ornsby again?" She set down the platter of stuffed mushroom caps, bit into one and dribbled it down the front of her shirt. She laughed, "Oh sorry, Mom. Now you'll have to wash it."

Megan motioned her unconcern with a wave of her hand.

Olivia turned on the radio, which played top-forty tunes in the background as she bounced around the room, nibbling off of the trays and humming.

"So Meg, this is the big thirty-nine!" Holly put her hand on Megan's knee. "How does it feel? I mean, you are so much older than the rest of us."

"Yeah, right!" Megan placed her hand on top of Holly's, thankful for the warmth as it seeped into her own cold skin. "I think you're a little older than me."

Holly got up and walked around the living room, inspecting photos of the four of them, admiring Olivia's vase from first grade art class, and ignoring Megan's comment completely.

"Hol-ly!" Megan sang. "*Aren't* you older than me?"

Holly spun around. "Actually, no. You see, when I was born, you were not, but then you were and we skipped a year and then I was no longer older than you. Don't you remember the old skip-a-year thing that our parents did?"

"What skip-a-year thing?" Olivia asked, perched on the arm of the couch next to her mother.

"Well, you know that Grandma and Mrs. Blackwell were great friends, right?" Megan said.

"Yeah, you and Holly were playmates when you were little."

"Right. What you don't know is that when I was born, our parents decided that they wanted us to be best friends, like *they* could decide it *for* us. So Mrs. Blackwell told Holly that she was one year old for two years in a row, and basically just pretended that she was the same age as me. It fell into place when we were about five or six, I think. Right, Holly?" Megan looked at Holly, who was lying on the chaise lounge next to Peter.

"Yeah, right around there."

"No way!" Olivia interjected. "So she just pretended you were the same age and it went on that way forever?"

"Yup, pretty much," Megan said. "Grandma and Mrs. Blackwell enrolled us in school the same year. Back then there weren't as many rules and regulations. No one gave it a thought if your kid started school a year later than was normal, and then each year they would send notes to the principal asking to place us in the same class."

"That worked until about sixth grade," Holly said, "until we talked so much that we became problematic."

"Then," Megan said, "we would just meet in the bathroom several times each day, or pass notes through other kids."

"That is so cool!" Olivia looked from one to the other. "And Holly, did you know how old you *really* were?"

"Well, not until many years later. I needed my birth certificate to drive, and when I saw it, I told my mother it was wrong, that she had to get it fixed."

"You were so pissed!" Megan remembered how Holly had screamed at her mother for not telling her the truth, and how badly she had felt—like it had been all her fault.

"Yeah, but only for a day or so, then I wanted to be your same age again," Holly said.

Megan remembered that decision fondly; Holly had snuck into her bedroom window in the middle of the night and had crawled into bed with her. Holly had looked her in the eye and had told her that no matter what her birth certificate said, she was always just the same as Megan. The memory sparked an affection that filled her with warmth.

"Wow," Olivia said. "Your moms were really cool. *My* mom would never do that!" She looked at Megan, who passed an intimate look to Holly.

"I might have, if the right situation had occurred," Megan said as she squeezed Holly's hand.

Megan snuggled into the couch, the afghan draped across her legs, the pillows embracing her petite frame. The din became a dull hum, and she was enveloped by the kindness that emanated from her closest friends. The lavender fragrance of candles, burning quickly down their wicks, mixed with perfumes and baked goods and filled the air. Scents of the ocean wisped through the open window, intertwining the many smells into one of comfort and happiness. *How did I get to this place?* Megan wondered. After thirty-nine years, she still couldn't believe that she was now the age that she'd always remembered her mother being. *When did this happen?* When had age crept up on her, like a flower that had bloomed, vibrant and beautiful, and quickly browned around the edges, struggling to simply keep erect. *There is no going back.* Gone was the energy that once revolved around what could be—wants, desires, and aspirations—and it was replaced with thoughts of what was best, what had to be.

Her small, veined hands felt cold, and she rubbed them together. Her olive skin had lost its sheen. It was slightly more wrinkled than what she had believed it was, what she had envisioned and held onto in her mind for the past few years. Her legs, she knew, were no longer strong and lean, but wilted and frail. The reality was like a weight in her heart. She had chosen to ignore it for so long that the realization hit her fast and hard, like a punch to the gut. She had truly thought she could beat it, age gracefully, and maybe even glow.

Peter popped up off his seat, "Okay, ladies, enough of this. Let's get down to the real thing, the cake."

"Shouldn't we wait for Jack?" Megan asked.

"No way! He'll get here when he gets here. Don't let a man's tardiness ruin our good time! Besides, you know Jack, he may not make it until the morning," Holly said, offering Megan her hand.

Megan took it gratefully and was surprised by the ease with which Holly lifted her to her feet.

Olivia dimmed the lights. Holly held Megan's hand, warming it as her thumb caressed her friend's thin skin. Holly swallowed hard, fought back the tears as they rushed forward. Her sadness sat hard and fat in her throat, as if she had swallowed an egg. The four of them stood around the lightly-textured countertop, brown sprinkled with beige and greens, like Megan's eyes.

Peter was the first to speak, "Well, Meg, this is your chance. Make it a good wish this year!" He looked at Holly and Olivia, who each looked down, unable to meet his eyes.

"Wait!" Olivia yelled, her smile revealed perfect white teeth like a fine strand of pearls. "We have to sing, remember?"

They all laughed, and Peter started singing Happy Birthday, softly at first, and careful, and then it grew louder and filled with joy as they each tried to sing the sickness out of their best friend's body.

Megan's eyes drifted closed. She could hear the singing and happiness around her, but separated her thoughts to be solely her own. She needed a quiet moment to make what she knew was to be her final wish. She envisioned herself as a sponge, absorbing every sensation. The muscles in her arms ached, her frail fingers clenched around her best friend's, like a lifeline. Her breaths felt shallow and weak. She took note of all of these feelings, and realized that they didn't fill her with sorrow. She accepted her frailty, accepted her pain, laced with a strange kind of loneliness, and accepted her fate. She relaxed her grip, and gave her wish to the powers that be, keeping her eyes closed for good measure.

Megan had only wished for two things in her life. Well, two things on her birthday wishes anyway, the important wishes, the ones that counted, the ones that God heard no matter how busy He was. She'd wished the same wish since she was eight years old, every night before she went to bed and every birthday before blowing out the candles. The wish had changed when Olivia was born. Her wish had gone from being solely about her to being inclusive of Olivia. Her heart sank, as she realized that this year's wish would be placed only half-heartedly, knowing that her first wish wasn't granted after thirty-seven years of wishing, hoping, praying, and making deals and promises in the dark, when it was just her and God. She really thought He had heard her wish for all of those years. She thought she and God had a special connection about that one wish, but she was wrong, as she had discovered a year ago. She was very wrong.

Yet here she was, putting her faith in Him yet again. Rethinking the first thirty-seven years of wishing, she held her eyes closed tightly and said in her mind, *Please, God, just half the wish. That's all I ask for, just half.* She wished her yearly wish, then, knowing it had already been broken, shattered like a glass fallen to the ground, she took a deep breath, and wished a new wish, *Please let her let go of me.* As a tear slipped down her cheek, she added quickly, *Let her move on with her life, but not forget me.*

She opened her eyes and returned to the present. She wiped the warm tears from her eyes, their salty remains landing on the cake. No one seemed to notice. Megan never saw the tears in her friends' and daughter's eyes.

Megan blew out the candles, and a wave of uncertainty thickened the air. Smiles and well wishes surrounded her. She felt the love that swirled in the air like a scent that she could smell, a taste that she could swallow. She realized, then, that though she had never wished it, the love she had assumed would always be there, taken for granted, and reveled in, was the most precious wish of all. That love, which had been there through the good years and the bad, would be Olivia's future, her stronghold, her vice. Megan said a silent thank you to God, and eked out a smile.

Holly wrapped her arm around Megan's shoulder, hugged her, and kissed her forehead. "Happy birthday, Meggie." Her smile came to rest softly in Megan's heart.

"You go, girl!" Peter said. "Let's have some cake!"

Olivia, who was already sneaking frosting from the bottom of the cake, licked her long, thin fingers and said, "I'll do it!" She cut huge pieces and handed out the heavy plates.

"Livi, I can't eat this much!" Holly said as she eyed the thick chunk of chocolate cake.

"Oh, come on, Holly. It's a party!" Olivia said.

"Well then, give it to me!" Peter said. He snagged the plate from Holly and took a big bite, leaving white frosting on his upper lip like a child would.

"Here, Mom," Olivia said. She handed her mother a large slab of cake, knowing she wouldn't eat it. "It's your birthday, live a little."

"Thanks, Liv," Megan said. Her hand brushed against Olivia's. "You guys mean more to me than you can ever imagine," Megan said. She looked around the room at her most cherished friends. "I couldn't have made it through my breakups, my heartaches, my *life* without you guys here to help me through. I just want to thank you guys for being so great. I love you all!"

Tears welled in Megan's eyes, "And Livi, you know you

are my heart. You are my reason for being, and my legacy. I love you, honey."

"We know, now drink up and let's have some fun!" Peter was never one for tears when there was fun to be had.

Eating cake and drinking a few too many shots of tequila, they laughed like goons and moved easily through their conversations, reliving moments in time, college events, and inside secrets, which Olivia loathed because she was not privy to them. When the sun dipped from the sky and the moon slowly took its place, when shoes were long ago kicked off, when neatly pinned hair had been pulled down for comfort, and when all of the excitement had died down to a familiar lull, Olivia, who was curled up in front of her mother on the couch, Megan's arm draped easily over Olivia's body, whispered, "Isn't it time, Mom?"

Holly answered in her own whisper, "I think it is, Livi." She had been sitting on the floor in front of the couch, and she reached her hand up behind her to hold Olivia's young, warm hand in her own.

"Well, let's get ready!" Peter whispered, his quiet tone was filled with mischief.

"Mom?" Olivia asked, hesitantly.

"I'm still thinking about it, Livi," Megan said, torn between spending every last second with Olivia and wanting her friends all to herself for this last ritual. She wrestled to find a balance between hurting Olivia's feelings and saving her own. She knew what was coming, and she wasn't sure Olivia should be there to bear witness.

Olivia jumped up, forgetting how frail her mother was, and threw her body right on top of Megan's, taking her by surprise, and sending an ache throughout her ribs and back.

Megan closed her eyes and relished the pain of her only daughter's weight on top of her. She reached up and brushed Olivia's hair off of her forehead.

"Livi, you know how special this is to me, right?" Megan asked.

"Yes! Yes!" Olivia said, her words burst with excitement.

"Okay. This is something we have done since we were kids, your age. So I need time to figure out if it's okay right now, for me, I mean. This is important. It is what centers us, what brings us each to the same place within ourselves, our own little world." She smiled, wondering how Olivia could possibly understand what she had just said.

"Mom, I've watched you guys out my window ever since I can remember. I know what it means to be part of this." She closed her eyes, willing the tears to stay at bay. "I want this so much, to be part of your world. Can't you please let me in?" Olivia kissed her mother's cheek and lay on top of her for a minute longer. A tear dropped onto her mother's hair.

"Livi," Megan said, her voice strained. She tried to move under Olivia's weight, and cringed with pain. "Livi?"

Olivia's head popped up, her eyes bright, her dimples made her appear even more youthful than her fourteen years. "Yeah?" She noticed the cringe on her mother's face and quickly jumped off of her. "Oh! Sorry, Mom!" she said. "Are you okay?"

Holly put her arm around Olivia's shoulder and squeezed, whispering in her ear, "You're a good egg, kiddo. Hang in there, we'll work on her."

Olivia's disappointment faded quickly. She beamed at Holly, taking her compliment and tucking it away with the others that she had held dear for so many years.

"Megan," Peter said, "why don't Livi, Holly, and I go set up while you relax here, inside?" He looked to the others for support.

"Great idea!" Holly said, busy tying a knot in her skirt so it fell just above her knee.

"Oh, great idea!" Olivia bent over and rolled up her jeans.

"You know," Peter said, "only someone like you could bend at the waist to roll up their pants! For God's sake, I have to bend my knees! I can't remember the last time I could actually reach my feet without bending my knees!"

The women exchanged a cynical glance, raised their eyebrows, and then looked toward Olivia.

"Whatever! Are you going to be okay, Meg?" Holly tucked the afghan around Megan and pushed the table with her drink close enough for her to reach. She put her hands on her hips as she surveyed Megan's perch.

Megan shooed them out of the room, "Go, go already. I'll be fine. It's not like I'm dying!" The words stung her heart as they left her lips, and her smile was lost among the shocked faces of her friends, who looked to one and other for support. "Come on you guys, go already, really!" Once they left the room, Megan took a long deep breath and closed her eyes. *Alone—finally.* The music calmed her. She opened her eyes and realized how much she loved her living room. She smirked at the thought, *living room*—the room where people do their living.

She eased off of the couch and made her way slowly up the stairs and down the long hallway to her bedroom. As she walked past her dresser, littered with scarves, papers she'd meant to go through, her hairbrush, strewn with hair gone from her head, she sighed. She'd had a happy life. She had lived her life just as she had wished to. Megan had cherished every day and hadn't let herself get wrapped up in the little things in life, like having a spotless house. She was comfortable. She had Olivia, and she was happy.

She pulled her hippie bag, as she liked to call it, from the bottom of her closet, where it lay safely tucked behind the few pairs of shoes and boots that she owned. She ran her hands around the outline of the multi-colored patches, the swatches of gold, orange, and red. She fingered the threads which clung for dear life, ran her fingers along the drawstring and the bottom, and finally across the fine gold threads that weaved their way in and out of the surrounding colors. She remembered finding the bag in Provincetown, the summer before Olivia was born. She reached inside the bag, unzipped the secret pocket that was stitched deep inside, near the bottom, and she withdrew her Yin necklace. As she fastened the clasp around her neck, she finally allowed herself to think of Jack.

At twenty-four, she had made a successful career out of painting murals, and had triumphantly tangled up her personal life. She had been dating Lawrence for many months, and they had discovered an intensity within each other that Megan had never before experienced—but had looked forward to. She may have even felt some kind of love for Lawrence—yet she had known she wasn't waiting to become his wife, which was why her reaction to the call from Jack Townsend had surprised her. Jack's desire to spend the weekend together, "To see what might be," enticed and confused her. She didn't know how to react to her own flittering heartbeat, or what to do with the excitement that grew within her as he revealed his plans. Having remained constant in each other's lives since childhood, years of camaraderie had taken place without a single meaningful kiss. *Why now?* Their history together had been just enough to tantalize her.

Megan had tried to think of Jack in *that* way. She had imagined his golden hair and finely-toned muscular body, his loose jeans hanging off of his perfect hips, his luscious chest muscles pressing against a slightly snug t-shirt, and Birkenstocks barely covering his strong, tanned feet. A chill had run down her spine while heat had found its way up her chest and settled in her cheeks. *This is silly*, she had thought. *I'll probably feel like he's my brother when we're to-*

gether. It'll be awkward.

Eventually Jack's pleading wore her down, "It's only two short days," he said.

"But we were together all the time through college, Jack. Wouldn't something have happened between us then? I don't know." Megan's hand covered her heart, which beat a little faster with every excuse she devised, challenging her own desires.

"We were distracted in college, Meg. I *have* to know. Every date I go on leads me back to you. Every face I see, I'm looking for your smile. Every time I—"

"Okay, okay," she cut him off with a quiet laugh and a silent blush, "I get it, Jack. I think I sort of know, too. I think that might be what's always happened with me, too. I am comfortable with you. I know you will always be there."

They spent a wonderful weekend knocking around Provincetown, enjoying the arts and the ease of being together. They climbed to the top of the Pilgrim's Tower, where Jack covered Megan's eyes as they passed each window because the height of the tower scared her. They ate too much ice cream and laughed as they had as children. They sat side by side, sated and happy, on a park bench watching the tide roll out behind the Provincetown Theater. What they hadn't done was share any sensual intimacy. It hadn't seemed to be a conscious thought by either party. In the evening, within the confines of their quiet motel room, Megan fell asleep in Jack's arms while they watched *Young Frankenstein*.

Saturday moved seamlessly into Sunday. Megan shopped at Shop Therapy and Freak Street, buying Jack a cool hippie hoodie and picking up a few cotton skirts and the patchwork hippie bag for herself. Jack bought cheap silver Yin and Yang necklaces, presenting the Yin to Megan, "For what might be," and keeping the Yang for himself.

As the sun fell from the sky, casting a purplish glow from above, they took a lazy drive into Orleans, eventually finding themselves eating cheese and crackers on Nauset Beach and making their way to the bottom of a bottle of White Zinfandel. Megan lay on her back, counting the stars and trying to ignore the growing pull in her center. She gazed at Jack, who leaned on his side, his head propped up in his large hand. He looked back at her sensually, expectantly.

Silently, they reached for each other. Their lips molded together with the ease of years of practice, although it was only their first real kiss. Jack's hands slid under Megan's blouse and a tingling sensation shot through her stomach and ran down her limbs to the ends of her toes. A soft moan escaped her lips. Her hands snuck under Jack's shirt. She became lost in his smell, his taste, the feel of his tongue in her mouth. She clawed at his muscular back. Under the cover of the night sky, they slipped out of their clothes and into each other. The waves played off the sand like a musical. Megan felt as though Jack somehow already knew every inch of her skin, yet at the same time, guiltily, her mind drifted to Lawrence.

Megan ran her right hand along the chain that now hung around her neck, and fingered the Yin necklace, pushing the memories aside. With her left, she swiped at the tears that fell down her cheeks. She then laid both hands across her emaciated stomach, trying to remember the feel of her swollen, pregnant belly, and the overwhelming emotions which had grown within her heart for her unborn child. She'd never forget the day when she finally gave birth: the excitement, the fear, and the exhaustion—the shock of Holly going into early labor while she recovered from her own delivery, the happiness of rooming in with Holly and the babies—and the sadness when Alissa Mae, Holly's baby, had died.

Megan realized that there was a certain fear when one brought life into the world, and a completely different type of fear when one prepared to die. She wiped the tears and the memories away and took a deep breath. She held her Winnie-the-Pooh stuffed bear against her chest, resting her head upon its worn fur. She thought of all the nights that Pooh made her feel safe, as if she weren't alone. She'd slept with the bear every night of her life, with rare exception: the nights with Lawrence, the night Olivia was conceived, the night Olivia was born, and of course the night of each of her birthdays when they held their rituals. She carefully placed the bear into her hippie bag and thought, *After fourteen and a half years, this ten-dollar bag has many secrets woven into the seams*.

She opened her wicker bedside cabinet and withdrew her meditation candles and incense, which she placed gently in the bag on top of the bear. Megan walked slowly across her room toward her closet, stopping at the doorway and turning again to survey her room. The plush blankets, textured wall hangings, and earthy tones comforted her. She turned and walked to the back of the closet, stood on her tiptoes and reached up, confirming its existence. The sides of her mahogany chest were smooth on her fingertips. She sighed as tears found their way, once again, to her eyes, and pain shot up through her bones. She reached behind her sweaters and grabbed her pink, lime, and tan chenille scarf, also from Provincetown, and wound it gently around her neck. She slipped on her favorite thick brown sweater, slung her bag over her shoulder, and walked with purpose toward her elegantly carved, cherry-wood bureau, which she had acquired by swapping one of her canvases of the Eastham Windmill during one of her summers vending at the Wellfleet Flea Market.

She made no effort to conceal the tears that streaked her cheeks. Deep inside her top right bureau drawer was a photo of Olivia sleeping when she was three years old. She remembered how Olivia had said she wanted to be a princess, and how she had taken careful measures to set up the house perfectly for her.

Megan had put up streamers and set candles in every nook and cranny, draped a red cloth down the stairs and into the living room, and made a tiara out of cardboard, fake jewels, and feathers, painted it white, and set it on Olivia's nightstand. She had bought Olivia a princess dress, the kind little girls wear on Halloween, and little gold sparkly dress shoes, which she had placed next to the tiara. When Olivia had awakened on that special morning, her world had been transformed. She had become Princess Olivia Taylor, ruler of Girl Land, and her mother had been dubbed her Lady in Waiting, available to satisfy her every whim.

They had eaten chocolate chip cookies for breakfast, marshmallows with chocolate sauce dribbled on them for snacks, and had surrounded themselves with peanut butter bananas and marshmallow fluff for lunch. Princess Olivia had demanded, in her tender little voice, to dine on spaghetti and marshmallows for dinner, complete with chocolate sauce. After that magical day, Princess Olivia's love of chocolate and marshmallows had withered out, as had her little bucket of energy. Megan had snapped the picture of Olivia when she had pooped out on the couch at seven o'clock in her princess dress, her shoes strewn on the floor, and her tiara toppled crooked on her head.

Megan tucked the photo inside her bra and picked up a framed photo from the top of her bureau, the one of her, Peter, Holly, and Jack standing in front of the Women's Nest. Four young, beautiful people, arm-in-arm, full of life and free of disease stared back at Megan. She ran her finger along each of her friend's faces. She tucked the photo next to the Princess picture and close to her heart.

Megan sat in the window seat of her bedroom and

looked out the window. Holly and Olivia gathered twigs for the bonfire, while Peter organized the pit. She watched the leaves blow in the gentle breeze, the tall pines bent with age, and she wished she didn't have to leave such a beautiful Earth. Her gaze turned toward the sound of laughter, and she smiled as she watched Olivia's lips curl up, just at the edges, as she joked with Holly. A laugh escaped Megan's lips at the sight of Peter, hands on hips, pointing to sticks and trying to focus Olivia and Holly, which Megan knew was a losing battle. Peter's desperate attempts to make the sticks stay upright, like a teepee, were comical. Megan covered her mouth. *God, I'll miss them.* She giggled when Olivia walked right into Holly and toppled them over, tumbling both to the ground in fits of laughter. Those were the images she wanted to take with her, the images of life as it unfolded, and the images of her daughter surrounded by her friends, safe and loved.

As an afterthought, she decided to give herself in death what she wouldn't allow herself in life. She padded across the plush carpet and kneeled by her bed. She reached deep under her bed and withdrew a small wooden box. Smiling, she laid her hand across the top of the box. After a moment, she lifted the lid and fingered through its contents. She knew just what she was looking for. She found her treasure, folded, and resting upon the rough bottom of the box. She withdrew it with shaking hands, and unfolded it with her delicate fingertips, careful not to rip the fine paper. She read the words under the newspaper photo, "Mr. Lawrence Childs

Donates $1 Million to the Center for Missing Children". She gazed into his electrifying eyes, which seemed to jump off the page, and put the article against her cheek. Megan closed her eyes and took a deep breath, relishing the smell of the stale newspaper. She had never before questioned her *desire* not to be married, and now, assumed fate had led her on this path. She *wanted* to wish things could have been different. She *wanted* to wish she could have allowed him deeper into her world. A part of her *wanted* to wonder what her life would have been like had she not gotten pregnant—but her mind did not travel in that direction. She had lived the life she had created—and the life she had loved. As much as she thought she should feel the need to revisit her decisions, that need was not there, and something about that lack of wonder made her happy. She gently folded the article against itself, kissed the outside of the folds, and tucked it into her clothing, next to the two photos.

A pang of guilt speared through her as she acknowledged what she had done. It had been over four weeks since she had taken her medication, allowing her body to quickly deteriorate and sparing her daughter and friends months of pain while they watched her die. That was what she wanted. That was how she was choosing to go.

Megan reached into the vase on her windowsill, the one that Olivia had made out of clay for her when she was seven, with hand-painted, uneven, tiny red and blue flowers painted on the sides. She felt the familiar shapes of the many pills she was supposed to be taking, sifted through them, and cringed, as if they had little thorns. She sorted through each pill until she found the forty Percocet, the ones that would allow her to leave this life as she knew it and enter into the next. Her heart pounded in her chest as she rolled them around in her palm, rubbing a few between her index finger and thumb. She looked at the horded pills, so little yet so lethal. She was glad that she had had the presence of mind to keep them after her initial surgery. Her doctor had never flinched when she had asked for more, a month later. Her head jerked up as a shriek broke through the air.

Olivia and Holly chased each other around the yard between the tall pine trees and the house. Just as Olivia caught up to Holly, she doubled back and Olivia was once again left trailing behind. Peter blocked off one side of the yard, his long arms outstretched as if he could cover the entire span. Holly positioned herself to stand guard at the other side, arms firmly crossed. They beamed with delight. Olivia hovered in the center, like a child caught in a game of Red Rover.

Megan put the pills in her skirt pocket and took her meditation CDs from the shelf, which she'd fashioned from a piece of driftwood she'd found near Cockel Cove in Chatham. As her tears subsided, she slung the bag over her shoulder and walked to her doorway. She stopped, turned around, and took one last look at her bedroom. She headed down the hallway, but could not bring herself to take her last look into Olivia's bedroom. Instead, she made her way slowly down the stairs, toward the shrieks and cries of happiness.

"Mom! Help me!" Olivia yelled as she chased Holly in circles around the bonfire pit.

"She's fine, Meggie! She's just being a brat!" Holly yelled.

Megan lifted her eyes toward Peter. "What is going on?" she laughed, which seemed to take much of her energy.

"Holly said she could outrun Livi any day," Peter motioned with his hands as if he were putting out a display of fine art, "so Holly slapped Livi on the behind and took off."

"Sorry, Liv. I don't think I'll be much help!" Megan's voice was soft, too breathy, and quickly caught her daughter's attention.

Olivia ran to her mother's side. "Mom, are you okay? Do you need to sit down?" Her hands felt warm and large on Megan's own.

"No, honey, I'm fine. I'm just winded, that's all," Megan said. She mustered up all of her energy to give them a good show. "Come on," she smiled, "let's do this right!" She turned to her daughter, not knowing how to tell her that this was when she needed to go inside, that it was her mother's time.

She didn't have to say a word as Olivia read her face and stormed toward the house.

Megan felt overwhelmed with guilt. She closed her eyes in an effort to gather her strength. *I need this time with them.*

Olivia will be fine. Struck by the smell of the evening—sea breeze, burning wood, and the crispness of the night air—Megan could not shake the feeling that Olivia needed to be by her side. She stood alone by the bonfire, and noticed that Peter and Holly had, in fact, done a great job of setting the sticks and rocks just right. Frustrated and confused, Megan sat back on her haunches and buried her face in her hands. She was unable to get her mind to settle on what was right and what was wrong. Death loomed in the night before her, and yet she was just throwing away the pieces of her life so that she could spend the next few hours enjoying her friends alone. She remained there, hunched over, the fire warming her, her head spinning, until she could no longer stand the thoughts racing through her mind. She stood abruptly, wobbled, and put her arms out to steady herself.

The rustling of leaves, snapping of twigs, hushed voices, and giggles drew her gaze toward the forest, where Peter and Holly were gathering more wood.

"Damn woods, you know all I can think about are the ticks and snakes," Peter's voice was tethered and annoyed.

"Come on, Peter. It's only nature. Suck it up! Pretend you are on a scavenger hunt," Holly said, "or that you're reliving the night with Tim Mate in college! You guys hit the woods, and I didn't hear any complaining back then!"

They both laughed so hard that Holly tripped over a log, landing on Peter's ankle and tumbling him to the ground. It was silent for just a second, until Holly overflowed with laughter.

"Damn, Peter! Watch your ankles!"

The laughter continued. A noise, like footsteps on leaves, came from behind the big oak tree on the side of the house.

"Guys! Did you hear that?" Megan wondered if they could hear her own loud whisper. She turned to see them righting themselves and brushing off leaves.

"Only thing I heard was my big ass landing on the ground," Holly joked.

"We all heard that," Peter said.

"No, I *felt* it!" Holly laughed so hard she fell down again.

The sounds of feet running through the woods made them all turn toward the oak.

"What the h—" Holly ran toward the sound.

"Careful," Megan said quickly, "it could be a bobcat, or a dog, or something—"

"Oh yeah, like bobcats laugh! I heard a laugh!" Holly was already deep in the woods, feet beating a path towards the laughter that had become unmistakable. "Gotcha!" She dove for the feet she saw just around the bend and grabbed a familiar, slim ankle, sending Olivia face first into a pile of rotten leaves.

"Thanks, Holly! What the hell was that for?" Olivia fumed. Her black sweater and faded low rise jeans were covered in leaves.

"It's for eavesdropping. What will your mother think?"

"I don't really care what she thinks! I wanted to see what

you were doing in your…your….club!" At fourteen, Olivia was tall and slender, but at that moment she was beautiful only to those who could see past her teenage angst.

"Well, you didn't have to spy, you little rat. All you had to do was ask." Holly reached out and grabbed Olivia's velvety hand, effortlessly pulling her to her feet. "Come on, let's find your mama and see what's what."

With a long sigh, Olivia answered, "Okay, but you know she'll just be mad. She doesn't want me at the bonfire tonight." Olivia folder her arms across her chest and huffed, "I already asked her, Holly, don't you remember?"

"Young lady, you don't know your mama like I know your mama. She doesn't have a truly mad bone in her body. Well, maybe a mad, like crazy-loco, bone, but not a real true I'm-mad-at-you bone—at least not one that lasts very long." She took a deep breath, "Let's just see what we can do." Holly rested her arm protectively around Olivia's shoulder, and couldn't help but wonder how Megan could possibly *not* want Olivia near her at all times, given her circumstances.

"Look who the cat dragged out of the gutter!" Holly presented Olivia, who appeared to shrink before her mother's eyes. She hid her eyes behind her bangs, and worried the leaf in her hand.

"Livi, what were you doing out there?" Megan's eyes sent a mixed message of anger and concern.

"I…I was taking a walk," Olivia lied.

"Aw, come on, Olivia," Holly interrupted, "she wanted to see our ritual." Over pronouncing "ritual" so Olivia would see that she was on her side. "What do you think?"

Megan sauntered toward the garden and began picking flowers, her back to Olivia and Holly.

"Olivia, you've seen us do this every year. You already know what we do," Peter said.

"No, I don't! I'm never allowed out here. No one is! This is your special time. It's like this big cloak-and-dagger club or something! Like you offer up sacrifices and wear garlic around your neck!" Her hip jutted out in a typical angry teenage stance.

"Come on, now, it's never that secretive. We've been doing this since we were your age. It's our way of....of—" Holly's sentence dropped off as Peter interrupted.

"Coming together, airing out our minds, cleansing our souls." Peter noticed Megan had inched further away. "Just ask your mother."

Megan turned and wondered how it was that in fourteen years she had never noticed how much strength her daughter possessed. How could she have let this distance come between them? "Olivia, come here." Yearning to say more, but unable, she pulled Olivia into her arms, and held her so close that she could count the beats of her heart. She had to protect Olivia from becoming too close to her, from seeing the outcome of tonight's ritual. "I'm sorry."

"See! I knew it! Whatever!" Olivia ripped herself from her mother's arms and stormed into the house.

"What the hell, Megan?" Holly demanded. She walked purposefully toward her and stopping within inches of

Megan's pained face. "You two were so close, what happened? You guys act like strangers! I've never seen you so cold."

"It's just that…I can't be close to her now. It's not the time. It will hurt her too much. I'm not myself, it's not like it was years ago." Megan's eyes filled with tears as she lowered herself onto her heels, elbows on knees, no longer having the strength to stand up.

"Meg, this is the time. There is no better time. She *needs* you. She needs to feel close to you," Holly said, suddenly seeing Megan again as a young girl, a mere shadow of her former self.

"It will hurt her too much. It'll make it harder in the end," Megan said, quietly.

Holly knelt down, and laid her hands on Megan's shoulders. "It'll be harder if she remembers you in a bad light. Let her in. She can handle this. She needs this. Let her know how great you are for God's sake." Holly looked at Peter. "We already know how great you are, Meg, she needs to remember you as we all do."

Megan stayed there, unable to stand, for a long time. When she stood, her legs felt unstable. Holly reached down to help her up, but Megan swiped at her hand, shooing her away. She steadied herself and took careful steps toward the house, unsure of each step, and unsure of her own emotions.

Megan approached Olivia's room with a pounding heart and a veil of confusion. She loved Olivia and didn't want to hurt her. Couldn't Olivia see that she was trying to create space so it wouldn't hurt so badly when she was gone? Then it hit her—hard. If all went as planned, tomorrow, she would not be there. What the hell was she doing? Olivia was her daughter! Megan stood up straighter, chiding herself for being so selfish. She smoothed her hair and put one hand on Olivia's doorknob, assuming she would be met with Olivia's pouting and angry face. She pushed the door open and took in the colorful dragonflies that hung from the ceiling, remembering the laughter that filled the room as she and Olivia stood on the bed and reached for the ceiling to tack them up. The bright quilted comforter displayed haphazard shapes and forms, covered by neon and fuzzy pillows in greens and oranges, and stuffed animals that had been slept with for so many years that they had become dingy and matted. Instantly, she recognized the feeling of emptiness in the room, and wondered if that was how her own room would soon feel.

She yielded to the pain that was burning in her stomach and accepted it as Olivia's anger, her hatred. She walked to the dresser and ran her finger along the edge, remembering when Holly had given it to Olivia. "Every little girl needs white furniture with gold trim," Holly had said. Megan smiled at the memory. She sat in Olivia's chair, and swore she could feel her daughter's body within her own.

She reached into the drawers, though she knew she shouldn't, and lifted out Olivia's diary. Her heart beat faster. She listened carefully for Olivia's footsteps. She'd never done this before, always believing that everyone needed a few secrets. The silence vibrated in her ears, and with shaking hands she opened the small leather bound journal, flipping quickly and carefully to the pages nearest the end.

April 16, 2009.
It's like Mom doesn't want me around so much anymore. She still watches tv with me and stuff like that, but sometimes it's like she wishes I wasn't here. I think she's getting sicker, but she said she's not. I think she's lying to me. Sometimes I hate her.

April 17, 2009
Mom isn't doing so good. She's been lying around on the couch and Holly had to come over again tonight to make dinner and take care of us. I wish I could take care of Mom, but whenever I try to she tells me that it's not my job. I like it when Holly is here. She would be a good mother. I wonder why she doesn't have kids. Anyway, she takes good care of Mom and me when she's here. She wipes Mom's head with a wet cloth and I hear her whispering nice things and then they laugh. She helps me with my homework and stuff, too. I hear Mom crying at night sometimes. I started to go into her room last night, but stopped outside her door and ran back to my room. I didn't want to embarrass her. I hope she's okay.

Megan flipped forward a few pages.

April 30, 2009.

Tomorrow is Mom's birthday. I got her the best present! Holly picked me up after school and we went and got a picture taken of me and her, then we bought a really fancy frame and we signed our name in ink, just like the stars do! I think she'll love it. She always calls me her shining star! I know Mom's going to die. She told me. I don't want her to. I will miss her so much! I keep thinking maybe she won't die, and I asked Holly when Mom was going to get better, but she just turned away and said she didn't know. I know she's not, but maybe if I ask enough she will. I love her so much. What will I do without her? Sometimes I feel so mean for being mad at her, but sometimes I am mad at her. I can't help it. Sometimes I feel like it's her own fault she's sick.

Mom's acting weird again. Today she spent all night sitting next to me, talking to me about Grandma and Holly and school and all sorts of stuff. I wish she didn't have to die. Maybe God is punishing me by taking her away. I asked her if she knew when she would die, and she just said that God will do whatever he has to and that she loves me. She said that she would always be with me, even if God took her away. She said that she would find a way to contact me if she died. We both cried. I was so sad. I don't want Mommy to die. But I don't want Mommy to hurt either, and I know she does. I hate God!

Anyway, Billy likes me now. His friend Charlie told me so.

Megan wiped her tears with her sleeve; the rough sweater lightly scratched her cheeks. She flipped backward toward the beginning of the journal.

May 2, 2004.
We had so much fun today! I stayed home from school today because I said I was sick (I think she knew I was faking!) and we played all sorts of games. She made brownies and we laid around in our pajamas all day! She didn't paint or get on the phone or anything! We watched movies on Lifetime, real grown up shows! Mom let me eat as much popcorn as I wanted. It was so cool!

Megan closed the diary and settled it back in the drawer. As she was closing the drawer, a paper pushed out from under it—stuck to the bottom of the drawer. Megan opened the letter, recognized her daughter's scrawl, and read it.

January 2007
Dear Mom, I'm sorry you are so sick. I wish you weren't. Sometimes I wish that I was you instead of you being you. Then you wouldn't hurt so much. I know it's selfish, but I wonder what will happen to me if something bad happens to you? I wonder where I will go and who will take care of me. Grandma is too old to have to worry about me. I wish I knew who my dad was. Maybe he would want to take care of me. Sometimes I'm so mad at you for being sick. I know I shouldn't be, but sometimes I am. Mom, please get better.

Please, please get better. I love you always and forever, Livi XXOO

Tears streamed down her cheeks and onto the letter, leaving small wet spots. She jumped as she heard Olivia walk into her room.

"Mom! What are you doing?" She demanded with her hands on her hips and a scowl on her face. "Did you go in my desk?"

Megan, too tired and too sad to fight, turned in the chair to face her angry daughter. "I was looking for you," was all she could manage.

Olivia snagged the letter from her mother's hand and sat on the bed. Tears finally sprang free from her angry eyes. "Great. Thanks for looking at my stuff. That's just—" She looked down and ripped up the letter. "It's a stupid letter. I wrote it when you first got sick. My counselor at school said it might make me feel better, but it didn't."

Megan moved next to her daughter, letting her head hang with the weight of a bag of flour. "Oh, Olivia, I'm so sorry. I didn't mean to get sick. I didn't mean to be a bad mom, or a mom who didn't pay enough attention to you."

"But you *did* pay attention to me, Mom!" Her voice carried through the house, her hurt raged in violent streams. "You paid *tons* of attention to me, remember? Before you got sick? It's just that now, now you don't…or can't…or whatever. Now it just sucks."

Megan's heart broke with each of Olivia's words. She

fingered the pile of pills in her pocket, thinking that perhaps now wasn't the right time to go. She needed more time to help her daughter understand her illness, to just be with her, emotionally and physically—and as much as she hadn't wanted to do it, she now felt an urgent need to tell Jack that he was Olivia's father.

"Livi, I'm so sorry. I want to be here for you all the time. It's just this damn sickness. I hate what it does to me and what it takes from you! It takes all of my energy—every bit of my strength. Sucks it right out of me and leaves me empty. There's nothing I wouldn't do for you if I could, don't you know that?" Megan reached out to Olivia, but Olivia stood and backed away.

"Yeah, I know, Mom, but it hurts. Damn it, I hurt too, you know?"

Megan heard the back door open as Olivia continued to admonish her.

"It hurts so much to see you sick and not know *when you'll get better*, or if you even will. It kills me, Mom! And you act like I'm not here sometimes—like you don't want me around—like tonight!" Olivia sobbed. She swiped at the tears that ran down her cheeks, but was unable to stop the flow.

Megan was taken aback at Olivia's words, when you'll get better. Did she not understand their talk the other night or was she just in denial?

"Oh, Livi! What can I do?" Megan asked. "I want you there tonight, but I'm afraid, too. What if it makes you closer to me, and then if…if…if something happens and you are too close to me, then you are left—" she couldn't continue. Sobs wracked her slight body.

Olivia stepped in front of Megan and knelt down, taking her fragile hands in her own young, strong hands. "But Mom, that's what I'm supposed to be, close to you. I'm your daughter." She laid her head in her mother's lap, and Megan rested her head on top of her daughter's. Together they cried. "I'd rather be with you than not with you…every day…until the end."

Megan heard footsteps recede down the hall. She lifted Olivia's sad face and cradled it in her hands. "Livi, I am very sick. I might even die soon, but there's one thing you must know." She kissed Olivia's forehead and took a deep breath, wiping her daughter's tears with her small hand, "One thing you must know, Livi, is how very much I love you. When I'm gone," she hesitated, letting the words sink in, "remember we talked about this, okay? Don't ever doubt my love for you because it is endless, like the sea. It will go on forever, no matter what happens in your life, no matter what mistakes you make. My love for you is solid, like a rock. I will never think anything less of you than seeing how perfect you are. You will make mistakes, Livi. That's normal, and my love will still be strong for you. Never doubt that."

Olivia nodded her head, unable to stop the flow of tears.

"When I leave this Earth, you will live with Holly and Jack. They love you." She pulled her daughter into her arms and held her there, feeling her heart beat against her own, taking in the light innocent smell of teenager and child blended as one, and hating God for taking her life away so early. The unfairness of it all boiled in her blood, fueled her anger. "Now, baby, let's go and have ourselves a ritual!" She smiled at Olivia, whose lips curled up around the edges at the thought of joining her mother's coveted club.

"Really, Mom? It's okay? I mean, you don't have to," Olivia said, her voice a mere whisper.

"Really. Get your CD player and let's get going, huh? They've probably all left by now."

"No way!" Olivia's happier tone slowly returned. "They probably drank all of your alcohol and finished the cake, but they'd never leave!"

"Yeah, you're probably right," Megan said. She waited for her daughter to collect her CD player and wash her face. Together, arm in arm, they walked downstairs.

Olivia whispered in her mother's ear, "I love you, Mom. You are everything to me."

"Do you think she's okay?" Peter asked Holly in a hushed voice.

"I don't know, Peter, it's a hard time right now. I pray every day that she'll get better, but I don't know. She said she won't, and without the meds, well," Holly hesitated. "She looks awful."

"I know. I just can't think about—" Peter's eyes welled with tears. Holly grabbed his arm and tugged him further into the woods. "Peter, honey, you have to pull it together. We can't let her see you cry. Straighten up, okay? I know it's hard, but we have to be strong for her—and for poor Olivia. Now let's go." With that said, she marched back into the yard and threw her wood into the pit. Peter came out behind her and placed his wood on the ground next to Holly's feet.

Holly greeted Megan and Olivia with a warm and pleased look. She squeezed between them, put her arm around their waists, and rested her head on Megan's shoulder.

"Happy birthday, chick. You know we love you," she said.

"I know you do. How could you not?" Megan pulled her sweater tighter around her shoulders and smiled.

Holly turned to Olivia and said, "Welcome to our little nest, Livi."

At that moment, a rush of sadness and joy intertwined and wound its way through Olivia's body, making her blush and glow all at once.

Megan lit the tiki lights, and watched Olivia walk toward the woods to gather flowers from the edge of the garden. Holly and Peter chatted about something near the fire—*life, no doubt,* Megan thought—not hers, just life in general. How things are, who's doing what, normal life issues. Megan longed for normal conversation, not hedged with worry, but now wasn't the time for self pity. She had a ritual to start!

"Okay, girls and Peter! Gather 'round!" Megan said, drawing from deep within to gain strength. "The time has come for us to begin." With the fire burning, the lights flickering, and all of them gathered closely together in a circle, Megan took out the blue CD from her bag and placed it in Olivia's CD player.

Holly beamed. She reached over and pressed Play. Their ritual Buddhist chant filled the air.

Each of them laid their special hippie blankets out around the fire, like petals jutting out from the stem of a beautiful flower. They sat cross legged and eager.

Olivia's heart pounded. *Oh my God! Oh my God! I'm here!*

"God, Meg, when can we change our chant?" Holly pleaded, hands in a praying position. "I love you, and I love our rituals. You make me spiritual, for God's sake, but can't our chant be peppier?"

"You can't change our chant! That's what a ritual is all about—the same thing year after year. Besides, it isn't supposed to be peppy. It's not a dance, it's a centering of our souls, and unification of our minds—a blessing of our beings. It is supposed to be peaceful and help you empty your mind of the clutter and chaos. Surely you want to be at peace for just a few moments in your life." Megan winked at Olivia, who sat silent and wide-eyed, granting respect to her mother's ritual, and absorbing it all. She did not want to miss a second.

"Yeah, once again you are right. I hate that. Besides, it *is* your day," Holly said.

They held hands and closed their eyes. Megan's skirt, another Provincetown favorite, billowed around her thin legs in the light breeze. Her calves, exposed to the evening air, tingled with a chill.

She began, "Thank you for bringing us together once again, oh Holy One." *We need these times, we live for them*, she thought. "Thank you for bringing me to my senses and allowing Olivia to be here and not letting me turn her away. Thank you for my wonderful cake, my treacherous friends, and for another year in which to keep our sanity by purifying ourselves tonight." She sensed the others sneaking knowing looks at each other.

Silently, they lay back on their blankets, eyes closed, and hands by their sides. Megan stole a glance at Olivia, who followed her every movement and moved carefully, desperately wanting to do exactly the right things at exactly the right times.

Megan waited in silence for a full two minutes before she began again.

Olivia was so excited that she could hardly lie still. She knew she must remain silent and not giggle. Her body tingled, waiting to see what they would do next.

"Oh Holy One, we need to relax, bring ourselves onto your plane. Relax our hair follicles, relax our foreheads." Megan paused, and another minute passed. "Relax our cheeks, our noses, and mouths." *Right about now*, she thought, *I usually hear sighs from them as they relax their faces and release their stress.*

Peter sighed.

Megan smiled.

"Release the darkness and let us be open to the light. Relax our chins, our necks, and our shoulders. Let them drop without weight. Relax our biceps, forearms, and hands. Let every finger lose its strength, relaxing into our blankets." Again she paused. "Relax our chests," this always brought a slight giggle from Holly, but tonight she remained silent.

"Relax our sternum and stomachs. Release the bad energy and let in the light. Relax our thighs." Again there was silence, the giggles sorely missed.

"Relax our knees. Let our calves bare no weight. Relax our feet, toes, and heels." Megan could feel the negative energy exiting her body through her toes, like darts being shot out of a bamboo gun.

"Our breath relaxes as we are open to the positive energy that You and your light bring us." Megan paused for three full minutes. She listened to the crackle of the fire and felt the heat of the flames warm her body. It was as if she had risen from the cold ground and was floating on warm air. It was an effort for her to remain awake enough to speak, but she knew she must.

The ritual was vital to her group. It was theirs and theirs alone. It was their way of blessing each other, blessing themselves, and coming together as one. After twenty-one years, they had grown to crave the ceremony. They longed for it as the day neared and missed it when it ended.

"Take the evil from our beings. Let it seep out from our pores and find its way into the fire where it will burn and live no more." Megan swore she could hear the fire simmer a substance, like food in a shallow pan. "Remove the broken heart, sorrow, and disease, and release it into the air. Allow it to disintegrate and hurt no more. Empty our beings so they may be open to the light. Replenish our souls with love, happiness, health, and passion. Let us feel. Let us remember what good life brings and forget the pain of the past."

Olivia reached over until she felt her mother's hand, and rested her right hand in her mother's cool palm. Megan felt a chill run through her and a tear slip down her cheek. She squeezed Olivia's hand, and held it as she had when Olivia was a small child and needed to feel safe.

"Bless our families, oh Holy One, and let them remain open to the light through our path," Megan continued. "We thank you for the journey, our Lord, and look forward to another hour, another day, and whatever it may bring."

Megan listened to each person's separate breath as they melted into one peaceful sound. She listened to the sound of leaves being stepped on ever so lightly, as if by a squirrel or a bird. It was a gentle sound, one that soothed her. It represented a knowing of life, a creature stirring. Her friends and daughter were still, entranced by their prayers, thinking their own thoughts, or perhaps not thinking at all. She listened to the wind as it brushed gently across the leaves. The sound reminded her of the walks she used to take with her own mother around the National Seashore—running down the dirt paths, her arms brushing up against the leaves as she passed by carelessly. Happier times, before her life's path had changed forever, before she really knew about inescapable hurt and pain, when her world was one of childhood bliss.

It took all of Megan's strength to will her words from her mouth. "We lift our flowers to our hearts." They all reached to their right, without opening their eyes, and gathered their flowers to their chests. Megan reached over and put Olivia's flowers in her hand, and without a word, gently placed it on her chest.

"With these flowers, oh Holy One, we say thank you for hearing our prayers." They sat up slowly, their bodies heavy with peacefulness, their eyes remained closed. Holly reached out and lifted Olivia to a sitting position.

Olivia snuck a peak, and smiled at the sight of each of her mother's closest friends looking so happy. She couldn't believe she was part of their ritual! She had waited her whole life, it seemed, to be included. For so many years she sat at her bedroom window, watching their actions, longing to be part of the group, and angry that she was never allowed. She had always wondered what was said around the fire, wondered if there were more to the ritual than what she saw. She had craved to be included in their secrets.

She looked at Megan. Her own mother, she realized, looked like someone she had never met. She seemed to be elsewhere, though her body was there, with Olivia. *She is beautiful*, Olivia thought. *Even though she's sick, she's still pretty.* Olivia closed her eyes, and took a deep breath, feeling sated in the night air.

They reach out with their left hands, and placed them on the shoulder of the person next to them. Holly guided Olivia to the position.

Megan began again, "With these flowers, My Lord, I ask that You give my friends peace, my family health, and the world enlightenment. For myself, my Lord, I ask for the knowledge of how to accept the light into my soul. Please Lord, let me find my way down this new path with dignity and without fear. If You could throw in a few ounces of health, that's always appreciated." Feeling guilty, she added, "But please don't give me health in place of one of my other wishes, they are far more important. And Lord, I beg You to watch over my Olivia, give her peace in her life and the strength to deal with whatever comes her way. Relieve her of stress and pain, and give her happiness and creativity in its place." She placed her flowers into the fire, and laid her right hand over her heart.

In unison they said, "Amen."

Megan could not see the tears which streamed down Olivia's cheeks, nor could she feel the squeezing of Peter's shoulder by Holly, as her friends silently, but together, said their own prayers for Megan's health.

True to form, Peter's voice was loving and warm. Megan imagined that it was the voice he used when he spoke to

Cruz late at night. "Oh Lord, my father needs your strength to deal with life's troubles. Please Lord, he is my rock, and I need him to have some happiness in his life. Please be kind to people and not make so many hardships on them." Peter cleared his throat. "I ask that You take care of Olivia, giving her strength and calm during this troublesome time. And please, oh Holy One, please let Megan be enveloped in the light. She has enlightened us, now please enlighten her soul."

Tears formed in Megan's eyes, as she realized how her friends filled every emotional gap in her soul.

Peter gently placed his flowers in the flame, and Megan was sure the night air had transformed into a warm lavender scent that permeated her skin. She felt the warmth spread through her body, and she could taste the scent, as if it were fine candy lingering on her tongue. *This is my heaven*, she thought. *This is my safe circle, my family who loves me for me and believes in me. At this very moment, I am truly happy.*

They said, "Amen."

Peter's right hand covered his heart and he squeezed Megan's shoulder lightly to let her know he was there.

Holly's voice was warm and gentle. "Oh Holy One, I'm not real happy this year, as You know. I'm pretty upset over what You have done to Meggie and Olivia." She sat quietly for a moment, letting her words find their way to the heavens above. "I ask, Lord, that You let Peter find happiness and allow Cruz to be his other half."

Peter sighed.

Holly continued, "Thank You, Lord, for giving me Jack. He is my soul mate." A breathy sound carried through the air, as if each person lifted a little smile. "And Lord, listen carefully now because this is the most important one of all, so sit your ass down and listen to me. This is really and truly important." Holly sighed, readying herself to hold back her tears and speak her mind.

"Lord, my friend Megan here, well, Meggie, she needs us. She needs our love, our advice, our harassment. Please keep her by our sides comfortably. There's no one else that can bring us to You as she does. These rituals are *hers*, my Lord. Please give her peace and surround her with light. Envelope her as we have enveloped each other. She's a special person. Please, Lord, make sure she has a special place." Holly took a deep breath. "Thank You, Lord, for bringing Olivia to us tonight. She's a welcome addition to our group. Please continue to watch over her and give her strength and guidance to carry on." Holly snuck a peak at Olivia just as Olivia snuck one toward her. She winked, conspiratorially.

Olivia tucked away the feeling of Holly's love along with her other stashed compliments, holding onto them as if they were treasures needed for some future journey.

"Please keep Jack happy and healthy, and keep our little nest together—always." Holly kissed her flowers and threw them into the fire.

The group said, "Amen" as Holly placed her right hand over her heart.

Olivia trembled with anticipation, uncertain about her

words, which tumbled from her mouth like pebbles from a high peak, rough and unsure, "Dear Lord, thank you for making me part of my mom's group. I've wanted this for so long." She took a deep breath, thinking of just the right words, wanting to sound more mature than her fourteen years might allow. "I really want my mom to get better. That's about all that I want right now." She tossed her flowers into the fire and her mother reached out and guided Olivia's right hand to cover her heart, leaving her own hand resting on Olivia's for just a moment longer. She felt her daughter's heart race, and willed her own strength, what little she had left, to become her daughter's.

Sparks flew from the bonfire, and the smell of flowers and ash wafted around them.

Together they said, "Amen!"

"With these flowers and prayers, oh Holy One," Megan began, "we become one once again. We wed for eternity, our souls, our selves, and our passions." This time they all shouted out, in almost a song, "Amen!"

Within seconds they were standing up, arms stretched toward the sky. Holly turned off the CD and the gay sounds of top forty music filled the air. They danced around the fire, held each other, jumped, sang, and rejoiced in the success of yet another ritual.

Megan's movements were slow, her breath encumbered, though her spirits soared. She felt herself deflate and prayed her strength would last just a little longer to get her through the celebration.

Her friends' hearts were lifted, and their faces reflected the happiness within their souls. They reached for one another, dancing in groups of two, alone, and falling into, finally, a dance of all four of them, arms flailing about, hips wriggling, and laughter filling the air.

Olivia sought out her mother, hugged her, and apologized for being selfish. Megan told her to think nothing of it and said she was glad she was there after all. She welcomed her to their group and wished her well in each of the future rituals to come. They looked into each other's eyes, forehead leaned upon forehead, and shared a smile reflecting years of love, treasured memories, and happiness. At that very moment, all of the ugliness and fights had disappeared, as if they had never existed at all.

As the excitement settled into an even pace of joy, Megan reached for her hippie bag and took out her gifts, four Runic Love Amulets. She wanted her friends and Olivia to find happiness and passion in their lives. She wanted them to be joyful and stress free. She hoped they would remember her as being those things as well. She slowly made her way around the fire to each one of them, placed the gift around their necks, and kissed them solidly on the cheek.

Peter held Megan's hands and slowly twirled her around. Holly did a gentle bump with Megan (a remnant of their childhood, dancing-in-the-basement days). The bump turned into a slow dance, even though the music was fast, as both women needed the closeness. *Holly gets me*, Megan thought.

Megan broke away slowly and walked toward Olivia, arms open. Olivia rushed into them. They immediately fell into their own dance of hugs and rocking, which evolved into the Batman, and they ended up both doing the Monkey, although Megan's Monkey was a bit hindered by the pain in her joints. Megan slipped the necklace around Olivia's neck and said, "You are my treasure, Olivia Leigh. I love you."

Olivia cried.

The four of them converged on one another, laughing hysterically, and moving in a mass of arms and legs. Hips swayed, breasts jiggled, and laughs took flight in the night air. Megan made her way to the back of the group, perched herself on her blanket, and watched her friends with delight.

They danced until they all fell to the ground, spent with exhaustion, and delirious with celebration. They chatted around the fire, warming their bodies and settling their minds. Not once did they let their minds drift back to Megan's illness. This was a time for replenishment, a time for relaxation.

They clung together on their blankets, overlapped like a litter of puppies, legs on legs, heads on shoulders, hands on backs. The night swathed them in darkness, save for the fire. Their voices trailed toward the sky. Every now and again a hushed voice could be heard saying a kind word, or a movement could be felt, a hug of tenderness, one body moving closer to another.

Olivia curled herself into a little girl again, and snuggled so close to Megan that their breaths fell into a symbiotic rhythm—Olivia's exhale became Megan's strength, and each of Megan's breaths comforted Olivia.

Holly and Megan faced each other and whispered as their energy dwindled. They lay so close that each time Megan breathed out, it became Holly's intake of breath.

Peter reached out to Megan and touched her. He held onto her, their hands familiar and comforting. Olivia's toes rested on Peter's leg, and she took great comfort in knowing he was there.

Sometime during the evening, Megan snuck her Winnie-the-Pooh bear out of her bag, and nestled it securely under her left arm. She was glad she had made the decision not to take the pills. She needed one more day to share her secret with Jack, one more day to see her daughter smile, and one more day to simply be. It was like this, as one, that they eased into sleep as the night air carried away their hopes and dreams, their cares and hearts, into the vast evening sky.

Chapter Five

The early morning sun illuminated the remnants of the campfire, and Megan watched her friends sleeping peacefully—knowing that shortly their lives would be forever changed. Olivia looked so peaceful that Megan wished she'd never have to wake, that she could stay in that peaceful state forever—leaving the truth of her new life unrealized. Megan's body was there, against Olivia's, but her essence, her energy, was gone—stolen from her body and taken with her soul for eternity.

Though Megan's heart ached for the pain her death would cause her daughter and most treasured friends, and she longed to have been the one to tell Jack that Olivia was his daughter, she felt horribly conflicted because she was also strangely enveloped by a sense peace and wellness. She had passed through her life with gracious friends and an amazing daughter, taking with her a small part of each of their beings, and stashing it away in her very own soul. She wept, not for her own death, but for the life she had shared with each of them and for the cumbersome job they would now have of putting her body to rest. Megan passed through on May 1st, the same day she had come into the world. She hoped that her friends would continue to celebrate that day for themselves in years to come, as they had for her.

Megan looked down and was not surprised to find that she was no longer whole. She had no body, though she had a form, a weightless cloudy shape that looked as if she were draped in a cloud. She felt healthy, whole, as if she were carrying the ten pounds she had always wished away, and that, surprisingly, made her smile.

Holly awoke feeling revitalized as she always had after their rituals. She breathed in the crisp air and let it out slowly. She moved carefully, trying not to wake Peter and Olivia. Olivia—she was so pleased that Megan had allowed Olivia to share in their ritual. It was time. Olivia was a young woman and certainly deserved to take part in their group. She was proud of Megan for changing her mind. Holly, of all people, knew how hard it was for Megan to make the transition from having *her* time with her friends, to including her daughter. *Her daughter*, the thought lingered in Holly's mind, and she looked down at Megan, whose eyes were staring not at her, but through her.

Holly squinted, darting her eyes to see what Megan was looking at. She reached for Megan, "Meg?" Her body was cold—not just cold from the morning air, but ice cold. A chill ran through Holly's chest.

"Meg? Meg?" Panicked, she leaned toward Megan's

body and touched her cheek. "Oh God. Oh God. Oh God." Tears streamed down her cheeks. She shook Megan, "Megan? Oh God! Megan!" Her voice rose.

Olivia stirred, her body still curled up like a baby cat snuggled against its mother. Holly reached out and gently placed her trembling hand on Olivia's arm, causing Olivia to turn toward her rather than her mother.

Olivia looked at Holly, saw the message in her eyes—and knew. She opened her mouth to speak, but could not. Her body began to shake uncontrollably; her hands flew up to the sides of her head. She spun around and looked at her mother. Her face contorted, and she covered her ears as if she could keep out the awful news of her mother's death. She shook her head vehemently. "No! No!" she cried. "It's not true!" She put her arms around mother's stiff body, feeling her cold flesh against her own warm hands. She lay flat against her mother's side, rocked, "No, Mom! No, no, no! I'm not ready!"

Peter watched the scene unfold in horror and shock. He was unable to speak, pleading with his eyes to Holly, begging for a different outcome, but her look told it all—Megan was gone. He moved silently to Olivia's side. He and Holly embraced Olivia. They didn't try to pry her away from Megan's body. They simply enveloped her, held her tight, and cried with her, each feeling his and her own private pain, their own private loss.

"Livi, honey, I think she knew," Holly said. The revelation only made Olivia cry harder. Holly wiped her warm tears, leaving wet streaks across her cheeks. "I think she knew it was her time, honey. She wanted to go this way, with all of us here."

Olivia sobbed harder. "No! If she knew she would have said goodbye! She wouldn't just…just leave me like that! She loves me!"

"Of course she does, Livi. She does love you, more than anything else in this world," Peter said through his own tears.

"She did say goodbye, Livi. Last night was her way of saying goodbye. She left you with us. She knew you would be safe with us here by your side." Holly took Olivia into her arms and rocked her, sharing her pain, soothing her with love.

"Why?" Olivia cried. "Why didn't she want me here then? If she knew she was going to…to...go like this, why didn't she want me here?"

"But she did want you here, Olivia. You are here," Holly said.

Olivia stood, her hurt turned into anger. "No!" she yelled, viciously eying her mother's friends. "You guys made her let me come! She said I couldn't! She said it was her time!" Olivia paced, her thin arms crossed across her heaving chest. "She didn't even want me here." Her last words were spoken as if they were meant only for herself to hear.

Holly knelt beside Megan, her hands steepled. Her tears landed on Megan's hair and sunk into its depth. She was unable to understand it herself. How could she explain it to Olivia?

"Oh, baby girl, my sweet baby girl," Peter said as he put his arms around Olivia. "I am so sorry, Livi, so very sorry."

Olivia fell into Peter's arms, giving into the sadness that coursed through her body and robbed her of her will to move. Her thoughts blurred together, her limbs hung heavily, and dizziness overtook her. She barely registered the sight of her mother's Pooh Bear before she blacked out.

Megan felt as if her heart were being torn into shreds. She hadn't thought of the immediate effect of her death, just of the months of pain that she would have spared Olivia. *Did I do the right thing?* Her tears flowed, though when they fell they formed a stream that wound through the sky and disappeared into a cloud, like a long silk scarf twisting and floating in the breeze. She marveled, momentarily lost in the wonder of the stream, and was called back to Earth by the sound of Peter's voice.

"My God, Holly, look." He motioned to the stuffed bear. "She did know. She must have known."

Holly's hand instinctively covered her mouth. She looked down at Olivia who hung in Peter's arms like a rag doll, closed her eyes, and whispered, "Oh, Meggie."

Peter laid Olivia on the couch and covered her with the afghan her mother had used just the evening before. Megan's scent of lavender and coconut remained in the fibers of the fabric and wrenched even more tears from the center of Olivia's heart. Olivia whimpered like a small child, spent of emotion.

Holly gave Olivia a Valium in an effort to help her calm down.

As she drifted off to sleep, thoughts of her mother wound their way around her tormented mind.

Peter and Holly went outside and covered Megan's body with a thick blanket.

"Shouldn't we call someone?" Peter asked.

"Yeah." Holly was still in a state of shock. "I don't know who we'd call. The morgue? The police?" She knelt next to Megan. "It just doesn't seem fair that she's gone. I mean, just yesterday she was here, alive. She didn't look great, but she didn't look like she was going to—"

Peter knelt next to Holly and held her while she sobbed.

"Why didn't she tell me, Peter?" Holly's voice was beset by sadness. "I'm her best friend, and she didn't even hint to me that this was so close."

"There's a lot about Megan that we will never know, Hol. She must have known. She never brought her bear to our rituals, and yet, we all know what it meant to her. It makes sense that she knew."

Holly swallowed hard and tried to stop her tears from flowing, tried to find her voice. She took Peter's hand in her own and closed her eyes.

"Oh, Holy One," she began. "Please embrace Megan and show her the light. She was the tie that bound us, and she is now yours." Holly's salty tears landed in her mouth, reminding her of the bittersweet evening before.

The pain in her heart was more than she could bear. She was drowning in her sorrow, each tear pushed her further into the depths of sadness.

From her perch just above, Megan watched the scene unfold. She was torn between relief at finally passing on and despair over what was happening to her friends and Olivia. She floated back and forth between them anxiously, watching her friends, watching Olivia asleep on the couch, her heart tearing over their sorrow. She wondered just how long it would take for Olivia to forgive her, to forgive God. Megan's thoughts drifted to the evening before. She could not remember taking the pills from her pocket and clearly remembered wanting more time with Olivia, even feeling ready and willing to fight for it.

Olivia had fallen fast asleep on the couch. Holly called Jack, her words almost inaudible through her tears, and Peter made the other necessary calls. Unable to remain idle and still in shock, they straightened Megan's house from the festivities of the night before in silence. When Peter was in the bathroom, Holly snuck outside. She uncovered Megan's face to have one last look, lay down behind her, and held her rigid and cold body against her own. She let her tears flow and the words come, without concern of how she sounded, without embarrassment of being seen.

"Meggie, my love, I am so sorry for everything. I knew, or at least I figured, for so long, but I couldn't ask you, not once you got sick. It took me thirteen years, but I finally put it all together. I wouldn't have loved you any less. I wouldn't have been upset. You didn't need to bear your secret alone. Why didn't you know that? Why didn't you trust me?" Holly quelled the mixture of anger and loss that coursed through her.

"I love her, Meggie, as I love you. I will be good to her." Holly took a deep breath, and held back the words that she still wished she could speak, *She is mine*. In a whisper, she said, "I am sorry, Megan. Thank you for being her mother." She closed her eyes and wept. Her tears fell from her cheeks to Megan's face, as if cried from her own still eyes.

Jack's deep sorrowful voice pulled Holly back to the present. He fell to his knees behind Holly and embraced her, tears sliding down his own flushed cheeks. Her body was still entwined with Megan's, and they lay there, the three of them as one. Jack's breath brought Holly strength, and that strength drifted up through the air and found its way to Megan, breezing through her like a rush of warm wind, lifting her full, thick hair and leaving a trail of heat, like a worn path running through her soul.

Holly rested her hand on Jack's arm.

Megan flinched in surprise as she felt his heat in her

palm, as if Holly's hand were her own. Jack's eyes opened wide, he squinted, and then as if he couldn't, or wouldn't, believe what he felt, he closed them again.

Olivia awoke to her mother's friends' hushed whispers in the kitchen. She looked outside at the afternoon sun, which had risen high in the sky, illuminating the remnants of the bonfire and the empty spot where her mother's body had been. She rubbed the fresh tears from her eyes and made her way slowly to the French doors. She put her hand flat against the glass and felt the warmth of her mother's hand against her own, which at first hit her like a bad dream, igniting a feeling of wanting to pull her hand back, as if burned. Not a second later, the feeling turned to one of a blessing. She put her other palm against the door and felt the same sensation. Tears flowed down both cheeks, and a sad smile crept across her face, *Mama?*

Megan floated just beyond the clouds, her hands outstretched, fingers reaching as if they were each a tiny hand. In the flash of a second, she felt the softness of Olivia's hands on her own. Just as quickly, it was gone.

When the heat subsided, Olivia tucked the feeling safely into her secret place, alongside Holly's accolades and love, and her memories of her mother. She knew her mother was with her now, as she always had been in life.

Olivia walked into the yard and sat down on the blanket her mother had used the evening before. She picked up her mother's bear and held it close to her chest. She didn't try to stop the sadness that brought a rush of tears and pain in her heart. She looked toward the sky and wondered, for a brief second, what happened to her mother's body, where it was taken, but the thought was erased by the understanding that it didn't matter where it had gone—she needed her mother alive, with her, not the empty shell that she once had inhabited. She closed her eyes and wondered what would become of her now. Who will she trust? Who will care for her? Who was she now? She felt lost, like a child who strayed at the beach, not knowing which way to turn or where to go next.

"Olivia, honey, come home with us, and we'll get a good night's rest. It will do us all good." Holly tried, for the fourth time, to get Olivia to go home with her and Jack. She was worried about Olivia, who had been silent for most of the day. She knew how hard it was to lose someone she loved. She knew that all too well—though with her loss, she could still see her loved one, and with Olivia's, there was a dark abyss.

Olivia refused to leave the house. She worried that once she left, she might never feel her mother again, or worse, that her mother would think she had deserted her. She knew her thoughts were not rational, but she also knew that she had to stay in her mother's house. Sure as the sky was up and the ground was down, she needed to be there. Olivia looked at Holly and whispered, "I can't."

Holly turned to Jack, "Why don't you go, and I'll stay with Livi tonight, Jack. Okay?"

Peter piped in, "I'll stay, too. I'm not ready to leave either." He winked at Olivia.

"I have to work tomorrow morning," Jack said to Holly. "I'll come by afterward, if you're sure it's okay that I go. I'm happy to get my stuff and stay here if you want, sweetie." He put his arms around Holly and held her tight.

Olivia watched them—and longed for her mother.

The evening was quiet. Holly moved through the actions that she had to, cooking dinner and cleaning up. She lit candles, hoping that the familiar scents might comfort Olivia. Every action brought a reminder of the hole in her life left by her best friend. The flicker of the candles reminded her of Megan's words, *When my light goes out, just shoot me.* She cried at the thought. The scent in the air reminded Holly of Megan's energy as she had rushed by her so many times over her lifetime. *Lifetime.* What did that really mean? Was this her lifetime? Megan's lifetime seemed so short to Holly. It was like they were little girls hiding in trees and making pacts just last week, and now Megan was gone. Gone!

Peter tried to cheer up Holly and Olivia throughout the evening, not quite sure what else to do with himself. He adored Megan and still felt as though she were nearby. He knew he was just missing her, and he wished for her to be near again. His efforts at normalcy were met with polite smiles that quickly faded into silence. Eventually he honored their feelings of sadness and loss with quiet.

At about midnight, Olivia broke the silence and said, "Quiet breeds too much thought." Which made Holly and Peter raise eyebrows and give a little laugh. That was one of Megan's favorite sayings. She'd liked chattiness and felt as though sharing thoughts was vital to healthy relationships and a fun life. They began sharing their memories of the wonderful things that Megan had done, the way she kept every moment alive and fun.

Holly shared with Olivia stories of their childhood games and sleepovers, the birthday parties they had crashed, and the boys they had had crushes on. *Oh the boys!* She spoke happily of their college days, how she and Megan had been roommates and Jack had attended a school nearby, and of their weekly gatherings at the Women's Nest. Her face softened as she spoke of those get-togethers, and she remembered the ease with which they would fall into conversations and pour over their lives and eventually their books.

Peter relayed his memories of how he had adored Megan when they first met and followed her around like a puppy, enthralled with the way she looked at life as an exciting adventure, one not to be missed. He told of his admiration for her lack of needing a man in her life, and how strong she was in the face of trials and life's harder side.

Olivia cried, mostly. She cried as she laughed at their stories and as she told her own. She told them how much she already felt the void in her heart, how she wished she could be held by her mother one more time. As she spoke, the candles flickered, as if there were a breeze, and the smell of lavender and coconut instantly became more aromatic. Olivia's face lit up, and with a little laugh, she stood and stretched her arms out to her sides, closed her eyes.

"Do you smell her?" she whispered to them. "She is here! She didn't really leave me. She is here!" She twirled herself around, and sure as sugar, Holly and Peter smelled her, too.

The two of them got up and sniffed the air, nodded, as if confirmation were necessary.

Olivia reached her arms up toward the ceiling, "I love you, Mom!" she yelled.

Megan knelt beside Olivia who was asleep on the couch. "It's okay, baby. I'm here, and I'll never leave you." Even as she spoke the words, she knew she was, in fact, fading. She could sense it. It was as if the little emotional energy she had was somehow lifting away from her. With no understanding of why she had been allowed to remain on the outskirts of life, she was thankful. She could only imagine that it was her own doing, that she had willed herself to stay, unable to pass through and fully let go of her life on Earth. Olivia's well being plagued her, and the struggle to remain around her was one she was willing to fight for.

Olivia woke with a start. Her dream had seemed so real. She looked around the room and felt as though she could reach out and touch her mother. She looked at Holly and Peter, fast asleep in the recliner and the chaise lounge.

"Mom?" Olivia whispered. There was no answer. "Mom?" she said again, then held her breath, waiting, hoping for an answer she knew she would not hear.

Olivia tucked her mother's bear under her right arm and headed upstairs toward her bedroom. At the top of the landing, she stopped, drawn toward her mother's room instead of her own. She took in the rumpled bedspread. *Why make sure it's perfect?* Her mother always said, *It's just going to get wrinkly anyway*. Olivia smiled at the memory. She walked slowly into the room, feeling as though she were entering forbidden territory, and not sure why she suddenly felt as though her mother's room, the room she had slept in, wept in, and played in, felt unexpectedly unfamiliar and off limits.

She put a dab of her mother's lavender and coconut moisturizing lotion on the inside of each wrist and breathed it in. She walked to the bed and lay down slowly. The floral smell of her mother's hair conditioner still remained on her pillow and comforter.

After fifteen minutes or so, restless and unable to fall asleep, she moved to the window seat and picked up the vase she had made her mother when she was a little girl. She rolled it around in her hand and the hidden pills spilled out onto the seat and tumbled to the floor like hail from the sky, little reminders of her mother's pain left behind.

Olivia's heart beat faster in her chest. Her breathing grew louder. Her sadness turned to anger, as she remembered that her mother had *chosen* not to take the pills and to let herself die. She threw the vase across the room and yelled, "God damn it, Mom! Why didn't you take these!" She kicked at the pills and swiped the remaining ones off of the seat with a quick slash of her hand. They flew through the air like unwanted trash.

Olivia ravaged her mother's room, driven by anger that hurt to her core. She pulled open her mother's drawers and looked...for what? For a note? For something that might give Olivia a hint of information, anything that she might have left behind? She threw the underwear and socks on the floor, carelessly trampled them as she hastily made her way to the bedside table and ripped open the drawer. She grabbed her mother's journal and tried to read, but was too upset to focus. Her tears made it impossible to see the writing clearly. She threw the leather-bound journal against the wall.

Megan tried to break through to Olivia as she felt, more than saw, her daughter's heart blackening with grief. She reached for her, mentally and physically, but was blocked by her daughter's anger. *Oh, Livi, please let me in!* She was forced to watch her daughter's pain eating her from the inside out. Megan was helpless and cried a stream so thick it formed a river.

Olivia came out of the closet holding her mother's small mahogany chest in her shaking hands. She'd seen the box many times before. It held her mother's most cherished possessions. She and her mother had gone through the box many times throughout the years. She was enamored with the box itself, and it had brought fresh delight each time her mother had brought it down for her to enjoy. Megan would draw out each item very slowly, making Olivia wait what seemed like an hour for the big reveal. Olivia's eyes would grow as big as hard boiled eggs with anticipation. Megan explained the significance of each item, and wove stories so grand that Olivia felt as though she were listening to a fairy tale.

She ran her finger across the top of the chest and remembered how special she had felt when her mother had shared her secrets. She felt a touch of her anger fade as she lifted the top of the chest in search of those treasured items.

Instead, Olivia was met with an envelope that read "Olivia Leigh" in her mother's handwriting. Her hands shook as she turned the envelope over in her hands, afraid of what it might contain and the emotions it might spark. She tucked the letter into her back pocket and cleared off her mother's bed. She picked up her mother's bear from the floor where she had cast it away in her fit of rage, hugged it to her chest, and lay down. Her first breath brought her mother's smell into her lungs. Her seventh breath brought her sleep.

Olivia was thankful that Holly and Peter had left her alone. It wasn't that she didn't want to see them, but she wasn't sure she was capable of being nice to others. She climbed out of her mother's bed and walked through the warm sunlight that streaked the floor and into her mother's bathroom. She put her mother's favorite foaming bath gel into the tub, turned on the faucet, and lit her mother's Jasmine candle that sat on a little shelf next to the window. She loved that the wick was half burned already. She loved feeling as though she were close to her mother, following in her mother's rituals.

Olivia undressed, and the letter from her mother fell onto the bathroom floor. She stared at it for a moment, filled with both curiosity and a growing anger. She watched as it unfolded slightly, as if it were trying to open itself. She laid it gently on the top of the toilet, closed the door, and lowered herself into the hot bath.

Her body relaxed as she remembered the ritual of the night before, the way her mother had calmed them all, working her way down their bodies and into their souls. She was happy she had been there. She was proud of her mother and her place in the ritual, the leader. She understood, now, why she had been kept away for so many years. It was a private ceremony. It was not for kids. The thought made her even happier. She was not a child anymore. They had allowed her to be part of the ritual. That must mean that she was growing up. She smiled to herself and let her arm flop over the side of the tub as the steam filled the bathroom and fogged the window and mirror.

Olivia peeked at the letter several times before finally

leaning forward and taking it carefully between her index finger and thumb. She looked it over. The plain envelope and delicate lettering of her name reminded her of her mother's natural way, her unstructured beauty, and her ease of being. She ran her hand across the front of the envelope, turned it over, and ran her hand along the back, leaving a wet streak all the way across.

With a heavy sigh, she sat up in the tub, dried her hands on the towel that lay on the floor, and carefully opened the letter. Before reading, she closed her eyes, took a deep breath, and then straightened her back, bracing herself for what lay within.

My Dearest Olivia,

I am so sad that you have to receive such a letter from me. I always thought I'd be here to watch you grow into the beautiful, caring woman that you are already becoming. There are no words to express my sadness to be away from you. But as you know, I am always with you, feeling your pain and your joy, helping to guide your way. All you have to do is be open to me. Let me in and I will be there.

Tears streamed down Olivia's face and into the tub. She blinked often to clear them away. Shifting her body, she began again.

I know you are angry with me for making the choice to stop my treatments, and for hiding it from you. But it was something I had to do. Trust me, please. I saved you months of torture, of watching me slowly die. You may think it would have been better to have me around longer, but I wouldn't have wanted you to go through the pain of watching my body and my mind deteriorate and see me in such pain. There is a point where ailing bodies deteriorate to the point that people become unrecognizable. There is a point where their minds do not function very well. A point where a person's body becomes like an infant again, in need of constant care. I did not want you to go through that. I'm not certain I would have been able to, either. I want you to remember me as I was, happy, loving every minute of life, dancing, reading, painting, and enjoying the textures and sounds of our cozy little nest. Remember how we danced at midnight every July 4th! Remember how, when you were little, you would cuddle up in my bed and tell me the bed was too hard and we would just move to another bed, until we ended up on the couch in front of the fire—where you wanted to start out anyway.

Olivia laughed to herself, swiping again at the tears. Her body shuddered as the water in the bathtub became cool.

Remember our late night pig-out sessions and watching Lifetime television. Please try not to remember my illness, remember me for who I was, not for what I had.

You are a beautiful, brilliant girl with such a wonderful fu-

ture. I am so lucky to have you as my daughter. Take life as it is dealt to you, Olivia, and let it make you stronger, not beat you down. Never let anyone take your dreams away from you, no matter how grand or silly they seem. Paint the world, Olivia, drink it in!

I suppose we need to talk about your father. Olivia, I have kept this from you because of so many reasons—they are hard to put into words, but the least of them is that I feel that this knowledge is going to be a burden to you—a burden that in so many ways, is equal to the blessing and peace of mind it will bring you. You will see that this involves more than just you and him. For that reason, I had to make the toughest decision of my life, and then keep the truth hidden.

Do you remember when you asked me about Lawrence? Well, I didn't really tell you the whole truth, and I am sorry. It still hurts to think about him. Lawrence was a very special man to me. I might have even been in love with him. We had been seeing each other for months when your father and I spent a weekend together. But, each time I was with Lawrence after that weekend, it hurt me—the guilt of my infidelity was too painful to bear—so I ended my relationship with Lawrence. When I told him that I needed some space, he was crushed, and truthfully, so was I.

When I found out I was pregnant with you, I went away. I needed to think things through without the pressure of my friends. I know this is hard to understand. I love Holly, Peter, and Jack. But that decision was so important to me, and it would have had such a severe impact on so many people that I had to go away and clear my head.

I told everyone I was going to Italy, as you have heard, but I didn't. I wanted to go where I could be comfortable, so I went to Provincetown. I didn't do much there. I painted, I read everything I could about childbirth and pregnancy—I devoured it, really, and I thought about if I was truly ready for a baby and if I loved your father enough to spend my life with him. It was not a one-night stand, Olivia, and I know that's what you are thinking. It was so much more. I love your father so much, and did then, too. But it was a different kind of love, Olivia. And I am ever so thankful that we had you. You were meant to be, Olivia. You are the meaning in my life.

While I was in Provincetown, there was no decision to be made as far as you were concerned. I wanted you. I wanted you with all of my heart and never wavered in my desire to bear you and be your mother. I wrestled with your father, though. He's a wonderful, brilliant man. He's caring, and loving, and everything I could want. But we weren't in love. We were two people who had wondered their whole lives what it would be like to be together and we took a chance and tried it out. But it wasn't true love, Olivia, it was friend-love. Three months after I arrived in Provincetown, I decided to come back and tell him about you. I had no hopes of marriage, but thought he might want to be involved in your life in some way. Olivia, one thing you must know in your heart – I truly believe God knew I would be taken early, and that's why he allowed me to get pregnant. We were not trying to conceive a child, but God knew I needed you, somehow, and God knew you were meant to be.

Your father is Jack, Olivia, Jack Townsend.

Olivia lowered the letter and whispered, "Jack." She closed her eyes and rested her head back against the tub, the smell of her mother's foam bath surrounded her. She thought of Jack and the way he was so loving with Holly. She remembered being on his shoulders as a young girl at the Labor Day parade in the center of town. She took a deep breath and continued reading.

With my decision to raise you alone, Olivia, the road ahead seemed lined with lilies instead of tangled with barbs. I knew I could make my life work with a baby—and I wanted to! I knew Holly would jump at the chance to help me raise you, and I also believed that Jack would agree that marrying for the sake of a child, and not for the sake of love, wouldn't have been the right thing to do.

When I came back, Jack and Holly were very much in love, and already talking about marriage. I couldn't crush Holly with my news. I was afraid if I told Jack, he might feel an obligation to marry me, and that's not what I wanted. Then, when I saw how happy they were, the answer became clear. I lied. I lied to protect them. I told them that your father was a guy that I had met in Italy. You see, Livi, they became close when I left—filling the void I had left in each of their lives. They were meant for each other, and you were meant for me.

Olivia set the letter down next to the tub. *Holly? My God, Mom. You and Jack were together before Holly and Jack. Oh my God!* A strange feeling came over Olivia and she began to shake. She wasn't mad at her mother, but she was confused. Jack was her father? After all these years? He'd been around for every event in her life, and he didn't know? *My God, he doesn't know now!* Her head reeled. She turned on the hot water and lay still until the water became so warm that it brought her back to the present.

She took a deep breath and began reading again.

I loved Holly and Jack too much to put myself in the middle. I feared it would destroy all of our friendships. But mostly, I feared it would ruin Holly's life. She adored Jack, and saw him as a gift from God, which he was for her. She needed him like I needed you. I held my secret.

What about me? Olivia seethed. *I could have had a dad!*

I thought that a situation would present itself, eventually, for me to tell them the truth. At times, I wasn't sure if I had done the right thing. But then Holly lost Alissa Mae, and didn't try again to have children for many years. I knew it would crush her to know that Jack and I had made you. So again, I decided I wouldn't tell them. A few years later I became ill. When I realized I wasn't going to recover, it all made sense to me. You see, Livi, I had you so Holly could be a mother. Now that I'm gone, she has you, Jack's child, and you have your father. Baby girl, God works in mysterious ways. In our case, he created a maze that led you to have a wonderful life with me and a wonderful future with a new loving mother and a father who deserve you. And you deserve them.

God damn it, Mom! Olivia didn't know if she was more angry at her mother for not telling her who her father was or for having Jack as a father. It was all so complicated now. Jack and Holly didn't know. She couldn't tell them, which only meant one thing to her. She would never have a real father.

I know you'll be angry with me, and I don't blame you. But as you get older, I hope that you will realize why I made the decision not to tell everyone. I did it not just for me and you, but for them, too. Holly loves you like her own daughter and has since the day you were born.

This letter, Olivia, is a gift for you. It is your decision what you do with this information. You can tell everyone, or you can tell no one. That is something that only you can decide. I will be proud of you no matter how you handle this amazingly hard situation.

I love you, Olivia. I may not have been a perfect mother, but I couldn't have loved you more than I did or than I do. Live your life, honey, don't mourn me too much. I'm okay. I had a wonderful life. I had you. Carry on our ritual, Olivia, it is part of who you are now, even though you haven't experienced it. It is part of me. Holly can walk you through the ritual. I want her to. I want you to enjoy it as much as I always did. And treat yourself kindly, Livi, respect your desires and dreams. Follow them no matter how many times they change or where they might take you. Be true to your spirit. Be kind to people, and they will be kind back. And remember, when you need me, just call upon me. I'm never more than a thought away.

I love you forever, Olivia Leigh. You are my treasure.
Mom

Olivia folded the letter and placed it back on the toilet lid. She wasn't sure if she was glad that she had read it or if she wasn't—a mixture of anger, sadness, and relief swirled within her young mind. She wondered when her mother meant for her to read it.

She closed her eyes. *Jack*, she thought. *Jack Townsend.*

Jack is my father. She lay back against the bathtub, closed her eyes, and felt as though she were whole. She knew who both her parents were—both—no more mystery. A strange sensation came over her body. The anger she felt moments before dissipated, and though she was beset with sadness about losing her mother, she was not depressed. She realized that in losing her mother, she had gained the knowledge of her father. *Jack.* She repeated his name over and over in her mind. *Jack. Jack Townsend. Jack. Dad?*

As her mind relaxed, and her guard was let down, she closed her eyes. Within moments, she felt the presence of another person. She opened her eyes with a start, and looked around the small bathroom, expecting to see Holly. The steam rose in front of the window, and it was there that she saw her. Her hair was once again thick and vibrant. Her face was full, her eyes alive with love. Olivia could not make out her body, for it was engulfed in the steam, had become one with it.

"Mom?" She whispered.

Her mother nodded in silence.

"Mom!" Olivia cried. She rose, the water dripped off of her naked body, her arms, her fingertips, her hair.

Her mother moved toward her, arm's reach away. Olivia found her beautiful, peaceful. She was stunned into silence. Her body shook from the cool air on her wet skin. She didn't reach for a towel. She could not move her limbs for she was entranced with the vision of her mother, so real, so lively.

Megan reached her arms out to her daughter, though she somehow knew they could not touch.

Olivia reached for her mother. Her hand moved right through her mother's arm, as if it were a cloud. Olivia screamed, "Mom!"

Megan spoke, and it was heard as a rush of air, like a breathy whisper, "My love," she said.

Olivia's eyes lit up. Her heart pounded.

Another breathy whisper, "I'm sorry."

Olivia cried, choking out her words, "It's okay. I love you, Mom." Warm tears made their way down her wet face. She didn't notice.

"You'll be okay," Megan said. "You have to live your life."

Olivia nodded, her throat would not release the words that her heart tried to put forth.

As her image faded away, Megan said, "It wasn't fair, the waiting. Please…forgive me." And she vanished into the steam, as if she had never existed.

Olivia reached out, wailing, "Mom!" she grabbed at steam. "Mom! Come back!" Olivia fell to her knees, sobbing, "I forgive you, Mom. I do."

Holly rushed into the bathroom and found Olivia kneeling in the bathtub, naked and shivering, tears streaming down her face. "Oh, Livi," she said, "let's get you a towel."

Dazed, Olivia whispered, "Mom!"

"I know, honey. We all miss her very much." Holly wrapped a large towel around Olivia and caught the faintest whiff of lavender and coconut. “Smells like her in here, huh?” she smiled.

Olivia, still unable to believe what she had seen, simply nodded as she gazed straight ahead and into the steam that was vanishing just as her mother had moments before.

“Jack, I found some things on Megan when she…the night...of our ritual,” Holly said in a hushed voice. She didn’t want to alert Olivia who was upstairs packing a bag.

“What did you find?” he asked.

Holly moved to the kitchen and took down a large wooden bowl that sat atop the refrigerator. She removed a smaller box and placed it on the table.

Jack walked over and gazed into the box. “What is it, honey?”

Holly reached in and took out a few photographs. She handed them to Jack and smiled.

His face warmed at the sight of Olivia’s sleeping face and her funny homemade tiara which sat crooked on her head. He looked up at Holly, fresh tears in his eyes.

“She had them tucked in her bra, right over her heart,” Holly said. “She knew, Jack. She knew she was going to go that night.” Threatened by tears, she busied herself at the sink.

Jack unfolded the newspaper article and was not surprised to see Lawrence Childs. His smile quickly faded as he remembered his many conversations with Megan about dating Lawrence. He could tell, from the first time he and

Lawrence had met, how in love with Megan Lawrence had been. It was not something he'd said—or even how he had acted. It was the way he had looked at her. The way his eyes had followed her every move with a longing—a desire—that one could almost bump into if they crossed between the two. Jack had asked Megan on several occasions why she didn't date him more seriously, though to be truthful, he was always glad she hadn't. His own selfishness now came back and lay on his shoulders like a heavy weight. Her answers were always a little vague and a little unsure, almost like a child's. *Oh, please, Jack, we're just friends. I wouldn't want to ruin the relationship we have.* She had a hundred excuses—if she had one. Jack wished now that he had pushed Megan harder. He would have liked to see her in love, really in love, with someone who loved her back, someone like Lawrence. She had deserved it. She had given to others and hadn't asked for anything in return. He refolded the article and set it gently in the box.

Jack ran his large fingers across Megan's smiling face in the second photo. She was in the center of the photograph with one arm slung over Holly's shoulder and the other around Jack's waist. Peter was crouched down in front of Megan, reaching up with his left hand, his palm turned to rest in Holly's hand. Until then, Jack had been able to hold in his emotions. The tears, however, could no longer stay at bay. They tumbled down his cheeks and onto the table.

Holly walked behind him and put her arms around his neck, rested her cheek against his back, and breathed in his scent. He turned and embraced her, unashamed of weeping for his friend.

"I remember when she did the whole princess thing," Holly said. "She was just so...there...for Olivia. You know? She was a great mother, Jack. How can I ever really take her place? What if I'm no good?"

Jack looked at her pained and beautiful face and cupped her cheek. She turned into his palm, soaked up the security of him.

"You are going to be wonderful, Holly," he said. "You are wonderful. Look how long you have been caring for both Megan and Olivia. It's almost as if you two were sisters. In fact, sometimes it was hard to see where she ended and you began. Olivia adores you, and you adore her. She doesn't expect you to be Megan. She just needs love, Hol, and you have plenty of that to give."

"I hope you're right. I'd hate to disappoint Megan. I do love Olivia, Jack. She's like the daughter that I could never have." Holly looked at Jack guiltily, ashamed of her own insecurities—and appalled by her deceit. She thought about Jack's words and hoped they were true.

"You will be magnificent, Holly. You are going to be a wonderful mother to Olivia." He hugged Holly around her waist, believing every word he said.

After a few minutes, Holly pulled back gently from Jack and said, "There's more."

He lifted his eyes in question.

Holly nodded and pulled a small plastic bag out of the

box. Inside the bag there was a balled-up piece of aluminum foil. Holly unwrapped it and exposed a mound of pills that she had found in Megan's skirt pocket the morning after the ritual. She held them out for Jack to see.

Jack asked, "What is that? Her medications?"

Holly shook her head. "I don't think so. I think they were something she could take to...you know...to die."

"No, n—" Jack said, shaking his head. "Megan wouldn't do that. We can get them analyzed. We can find out." He picked up a few of the pills in his hand and looked closely. "These are Percocet. Don't you remember when I took them for my torn Achilles?"

The truth of the situation set in, and tears sprung to Holly's eyes. She sighed. "There's no need to get them analyzed, Jack. She told me and Livi she stopped taking her meds so we all wouldn't have to suffer through her deterioration. She wanted to die quickly. I *know* what these pills are, or what they were intended for, at least. I have no question about it. I just thought you should know. I had to tell someone, you know?" Holly couldn't stop the flow of tears. She sat down in a chair at the table and buried her face in her hands. "Oh, Jack. I understand," she sobbed, gasping for breath. "I understand why she didn't want it to take a long time, but still. It still hurts. It still feels like we were robbed of her, you know? What if they find a cure in the next month? What if she could be here right now? Why did she choose to end it alone?"

Jack moved to hold her in his arms, and stroked her

back. "Holly, honey, you know they aren't going to find a cure in the next month. She did what she had to do. You, of all people, knew Megan best. You know," he covered her heart with his hand, "you know in your heart that she knew what was right for her, for Olivia. She wouldn't have done it if there was even a slight chance that she could recover. Even if she would have taken the pills, she would have known what she was doing. You have to trust that." He looked away, "Besides, she didn't end it alone. She was with you, and Olivia, and Peter." *But not me, damn it!* he chided himself. *I should have been there!*

"But she didn't take them, Jack. They were still in her pocket. That means that her body made the decision for her. That she didn't do it, right?" Holly asked, looking for something other than the truth to cling to, some shred of decency for her best friend, and purposely pushing the thought, *Or was she going to swallow them all?* from her mind.

"Yes, of course," he said. "Her body just let go, that's all. She was probably going to take them, but there was no need. She died in her sleep, right? Isn't that what you told me?" Jack said.

"Yes," she said. "We all had such a good time at our ritual. It was like she was healthy again. I forgot, for a while, that she was sick. She was like her old self, laughing and dancing around. She didn't complain or act like she couldn't keep up." Holly wiped her eyes.

"But that was Megan, wasn't it? That's who she was. The essence of her was life itself. She wasn't one to complain or ask for special attention. She always made sure everyone had a good time," Jack said. "I remember at summer camp when we were kids. I would tell her I was bored, and within minutes she'd have me laughing and running around. When we saw each other, summer after summer, it was like no time had passed at all. That's how she was, Hol. That's who she was. She went out of this world with all of the glory of her natural being. You should be happy about that. So what if she had pills in her pocket! It doesn't even matter, really, does it?"

"I guess you're right," Holly relented. "It wouldn't matter if she took it or if she didn't. She left us on her terms in any case—and she was happy. She left when she was ready. I just miss her so much already, you know? It's really, really hard—and poor Olivia." Holly's heart hurt when she thought of the emptiness in her, and realized it was probably not nearly as empty as what Olivia was feeling.

Jack held Holly for another moment and then looked back in the box. There, at the bottom of the box, twisted all unto itself, was Megan's Yin necklace. Jack smiled and fingered the rough chain. The memories that he'd hidden for so many years came rushing to the forefront of his mind, knocking to be set free. The feeling overwhelmed him, and he had to sit down.

The Yin rested in his hand like a fine stone, cool and rough. He wrapped his fist around the charm and put it to his forehead, and closed his eyes as the memories came flooding back.

The smell of the night sea air had wafted around them. He could still feel her hands on his back, softly at first, then rough, as if she couldn't get enough of him. He remembered the way her body was flecked with sand, and how it made her giggle—and how those giggles turned to sensual moans and gasps of pleasure. The memories of the weekend they shared, those three glorious days, brought on a blush that climbed up his neck and burned into his cheeks.

The ease of their togetherness, like it was something they had done many times before—and the ill-fitting feeling that had flittered around him that he had refused to acknowledge at the time—he had desperately *wanted* to be in love with Megan—and then she was gone. She had disappeared without returning his phone calls, heading to Italy to study painting with some other famous artist. He hadn't even thought to ask who it was she was studying under. At the time, he had thought it was just another of Megan's whimsical trips, one of her wild excursions that brought her such joy. She had done that, from time to time, as she had noted in her letters during the autumns and winters when they were growing up, and again throughout college breaks. He used to vie for those summers, to be able to incite such excitement in Megan. She had gone to California with an aunt, Montana with her mother, and even New Mexico on her own—spur of the moment trips. She would write such striking details upon her return that Jack felt as though he had shared her private moments and had taken the trips right along with her.

The trip to Italy, however, had nearly broken him. When she had left, he had felt as though even functioning were difficult. He had thought about her night and day, anxious to see her again. He had longed for her as he had never had for any other woman.

Then Holly had called. She and Jack had become friends when Megan had introduced them in college. Though there had never been any romantic interest on either side and the friendship was nowhere near as deep as his friendship with Megan, the camaraderie had been nice, and he had looked forward to seeing her and commiserating about the vast hole their mutual friend had left in him.

In an effort to quell their loneliness, each had allowed the other to fill the void Megan had left in their lives. It quickly became apparent that Holly had no idea that Jack and Megan had been together. Jack decided not to divulge it to Holly after all, believing that Megan probably had her own reasons to keep it a secret.

As it turned out, he and Holly shared much in common, and a quick jog had turned to dinner, which turned to lunch the next day and a visit to a museum the next. Five nights later, dinner led to dessert of another kind, which led to breakfast the next morning—and every morning thereafter. They couldn't have stopped what was developing if they had tried. They had fit so well together that there had never been any question of it being right or wrong. There had never been any discussion of it at all. It just was.

Jack realized that while he *wished* he could have been in

love with Megan, he was not. He was in love with Holly. She was level-headed, loving, positive, and though she was not creative, as Megan was, she was interesting and intelligent and supportive and not afraid to love, which was the one fault that he could tell Megan possessed. He had always felt as though there were a wall that Megan erected, something to keep others out of her little world. And yet, he had fallen for her over and over again during each summer when they were growing up, and the night on the beach, when he had held her in his arms, although he had felt as though he had made a fissure in her wall, he knew he had not broken through—his heart and hers had not become one.

From the evening that Holly had shown up at his house to fix him dinner, and he had watched her from behind, her brown hair brushing her shoulders as she reached into his cabinets, Jack felt as if she'd done it a thousand times before, as if she had always been there, as if she belonged there. When they touched, his heart was satiated and happy, not lustful or panicked. To Jack, that feeling of fullness made him whole.

Jack wondered, as he held Megan's Yin in his hand, if the trip to Italy was not an artistic jaunt at all, but one of contemplation. The thought lingered in his mind as Holly walked behind him and placed her hands on his shoulders.

"She was wearing that," Holly said.

The statement took Jack by surprise. He hadn't seen Megan wear the necklace since the day he put it around her neck. He opened his palm and stared at the Yin.

"I wonder what it meant to her, where she got it," Holly said, curiously.

Jack held his breath, as tears hedged the corners of his eyes. *Megan never told her either*, he thought. A lone tear found its way down his face and into his palm. He squeezed his eyes shut and shook his head.

Holly misread Jack's actions, "I don't know either. It must have really meant something wonderful to her." She rubbed Jack's neck.

Jack felt both guilt and happiness. The thought of Megan wearing her Yin meant much to him, touched him in a way that he hadn't thought of for many years. If she knew she was going to die, did she want to be buried with it on? Was it meant as a sign to Jack?

Holly interrupted his thoughts, "Maybe it's from the guy in Italy."

Jack's breath caught. *Could it have been?* The thought had never even crossed his mind. He and Holly had been so intertwined when Megan came back, and Megan had acted truly happy for them. There was never any animosity or awkward feelings or glances. No, certainly he was reading too much into this.

"What do you think?" Holly asked, as she came around the table and sat next to Jack.

"I'm…not sure," Jack mumbled. He quickly wiped his eyes with the back of his hand and closed his fist again. He looked at Holly and wondered just how to tell her. He'd never lied to her before, never had a need to, though he never told her about he and Megan, either. *Does a lie by omission count?* He looked into her trusting brown eyes, which looked back at him with warmth and love, and could muster nothing more than a shrug. Disappointed in himself, he let his eyes drift away from Holly and to the refrigerator. It was there that he saw the photographs of Olivia and Megan in all phases of life. He'd seen them a hundred times before, but it occurred to him that he'd never really looked at them. He moved toward the pictures.

The smiling, happy faces of Megan and Olivia stared playfully back at Jack. Photos of them building a snowman, arm in arm in front of Megan's murals, Olivia in last year's school play—and then he saw, really saw, Olivia's face. Her dimples mirrored his own, her hair fell straight, in stark contrast to Megan's curls. Jack reached up and touched his own fine hair. *I'm reading too much into this. She could look like Peter, or even Holly for that matter.* Jack turned his back and walked away.

He gazed into the yard, unable to stop his mind from wandering down that path. *Could Olivia be my child? Why wouldn't Megan have told me?* He quickly did the math in his head, something he had never thought to do, and realized, with a shock, that Olivia could, in fact, be his daughter.

Compelled by something he did not understand, yet felt bound to follow, he placed his hand against the glass of the kitchen window. A flow of warm air whipped through him, though the window was closed. As he stood paralyzed and perplexed, *It was for the best*, filtered into his ear like a whisper.

Chapter Six

Olivia walked outside dressed in her black knee-length silk dress, the one her mother had bought her when they had gone to see *Rent*, the musical. The morning was brisk, and she thought for a moment about walking back inside and grabbing her sweater, but decided against it because her high heels were hard to walk in and she was already halfway to the car. She took in the light blue sky and the few clouds that meandered slowly above her, wondering if her mother was nearby. She couldn't shake the feeling that cremation couldn't have been what her mother had wanted. If she were cremated, would that mean that she was really gone, *truly* gone, forever? She never had a chance to ask her mother what happened to someone's soul after they were cremated, but she'd assumed it wasn't good. This unknown rode heavily on her shoulders. She fiddled with her dress and began to sweat under her arms which annoyed her. Nerves! She hated them. Even on a chilly day she would be the sweaty girl! Urgh!

"Come on, Jack, we'll be late," Holly said.

Jack finished tying his tie and rubbed his hands down the front of his black suit. "I'm coming," he said, quietly. He looked at Holly, whose blue dress against her tanned skin took his breath away. Jack hadn't been able to think of anything other than Megan and their weekend together since the other night in Megan's kitchen. He couldn't help but wonder if Olivia was his child. It would be just like Megan, given the circumstances when she had arrived back in town and found that he and Holly were a couple, to withhold that information in an effort not to hurt them. *God damn it.*

He reached into his pocket where he'd safely stashed Megan's Yin necklace. "Do you think Olivia is okay?" he asked.

Holly rushed around the bedroom, agitated. She dropped to her knees in the closet and tossed out shoe after shoe, looking for her high heels. "Aha!" She slipped them on and found dangling earrings to match her dress. "Ready!" She slowed for a moment and looked out the window. "Would you be if Megan were your mom?" she asked.

"No, I guess not," Jack said. He stood behind Holly at the window. They watched Olivia, sitting in the back of Jack's car, fiddling with the edge of her dress. "Poor girl."

Holly patted his hand and walked toward the door. "We all miss her. We'll help Olivia, Jack. We'll get her through this." *If only you knew. You could help her more than anyone else. How do I tell you that Megan raised the daughter that I never could?* Holly nestled the thoughts back into the confines of her busy mind and headed toward the stairs. Her own guilt kept her tears at bay.

"Holly, are you sure this is what Mom wanted? I mean, cremation is so...final," Olivia said from the back seat of the car.

Holly turned to face her and was momentarily struck by her beauty. She had to blink a few times to ward off her tears. "Yes, Olivia, I'm quite sure. Ever since we were young, your mother had a real aversion to being buried. We used to walk through the graveyards near my mom's house, and your mom would talk all about what happened to the bodies after they were buried. She said it grossed her out. Let's just say she really didn't want to be in the ground." She smiled at Olivia.

"That sounds like Mom." Olivia looked out the window at the passing trees. "But what happens to her after? You know, after they cremate her, what happens to *her*?" The pain in Olivia's voice tugged on Jack's heart.

"It's simple, Livi," he said. "Your body is like a peanut shell, and your soul is like the peanut. Once someone passes on, their soul, or the peanut, lifts from them and moves into their next life. The body is like the empty shell. It's a physical structure, but it's empty." He looked in the rearview mirror and watched Olivia contemplate his words.

"I guess you could be right," she said.

"Where did you hear that, Jack? That's a wonderful way

of explaining it." Holly looked at Olivia. "He's right, you know, he's exactly right. The body is simply an empty frame. The important part, the soul, lives on."

"I heard it," Jack began, glancing again in the rearview mirror, "from Olivia's mother."

"Mom told you that?" Olivia asked.

"Mm-hmm, it's funny, I hadn't remembered that until just now," Jack smiled at Holly.

"When did she tell you that? That's pretty deep," Holly said.

"Not for Megan. Remember who we're talking about here," Jack said, and they all agreed with a little laugh. "We must have been about twelve or so. It was at summer camp. The camp mascot was this dog, a huge Newfoundland that had thick chocolate brown fur." He looked in the mirror at Olivia again. "Its fur was exactly like your mother's hair."

Olivia smiled.

"Anyway, the dog had been there every summer, for like a hundred summers. That summer, it died. We were all really sad. He was the biggest, happiest dog we had ever seen! His name was Lacky, like the camp, Lakamar. Anyway, when he died, all of us kids got together and held a ceremony for him. Megan, of course, was the leader. Even back then she could hold a wicked ritual!" Jack adjusted himself in his seat and took a deep breath.

"So there we were, all gathered around the bonfire by the lake, and your mother, Olivia, was hosting this service. She took us back through each summer with Lacky. She must have talked for forty or fifty minutes, way too long for a bunch of kids, but she held our attention like she was a real live movie. Anyway, she described the summers with him and how wonderful he was, and in the end, when everyone was brought to tears, she put her hands on her hips and said, 'We can't sit and cry over Lacky! Why, he's still here with us! Don't you feel him?' And everyone concurred, nodded, and she dove right in again. 'His soul is right over there!' Jack pointed for emphasis. 'His body might be lifeless, but it's just like an empty peanut shell. His soul has already moved on! His soul is everywhere!' Everyone cheered and laughed, and suddenly Lacky's dying wasn't so bad anymore. We all felt like he was right there with us, thanks to your mom."

Olivia imagined her mother at twelve years old, taking charge of the group and making everyone see the bright side of the dog's death.

"That sounds like Megan!" Holly said with a smile. "Livi, are you okay with our decision to hold a small ceremony now and a private ceremony later?"

Olivia looked up from her lap, "Yes. That's what I want. I think everyone who knew Mom needs to be able to say goodbye," she looked out the window again, "but I think she would have wanted us all to say goodbye privately, too."

Peter straightened his tie and tried to mentally prepare for Megan's ceremony. He still could not believe she was gone. It was as if her life had happened in fast forward, at least that's how it felt to him. He felt cheated, ripped off, like he didn't get enough time with her, but then he felt guilty for feeling that way, after all, he was not Olivia, the one who really deserved more time with her.

There was something about Megan, something more alive than he'd ever felt in any other human being. She had kept her eye on what she had wanted out of life, and had never let people dissuade her from following her dreams.

Peter inspected his face in the mirror, which to his surprise, looked to him much as it did when he was younger. He put his face closer to the mirror, peered deeper into his own eyes, and wondered why he saw emptiness there. It was no wonder at all, really, he mused. He knew why he saw emptiness in his own eyes when Megan's reflected a full life up until the moment she died.

"Damn it," Peter murmured as he walked away from the mirror. On his way to the door, he passed by a photo of himself and his father. He picked it up and touched the delicate lines of the antique frame. He remembered when the picture had been taken, a few months before his mother left him and his father. He looked closely at his father in his white t-shirt, khaki pants, brown shoes, and full head of hair which was slicked back with something like Brylcreem. Peter wondered why his mother had left them. Was it really so bad for her, taking care of them? He peered into his father's eyes for the answer, but saw nothing of consequence. He saw a contented man.

Peter had few memories of his mother. Sometimes he couldn't decipher what was real and what was merely hope.

She had not been beautiful, that he remembered. She had been an average-looking woman with short dark hair and a fine figure. He didn't remember her hugging him much, though he remembered his father's full embrace, long, strong, and often. His mother, it seemed to him, was always milling around the kitchen or ironing. He remembered that sometimes she read books to him.

Peter did remember longing for a real mother, though, and the memory was painful. He remembered visiting his friends' houses where the mothers were always baking cookies, setting up crafts for them, or playing games. He remembered long hugs his friends would receive, with a firmly planted kiss on his forehead; his friends always cringed and tried to pull away, and all the while Peter was hoping the mothers would grab him and slather him with that kind of love.

"Why'd you do it, Ma?" Peter whispered, though he knew he could ask the question one hundred times and never receive an answer.

He had asked his father once, and only once, "Dad, why did Mommy leave us?"

His father's stern response had told him the subject was off limits, "Your mother didn't leave us, son, she was running away from herself."

That answer left Peter wondering how someone could run away from herself, and why she would want to. He pictured someone running in circles while peeking behind her, like a dog chasing its tail. For years this vision haunted him.

His grandmother wasn't much help, either. "There are

just some people in this world that weren't meant to be tied down," she had said, "and your mother was one of them."

That comment left him with even worse visions of his mother tied down somewhere in the house when he wasn't around, which led to him worrying that his father was some kind of monster that he hadn't found out about yet. But that fear faded fast, as his father always woke him with a kindness that lingered through the days and into the nights. It was a kindness that permeated his being. When he went to school, he knew his father would always be there upon his return. He didn't worry that he might disappear as his mother did.

His father's job at the steel mill was flexible, so he could work while Peter was at school, and then again at night after Peter was in bed sleeping, when Mrs. Waters would come and sit at the house, but Peter hadn't known about the latter. He hadn't known that his father went back to work while he slept. He was told after a few years had passed since his mother had left. His father had mentioned it in passing, having assumed it was prior knowledge for Peter.

At first it had scared Peter a little to know that his father had left him at night, but then, he came to revel in the fact that his father always came back, which was something his mother never did.

As his mind vacillated between thoughts of Megan and of his father, he realized that he had been living his life just as Megan had pointed out. He'd been afraid to commit. Peter placed the frame gently back on the table and whispered, mostly to himself, "Goodbye, Mom." He then picked up the phone to call Cruz.

Megan hovered above and watched the small gathering take shape. She was pleased that they had chosen the Nauset Lighthouse property to hold the gathering. Never one for conventional religion, she would have been disappointed if the ceremony had been held at a temple. Megan held her breath as Holly and Jack arrived with Olivia in tow. She was so beautiful, and yet her face, her eyes, looked as though she had aged five years in a few short days.

Oh, my baby girl. I am so sorry. Megan reached out, yearning to touch Olivia, to make her feel safe and happy once again, though she knew it was a hopeless feat. She could not touch Olivia from her new world.

Sadness permeated Megan's form, as if a heavy cloud had overwhelmed her and weighed her down. Tears streamed from her eyes as she realized that her lower form was rapidly turning a sad shade of gray. She somehow knew this was reflective of Olivia's sadness. She also knew that she could not fix her daughter's despair. She was gone. Gone! Her tears turned to sobs, and were quickly swept away into a path as rough as a raging river, snaking its way to a nearby cloud. She watched the sun disappear and felt, more than saw, Olivia look up toward the sky.

Megan didn't know what remained in her form that was now her body, but if she had a heart, it was lifted at the thought of Olivia finding her above.

Holly and Jack were unaware that Olivia had stopped walking, and they continued toward the lighthouse. Olivia, however, stood in the dune grass, just past the parking lot, and looked up at the shadowy cloud, unable to put her arms around the emotions and feelings that swam within her. Sad? Nervous? Angry? Mostly, she just felt empty—empty as a dark well with no water to fill it up. Somehow, she thought she would be prepared for the day. She'd seen the need to say goodbye, and she had thought she'd be strong enough to see it through without hysterics. She knew it would be hard, but she hadn't imagined the despair that she now felt; nausea, pain, and tumult boiled in her belly.

The sky changed from a gloriously sunny day to suddenly murky and gray. *Funny, that's just how I feel,* Olivia thought to herself. She felt her mother's presence. She could not say why, or how, or even what made her feel that it was her mother. Yet somehow she was certain that her mother was near. She looked to the sky and mouthed, *Mom*. She knew, then, that she was not alone, and her pain subsided. She was not empty. Her mother was nearby.

Peter reached his hand across the front seat and said, "I'm glad you are here." He smiled and squeezed Cruz's hand.

As they rounded the curve into the parking lot, they saw Olivia standing alone in the grass, looking up at the sky. Peter maneuvered the car into a parking space.

Cruz's voice was deep, reassuring. "Of course, Peter."

His eyes peered directly into Peter's heart. "I'm always here for you. Don't you know that?"

Peter could not bring himself to speak. His heart was soft, his emotions raw. He had lost one of his best friends, and because of her, he had begun to open himself to another. He stared into Cruz's eyes for a full two minutes before Cruz broke the gaze and nodded towards Olivia.

"Do you think she's okay?" Cruz asked.

"I'm not sure. I'm not okay, I can't imagine that she is," Peter said.

"Let's go. She needs someone right now, and you are special to her."

Cruz's understanding warmed Peter, who realized he'd made the right decision to trust Cruz. He hugged Cruz, thanked him.

Together they walked toward Olivia, who looked as though she were in a trance. She stared up at the clouds, her long thin arms hung loosely at her sides. The wind blew wispy strands of her hair across her face. She looked surprisingly peaceful on what was sure to be a heart-wrenching day. Peter caught a glimpse of Holly walking toward Olivia and held his hand up as if to say, "I've got her. It's okay." Holly smiled, waved, and walked back toward Jack.

"Hey, baby girl," Peter said gently, placing his hand on Olivia's shoulder, and turning his own eyes up toward the sky.

Olivia's body stiffened. "That's what Mom always called me," she whispered.

"I'm sorry. I just say what I feel when I see you," Peter said with a soft smile. He reached out and took Olivia's hand. "Are you okay? Is this going to be too much for you?" he asked.

"She's here, Peter. It's okay," Olivia said and looked again toward the sky.

Cruz and Peter exchanged a look of concern.

"Of course she is," Peter said gently. "She will always be here, Olivia. She is part of you now. You carry her in your heart." He reached up and carefully wiped a tear from Olivia's cheek.

Olivia, still looking up toward the sky, said, "Peter, she's *here*. That's her," she pointed to the gray cloud. "She took my feelings and made them real. She made today gray instead of sunny."

As Peter opened his mouth to speak, Cruz tenderly touched Peter's arm and shook his head. He moved closer to Olivia and looked up at the sky with her.

"You know, honey, I think you're right. Peter's told me about the connection you two have always had." Cruz kissed the top of Olivia's head and put his strong arm around her lower back. "She loves you, sweetie," he said.

Olivia curled into him, and let her tears fall onto his white shirt. She looked up, sniffled, and cracked a slight smile. "How come I only see you a few times each year," she asked, "and you still know how to make me feel better?"

Peter placed his arms around her, and together, Cruz and Peter embraced Olivia. They absorbed the impact of her sobbing body, hoping to lessen her pain.

Megan felt her energy drain as her form returned to its previous color. She felt light headed and could only liken it to the way she felt after being ill and not eating for a day or two, the listless, weak feeling that kept people in bed for an extra day. Was this what it would be like? As she eased into the other realm, would she simply become less *there*? She feared this, though she knew it was inevitable.

Below, Peter, Cruz, and Olivia slowly parted. Each gazed up at the sky with wonder as the cloud changed from gray to white. The sun peeked out just slightly from behind. A knowing look passed between the two men.

Hand in hand, they walked toward the lighthouse where friends and family had gathered. The tears on their faces slowly dried from the cool ocean air. Peter and Cruz guided Olivia to a seat between Holly and Jack who immediately reached out to her. Jack put his arm around her shoulder and Holly squeezed her hand. Peter and Cruz settled in next to Jack. Jack took Peter's hand in his own.

Jack smiled at Peter and pulled him closer. He leaned down and whispered, "It's about time he became one of us."

A flush rushed up Peter's chest to his face, and he smiled. Peter glanced at Cruz, who was still wiping tears from his eyes, and he took Cruz's thick, strong hand in his own. Warmth ran through Peter. He knew he was in the right company. He had done the right thing.

Megan watched her friends from above, linked like a lifeline, and reveled in her daughter's safety. She shed tears of happiness, a gentle trickle across the sky, above the clouds, for only Megan to see.

She marveled at how many people had shown up for the gathering. Throughout her life she had believed that she'd been somewhat invisible. She had lived her life in what felt like a closed circle of people. She couldn't imagine that she'd touched so many lives, that she was memorable to so many.

Megan spied Lawrence Childs amongst the crowd. A rush ran through her like a school girl waiting to be asked to dance, bringing new energy to her tired form. Touched that he would come, her hand instinctively covered her heart.

She was surprised to see two of her college professors and many of her high school friends. She wondered how they could have heard so quickly of her passing. Moreover, she wondered why, after so many years, they would make a special trip to bid her farewell.

Various relatives had come to say goodbye. Uncle Carl and Aunt Bettie, Uncle Mark and Aunt Eva, and their children sat teary-eyed and sullen. Almost all of Megan's cousins were in attendance. They whispered amongst themselves, wiped their sad eyes, and took turns paying their respects to Olivia.

Megan's biggest regret was that her mother was not there. Her mother's health was not strong, but her love beat on like a bass drum. The three-hour trip would have been too much for her mother's frail body to take. At seventy-five, she was cruelly stricken with Relapsing-Remitting Multiple Sclerosis which caused her great pain. When Megan had swooped down the day before, she had found her mother completely fatigued, in great pain, and grasping to stay coherent. Her cognition had become even more fragile. Seeing her had made Megan weep so hard that she had ached, she had stayed a deep shade of gray all night. Megan's newfound knowledge that her mother would soon be with her, and that her mother's deteriorating body and pain would vanish, as hers had, lessened her anguish and helped to bring her form back to its transparent state before the arrival of her family and friends.

Holly stood before the group to begin the ceremony. When she opened her mouth, however, she had to close it and swallow back the tears that vied for release. She looked down, curled her lips inside her mouth and clenched them with her teeth. *Do this for Megan.* She took a deep breath and began, "Thank you all for sharing in this special day with us. Megan would be so pleased to see each of you." A forced smile appeared and quickly faded to a quivering lip. "I'm not sure I can put into words what I feel for Megan. She is like my other half. She is my true sister. I will not say 'was' because, to me, Megan lives on. She lives on in Olivia." Holly took another deep breath and gave in to her tears. "She lives on in me, and Jack, and Peter, and I am sure she lives on in each of you, as well." Holly paced slowly by the rows of flowers at the base of the lighthouse, her fingers trailed along the petals. When she began again, her eyes sparkled behind her tears. "Megan is life itself. That's how I think of her. She was a whirlwind when she was on Earth, and I'm sure she is creating something wonderful in her afterlife. Megan grasped each day. Even when we were little, she lived each moment as if it were an adventure, a blank page in a book waiting to be filled with something exciting." Holly stopped to catch her breath and looked at Olivia, who was holding Jack's hand while tears streamed down her face. Holly cocked her head and furrowed her brow, as if to say, *I know, honey. I'm so sorry.*

Holly spoke softly, "Once Olivia came along, Megan lived every second of her life for her. It started before she was even born. Megan inherently knew how to be a wonderful mother and gave her free time up to Olivia without concern for herself or her own needs. She relished her. Every breath she took, she took for Olivia, and it paid off, because Olivia is a vibrant, wonderful young woman."

Olivia flushed, openly crying.

"I'd like to thank Megan for letting me be part of her wonderful world, and part of Olivia's." Holly raised her eyes toward the sky, and reached her arms up, as if by doing so she could embrace Megan one last time. "I love you, Meggie! Thank you for being you!"

Reverberations from the applause could be felt all the way up in Megan's world. She reached down toward Holly, and whispered, "No, Hol, thank you!"

Holly closed her eyes just as Megan's words swept into her ears like a rush of warm air. Shaken, she opened her eyes quickly and brought her hands to her mouth. As her knees began to buckle, she felt Jack's strong hands on her waist from behind, guiding her back to her seat, where she instinctively held Olivia's hand in her own.

Megan was touched as each of the guests came to the front, as they felt compelled to do so, and spoke of who she was and what she had meant to them. Much of what was said surprised her. She hadn't thought of herself as being *interesting*, or *prolific*. She certainly didn't feel as though she had reached out in any significant way to the people who spoke so warmly about her. That saddened her, too. Was she all that they made her out to be? Had she not been and they merely wished she were? Had she been a good friend, a good student, a caring partner on projects? Her head swam in circles.

Lawrence Childs stood before the group. For the first time, she saw, really saw, the emptiness in his eyes. Those eyes that were always so full of life and seemed so endless, appeared dull and sullen. The fact that he had come forward was not a surprise to Megan, but as his story unfolded, she was completely taken aback. She listened intently, watching him move his arms about, as if he were directing a symphony. His navy blue suit moved through the air with a comfort that she rarely saw in other people when she had been on Earth, yet Lawrence had seemed to emote from the very moment they met. His voice was soft, yet intent, as though each word was vitally important.

Lawrence told of the first time he had seen Megan, which had not been at the flea market, as she had thought.

"I feel a little like an imposter, when it comes to Megan." His voice instantly made her form turn a vibrant red. "You see," he looked down at his hands, then back at the crowd, "I adored her. At first, it was her talent that had caught my eye. When she was a sophomore at the Rhode Island School of Design, I happened to be visiting one of my old professors. He brought me to meet Megan's art professor, and it was there, in his class, that I first saw her art on display." He looked to the sky. A tear slowly made its way down his flawless cheek. "It took my breath away. I went back each day for a week to the classroom. I…I spied on her," he spat his confession, embarrassed and hushed. "I lingered outside the classroom just to catch a glimpse of her." He looked at Holly, and then to Olivia and Jack. "She never knew, but once I saw the creature that brought such beautiful art to life, well, her energy captivated me. She was like a burst of sunlight on a dreary day."

Megan tried to pull memories from that time from the recesses of her mind. She was unable to recall ever having seen Lawrence on campus. She tilted her head and listened for more.

"I followed her art through her teacher, her progress, and her shows. When I finally got up the courage to approach her at the flea market, which was years later, I actually had a hard time speaking. I remember taking her hand in mine and feeling this..." he looked again to the sky, and brought his right hand to his chest, "well...she stole my heart the moment we touched. She was more than beautiful—she was life itself, vibrant and interesting. Megan brought her deepest thoughts out through her artwork, her murals. And what I learned, as I watched her grow over the years, is that she didn't compromise her values or her opinions. She lived them. She valued herself and her dreams." He grasped for just the right words. "To encounter Megan was to encounter an amazingly spiritual being. Lord forgive me, I never let Megan know how I felt." Lawrence stopped speaking to wipe his eyes with his handkerchief. He held a hand up to the silent crowd, "I'm sorry. I don't know why I feel like you need to know this, but I do. I've been silent too long. I've lost the woman whom I have come to believe was the love of my life."

There was a collective gasp. Holly put her arm around Olivia. Jack looked behind Olivia and winked at Holly. She couldn't help but feel sad for her friend, having missed out on such a wonderful man. She wished Megan could have been completed by finding her soul mate and experiencing the love and happiness that she had deserved.

Lawrence began again, "Around Megan, I was another person altogether, and yet, this warm, loving woman, who so touched my life, also scared me. I felt so much for her, and I didn't know how to make it okay. I suppose I just want to say to her, to Megan, you were an inspiration to me. You touched my life. You gave me a friendship without demands and filled my heart with happiness. It made me happy to see you whole, you and Olivia. I'm a better person for knowing you." He lowered his head. "Megan was so confident in her life, so complete, and shortly after we met, she was pregnant with Olivia." Lawrence looked around at the questioning eyes that looked upon him. "I wish Olivia had been my child," he took a deep breath. "I wish that Megan and I could have remained together, had a family."

Olivia let out a little laugh and instinctively darted her eyes toward Jack. Holly and Jack tightened their embrace around her shoulders.

"I didn't want to disrupt Megan's life. I always thought, at some point, we might find each other in that way, and I would tell her how I felt, but the time never came. In all the years since, we were so comfortable in our relationship for what it was, that I was scared to step out of that—scared that I might mess up and lose what was so perfect. I was satisfied with the part of Megan that she gave me, and afraid to ask for more." He took two steps forward and bowed his head, his hands clasped under his chin. "Thank you for listening. I should have said all of this to Megan. I do love her, even now, when she is beyond my reach." With this confession, he walked slowly to his seat.

There were hushed whispers as he made his way around the chairs, the murmurs reached the heavens and snapped Megan out of her trance-like state. The river flowing below her was as blue as Lawrence's eyes, and rushed in a calm, even flow toward the clouds. Megan worried that it might dampen the afternoon and whooshed herself through the air in one fluid, graceful movement until she lay across the cloud. The river redirected above her form, never touching it, as if instinct drove it higher into the sky, and it disappeared into the vast abyss far above the clouds.

Megan swooped down toward Earth, trying to reach Lawrence. She was close enough to feel his heat, yet he was oblivious to her. She reached out to touch his arm.

He rubbed his arm, as if a bug had landed there. He looked down at the spot he has just rubbed, and peered intently, looking for the prickle that he felt.

She tried again, reaching out and placing her palm on top of his. She closed her eyes, somehow understanding, knowing that he had to believe, really believe, in order to feel her touch. She was not sure how she knew that, but she had no question it was so.

Megan's scent reached his senses, and Lawrence found himself looking for her, expecting her to be right beside him. He took a long, deep breath, but the scent was gone, as if it had been swept away with the wind. She realized she wouldn't be able to reach him and regretfully, pulled away.

When the din around the lighthouse quieted, and it was clear that everyone who wished to speak had done so, Jack came forward. His eyes were red, his face strained, saddened. He stood silently for a moment, his hand clasped in front of his mouth, his eyes closed. The guests were silent, waiting. He looked up and took in all of Megan's friends and family. His heart panged with hurt and sadness. Jack closed his eyes again and took another deep breath, inhaling the taste of the ocean and remembering their one intimate weekend together.

Just as the whispers began, Jack opened his eyes and looked toward the sea. He smiled. His words came lightly, warm, and full of love. "Thank you for coming to say goodbye to Megan. She was a special person to us all." He looked at the faces of those who had known Megan, who loved her. He saw smiles and tears, and understood both. "Megan was someone that took no figuring out. The person she was was the one that she let us all see." He looked at Lawrence, "She loved you, Lawrence."

Lawrence bowed his head, closed his eyes, and nodded.

"She loved each of you." He stretched out his hands, palms up, and brought them around his body to rest at his sides. "Megan knew she was going to pass on. She tried, even in death, to make life less painful for each of us. She was protecting us." Jack eyed Olivia, who was listening intently to his words. He winked, and she smiled and then looked down, absently fingering her tear-soaked tissue. "Megan isn't gone, you know. She is still with us. She lives on in Olivia and in our hearts."

Jack walked to the tiger lilies that were artfully arranged at either the side of the first row of chairs. He took a flower in each hand and passed it down the row of people, who in turn passed it along to the next, and so on. He continued this with each row until each person held a beautiful bright orange-and-salmon lily in his hand. The tall stems raised the flowers high. Jack walked back to the front of the group and held the flower up above his head, toward the sky.

"These were Megan's favorite flowers." He lowered the flower and held it against his heart. "I remember when we were kids at summer camp. She would sneak off to the woods just to find them and stealthily sneak back with a bundle of lilies under her arm." He laughed at the memory, at the happiness it had brought her. "She did this at least once each week, year after year. Each and every time she was scolded by the counselors for sneaking off, but she didn't care. Megan would give each counselor a flower and apologize. She always kept one for herself and one for me. She had those hidden, though. She stashed them at the edge of the forest. She would sneak out late at night and retrieve the flowers, then come to my bunk, the boys' bunk, sneak in, and lay one next to me while I slept." He looked down. "I hadn't remembered that until just now." Jack looked toward Holly, whose face was wet with fresh tears. "Megan let us all know she loved us. She had her ways, even without words. I think she would have liked to say thank you to each of you for seeing her off. She would have given you these flowers herself had she been here. It was her way—silent, meaningful. Thank you." He raised the flower to his nose, breathed in deeply, and walked back to his seat.

The ceremony came to an end, and the guests mingled

in small groups. Megan felt Olivia's sadness before she saw her. She swooped down and scanned the beach. *Where is she? Olivia? Reach out to me.*

Olivia was hidden in the dune grass on the side of the lighthouse that faced the ocean, tucked tight within herself—her knees pulled in to her chest, arms wrapped around them, her head buried in between. *Oh, Mom*, she thought. *You are really gone. What am I going to do without you?* Tears streaked her sullen face. *I can't do this, Mom. I can't go on without you. You shouldn't have left me. I thought I could do it, but I can't. I'm not strong enough!*

Megan was drawn to her. It was as if a force were pulling her form through the clouds and toward the lighthouse. She passed the enormous light on the top, which was dormant in the summer sun. Her form glided around the lighthouse, worked its way toward the grass on the far side. She swept down behind Olivia, recognizing the top of her silky hair and holding back her own tears at the sight of her daughter's pain.

You must go on, Olivia. I filled your heart with love, as you did mine. You have a wonderful life ahead of you. Live your life. Please, live your life. I am here for you. I will always be here for you.

Megan reached out and tried to touch Olivia's shoulder. Though Megan could not feel her daughter's youthful skin, she saw Olivia's muscles in her arms grow tense. *Good. Feel me, Livi. I'm here. You're okay.*

Olivia felt warmth on her shoulder. She sniffled as she

lifted her head slowly. The faint smell of lavender and coconut wafted through the air. *Mom?* "Mom?" she said softly. Her heart pounded in her chest. Her body began to tremble. She turned her head swiftly from side to side, waiting to see her appear. "Mom, are you here?" she asked anxiously.

Yes! Yes, baby, I'm here!

"Mom? I...I felt you," Olivia whispered as she stood and looked around frantically.

Megan put her hands on Olivia's shoulders again, hovering in front of her, willing her to feel her presence. *I'm here, Livi. I'm here!*

Olivia smiled, sighed, oblivious to her mother's words. Her eyes darted from left to right. "I know you're here somewhere, Mom. I can feel you," then added, sadly, "but why can't I see you?"

"Peter, I'm so glad that you brought Cruz with you," Holly smiled at Cruz, then at Peter.

"It was about time, huh?" Peter squeezed Cruz's hand.

"Megan?" Holly asked, knowingly.

"Yeah, Megan. She made me realize that life doesn't go on forever. I can't sit around and hope Cruz will stick by me for however long it takes." He put his arm around Cruz.

Cruz squinted his dark eyes and said, "You know I'd wait. You and I, we're like...I don't know, peanut butter and chocolate, I guess. We go together whether you want us to or not." He smiled.

"Well, I'm glad you are sticking around, Cruz, because

Peter can be a royal pain in the ass! I'll need someone else for him to bother," she laughed.

"That's not fair, my mother—"

Holly interrupted, "I know, your mother left you when you were small. Peter, I feel for you, I really do, but it's about time that you let that crutch go and decide to let Cruz in." She put her arm around Cruz, who nuzzled into her and let go of Peter's hand. "Really let him in, Peter. He's a great guy, and he's not your mother!"

Peter kicked at a stone. "I know. It's hard to trust. I should probably go back to therapy or something."

"Whatever it takes, P," Cruz said encouragingly.

"Guys, where's Olivia?" Holly asked, suddenly aware of her missing presence.

"I saw her earlier. She was walking around the lighthouse." Cruz started off toward the lighthouse. "C'mon, we'll check it out."

Peter took his hand. Holly hurried beside them.

"Jack," she called out, "where's Olivia?"

Concerned, Jack looked around, motioned with a shrug, his palms held up. "I'll look around," he yelled.

Olivia heard a rustling of feet through the dune grass. She turned toward the sound and wiped her eyes.

"Hey."

Olivia turned at the sound of the boy's voice.

"Over here," he said.

This time Olivia followed his voice. Behind a bundle

of bushes she saw a boy who appeared about her age. He smiled, flashed a row of perfectly straight white teeth and deep-set dimples. Olivia smiled back and answered tentatively, "Hey."

"They're coming to find you," he said. "If you hurry, you can hide in here with me."

Olivia thought for a moment about the last time she went with a boy she didn't know. A chill ran down her back. Her hesitation reflected in her immediate frown. She looked toward the encroaching voices and back at the boy. *He looks nice.* "What are you doing back there?" she whispered loudly.

"Watching you," he said. Jason peered out of the bushes at the people milling about, the flowers, the chairs set up like little soldiers. Then he noticed the clothes—everyone was dressed in black, "Was there a funeral or something? You look so sad."

"Yeah. Well, kinda anyway." She walked slowly toward the bushes.

"They're coming! Quick, back here!" he said and ducked behind the bushes.

Olivia lifted her dress away from the prickly leaves and crouched behind the bushes. She was eye to eye with the lanky boy.

His hazel eyes danced with delight and mischief as he flicked his chestnut hair off of his forehead with a quick jerk of his head. His long bangs fell immediately back in place just above his brown eyes. "Hey," he said quietly.

His voice sent chills down Olivia's spine, landing in the pit of her stomach. "Hey," she whispered back.

"You okay?" he asked.

"Yeah, sure," Olivia said. "Why are you here? In the bushes, I mean."

"My name's Jason," he said. He reached out and shook her hand.

"Olivia." His hand was warm. His long boney fingers were much longer than Olivia's. He held her hand for just a second longer than was necessary, and despite herself, butterflies rushed through Olivia. She cleared her throat.

"What are you doing here?" she asked again.

"I live over there." He pointed to a Cape Cod-style home with additions on both sides and a large deck that overlooked the water. "I saw you guys come into the parking lot, so I came to see what was going on. I watched the service, or whatever it was." Jason looked at the lighthouse and the people milling around it. He whispered, "Why were you alone?"

Olivia watched Holly and Peter, wondering, she knew, where she could possibly have gone. They would be frightened for her safety. She felt badly for hiding, but desperately wanted to be alone—but she was not alone, and suddenly she felt as though it was okay not to be alone. "I just wanted to be." She looked back at him and felt that funny tingle run up her body again.

"I know what you mean," Jason said. He turned his back to Olivia and motioned for her to follow him.

"Where are we going?" Olivia asked. She wasn't sure she

should follow him. She looked back over her shoulder at Holly who was beginning to get frantic. "I should tell them where I'm going," she said and turned toward the lighthouse.

"I thought you wanted to ditch them," he said.

"I didn't really want to ditch them. I just didn't want to be with them—or anybody really." She saw his face deflate, his smile quickly fade. "I don't mean you. I mean, I didn't know you. I'll still hang out, but just let me tell them so they don't worry."

Immediately his smile returned, his face lightened. "Okay. Want me to come?"

Olivia nodded. *A friend, maybe I'll have a real friend.* "Sure, come on!" She rushed out of the bushes. When she reached the clearing, she found herself facing Holly's back. "Holly!" she yelled, happily.

"Olivia! I was so worried!" Holly watched the boy emerge from the bushes. He was tall and handsome in a mischievous boyish way, with an innocent face and beautiful eyes. She smiled, hesitantly, "Who is this?"

"This is Jason," Olivia said. "He lives over there." She pointed to the house on the knoll. She brushed the dirt off her dress and smiled at Holly, a particular smile that Holly had rarely seen. It was an effortless smile, filled with teenage hope.

Holly extended her hand to Jason, "Hi Jason. I'm Holly."

Peter and Cruz eyed each other knowingly and protectively sidled up beside Olivia. Peter bent down and whispered, "He's a cutie!"

Olivia blushed.

Jason shook Holly's hand. "Hi. It's nice to meet you." He said hello to Peter and Cruz.

Jack sized up Jason, letting his eyes rise up and drop down slowly, with a cautious gaze of protection. "Jason," he lifted his chin in a quick nod.

Holly elbowed him in the side and gave him a look that said, *Ease up*.

"So, Jason," Jack tried to sound pleasant, though his heart screamed, *Protect!* "What were you doing over there?"

"I saw ya'll come into the parking lot and wanted to see what was going on," he said easily, then looked down and added, "I'm sorry. I didn't realize it was a private ceremony."

"That's alright," Holly said and smiled at Olivia.

"Holly, we were going to take a walk. Is that okay?" Olivia's eyes were bright and pleaded for a little teenage time.

"Um, sure, but stay close by, okay? We're going to go back home for brunch pretty soon." She took Olivia's hand and turned her away from Jason. Holly whispered, "Are you sure you are alright? Do you want me to go with you?"

Olivia shook her head quickly, and her smile stretched from dimple to dimple.

"Okay, then. Just be careful. Oh, and take my phone, just in case. Jack's number is speed dialed into it on number two." She pressed the phone into Olivia's palm which she noticed was trembling.

"Thanks," Olivia said, and turned to Jason. "Ready?"

"Sure," Jason said. He reached out to shake Jack's hand again. "Nice to meet you, sir. Don't worry, we won't go far. There's a cranberry bog I want to show her. It's right over that hill." His tan, thin arm pointed over the crest of the hill.

Jack nodded. The pull in his heart was new to him. He felt like a father bear protecting his young and wondered why it was hitting him so strongly. He looked back at the empty chairs and quickly remembered.

Holly sidled up next to Jack and rested her body against his. His arm quickly circled her shoulder, pulling her closer. "It's okay, Jack. She needs this."

"Yeah," he sighed, and kissed her forehead. "I'm sure she does, but it feels weird. All of a sudden I want to protect her. I've known her all my life. Why now?"

"Because Megan's gone." Holly looked up at Jack and into his caring eyes. "She's ours now, Jack. We are supposed to protect her."

"This is hard, Holly. How do we know he's not going to hurt her?"

Holly laughed inwardly. She loved the paternal nature that was coming out in Jack. "We have to trust our instincts and Olivia's." She draped her arm around his waist. "She's a smart girl, Jack. Just look at who she learned from. What she did before, that was rebellion. What she's doing now, this is normal. This is good."

"I guess," he said. Jack took her hand and they made their way back to the other guests.

Olivia followed Jason through the bushes and over the crest of the hill. She watched his tall thin body move effortlessly. He was nimble, weaving his way around the prickly areas and holding branches up for her to walk underneath. The butterflies were back, and every time he looked at her they tied her stomach in knots. She was glad for the silence, not sure if her voice would fail her if she tried to speak.

As they moved further away from the lighthouse, a wave of guilt passed through Olivia. She stopped, look behind her, and in the space of a breath was gripped by teenage confidence. *Mom would understand.*

Jason reached out to help her up the last step of the hill. He lifted her with ease. Thoughts of her mother and the others were tossed aside, replaced with the beautiful scene before her. Thousands of flowering plants covered the water. Little flowers sprouted up through the thick, lush greenery. Though it was too early for the actual cranberries to grow, the vegetation was glorious.

"This is my grandfather's bog," Jason said with pride. Her smile made his heart race. *Wow, she sure is pretty.* Jason swallowed hard, and looked away to quiet the stirring in his body.

"Really! That's so cool!" she said. "Can we go closer?"

Jason took her hand and walked her down the hill. He felt her hand shaking in his own and wondered if she felt his as well. He bent down to take off his flip flops. "Take your shoes off, it's pretty mushy."

Olivia bent down and took off her heels, placing them on the grass beside his sandals.

"We can't go in, but we can get close," he said, and they walked to the edge of the bog.

"My granddad brings in beehives during June and July. You have to be careful. The bees pollinate the flowers." He pointed to an area about three feet to their left. "See! Look there! See all those bees?"

Olivia squinted, gave a little shriek. "Oh! Wow!" She instinctively took a step backward. "I hate bees!"

He stepped back with her. "Don't worry. They're so interested in the flowers that they won't come near you." They stood in silence for a few minutes. Jason's heart beat so hard he was sure she could hear it. "In a few weeks the cranberries will grow. The whole place will be red, like a red sea or something. Then in early fall, Granddad harvests them. It's really cool."

Olivia couldn't quiet the storm that swirled in her stomach. She put her hand across her belly. "I want to see them. I've seen pictures, but I've never seen the real thing."

"Well, where do you live?" He silently hoped it was nearby.

Olivia looked away, not sure how to answer the question. "I live about an hour from here, but I'm moving closer."

"When?" Jason asked, unaware of her pain.

"I don't really know. Soon, I guess." Olivia's mind drifted

to her mother. Guilt replaced the excitement in her stomach as she realized that she was happy while her mother was gone. She couldn't believe she was actually contemplating the possible happiness of moving here, while her mother wouldn't be by her side. Her legs suddenly felt heavy, and she moved back to the grass and crouched down, resting on her heels.

Jason turned around. "What's wrong?" he asked.

"Nothing. I guess I'm just tired."

Jason felt her change. Her easiness had turned heavy, her face looked sad. "What's up, Olivia?" He settled on the grass beside her, their knees barely touched.

The feel of his skin on hers sent a tingle up her spine. Olivia wanted to move her knee away from his, feeling badly for feeling so good, but she couldn't. She liked the feeling. She wanted to feel it, to feel happy. *Shit! What am I going to do. I'm sorry, Mom.*

"I...I heard you," Jason said tentatively, "before."

Olivia looked up at him, her green eyes like emeralds glistening in the summer sun. "Hm?"

"I heard you. I'm sorry. I didn't mean to spy on you. When you were at the lighthouse, I—" he quickly looked down at his hands, tore a piece of grass from beside him, and began to rip it into small pieces, "I heard you crying."

Olivia blushed and turned away.

"Why were you sad?" he asked.

She couldn't look at him. She wasn't ready to talk about her mother. *I'm such a fool. What am I doing here? I should be back there thinking only about Mom.* She sat in silence.

"You don't have to tell me. I'm sorry I asked," Jason said quietly.

"No, it's okay," she said. Tears pooled in her eyes.

Jason looked up at her. "What is it? Did I do something?"

"No, no," Olivia said, shaking her head as the tears tumbled down her cheeks.

Jason reached up and wiped them with his thumb, slow and careful.

"I'm sorry. I shouldn't be here. I'm such a mess." Olivia stood to walk back to the lighthouse.

"Wait!" Jason was up on his feet in a second flat and reached for her arm.

Olivia froze when he touched her. She felt the heat of his hand all the way to her toes. She covered her eyes, embarrassed by her tears. "I'm sorry. I just—" She couldn't stop her tears which flowed in between her fingers.

"What? What is it Olivia?" Jason asked. "You can tell me." He felt bad for Olivia. He wished he could take her in his arms and hold her, yet he knew he couldn't. It would have been too awkward. "Olivia," he whispered, "you can tell me." He bent down and craned his neck to look up under her hands and into her wet eyes. He smiled.

She wiped her eyes and turned around. She sunk to her knees in the grass and took a deep breath. Her eyes drifted up and away from Jason's face, up toward the clouds. "It's my mom."

"What's your mom?"

Olivia pointed to the gathering beyond the lighthouse.

Jason quickly thought back to what he had seen earlier, the way everyone had watched Olivia so intently, how she had cried continually. Realization dawned abruptly. How could he have been so stupid?

"Your mom," he said.

Olivia took a deep breath, hoping with every fiber of her being to smell lavender and coconut, but instead was filled with the fresh smells of summer: dune grass, sea water, and wet sand. She turned to Jason. The rush of tears slowed to a trickle.

"Yeah," she whispered.

"I'm so sorry," he said. "My parents are gone, too."

Olivia whipped her head toward him, her eyes opened wide. "They are?" Her heart pounded.

"Yeah, two years ago. That's why I live with my granddad." Jason lifted his eyebrows, as if to say, *I get it*.

"I'm so sorry. How?" Olivia turned her body to face his.

"You may have heard about it. We were on our way to Virginia Beach for a family reunion. We were driving through Maryland. It was really foggy. My mom wanted to stop, but my dad had been driving for like twelve hours and wanted to just get there." He looked away.

Olivia watched him swallow. The lump in his throat moved up and down. His jaw clenched.

"It was like all of a sudden the lights went out. We were driving through this fog that was pretty thick, but then suddenly you couldn't see even the car ahead of you. My dad said he'd get off at the next exit, but we never got the chance. By the time we saw the lights ahead of us, it was too late. He slammed on the brakes, but the tractor trailer behind us couldn't stop." Jason looked away, blinking away fresh tears. "The guy said afterward that he didn't see our brake lights until he was almost right on top of us. Anyway, there was a fifteen-car pile up, and we were right in the middle."

"My God, Jason, I'm so sorry. You were with them? You didn't get hurt?"

"It's so weird. When he slammed on the brakes, the truck came from behind and actually came on top of the car. It crushed them right away." Tears streaked his face. "I...I guess I got into a ball, you know, wrapped my arms around my knees and ducked my head, like they teach you in school. The truck tires were on both sides, and I guess I passed out. When I came to in the hospital, they told me that it was like there was an angel looking over me. The only part of the car that wasn't crushed was right where I was, between the tires."

"You must have been terrified." Instinctively, Olivia reached out and covered his hand with hers.

"I was in shock, I think. They didn't tell me about my parents until two days later. I kept asking to see them, but they kept me pretty sedated, so really I slept most of the time." Jason turned away from Olivia, feeling the same sinking feeling in his gut as he had two days after the accident.

"When my granddad got to the hospital, he stayed with

me. I remember that. Every time I woke up, he was there, sitting next to my bed. I'd ask him about my parents, and I guess before he could answer, I'd be asleep again, but when I woke up, really woke up…he looked like he got ten years older in the three months since I had seen him. I remember wondering why he looked so old. Then he told me. He said they died instantly."

"Oh, Jason, that's horrible. I'm so sorry. That is just... too much."

"It's no different than you, really. Your mom is gone, too."

"Yeah, but it wasn't...like that." Olivia felt badly for Jason. She stood and stared out at the bog. "She had cancer. She was really sick, but she didn't come out and tell me until near the end."

"Cancer sucks. It seems like it's everywhere," he said as he walked toward her.

"Yeah. It's just so unfair, you know? I didn't know who my dad was, either, so I'm kinda left alone. For the first time ever, I think I'm really lonely. I miss her so much."

"You didn't know who your dad was? Were you adopted?" he asked.

"No. My mom had me, but she never told me who my father was. I know now, but I just found out. I mean, she left a note, so I know who he is, but I'm not sure that I want to say anything." She faced him and saw compassion in his eyes.

"Why don't you want to say anything? Are you afraid he

won't want you?" he asked.

"No. I'm afraid of what knowing I'm his will do to his family," she said.

They exchanged a look of understanding.

"A note? Why didn't your mom just tell you?"

"I don't think I was supposed to find the note. I sort of went crazy in her room and found it in her box of personal stuff that she kept. She always said she didn't want me to know until I was older, but—whatever!"

Side by side they made their way back to the lighthouse. Olivia saw Holly in the distance and waved. Holly waved back. Relief was evident in her smile.

"I better go. It looks like everyone is leaving," Olivia said. She played with a twig she had picked up on the trail. "Thanks for letting me see the bog."

Jason didn't want her to go. He had many friends, but none as pretty as Olivia. Beyond being pretty, they had something in common that bound him to her in a way that other kids his age couldn't understand. "When are you moving again?"

"I'm not sure. Soon, probably," Olivia said.

"Well, I guess I'll see you 'round then."

Olivia's heart sank to the pit of her stomach. *He didn't even ask for my number. I guess he doesn't like me. Who would? I'm a mess. I shouldn't have cried.* "Yeah, see you 'round." She forced a smile and turned to walk away.

As she neared Holly, she heard his footfalls behind her. Her stomach leapt into her throat. *Yes!*

"Olivia!" he yelled, just as she reached the empty chairs.

She spun around, smiled.

"Wait!" he yelled again. When he reached her he put his hand on her forearm, and once again electricity shot through her.

"Yeah?" she laughed.

"Can I," he looked at the ocean, "can I, um, get your number maybe?" Jason couldn't stand still, his feet moved from side to side as the distance between his question and her answer lengthened. His nerves were on fire.

"Sure."

"Great!" His eyes lit up. He continued to move from one foot to the other. "Great!"

Excitement hung in the air between the two.

"Oh, I don't have a pen," Olivia said, "or paper."

Jack looked around, then pointed his finger up toward the sky and lifted is eyebrows. "You have a phone, right? You have Holly's phone?"

"Yeah," she laughed, "but that won't help you."

"Sure it will." He dug deep into his shorts pocket and pulled out a cell phone. "Text me your number."

She giggled. "Okay. Good idea." She texted him her cell and home phone numbers, then Holly's number, then her name.

He laughed as it came through on his phone. "Which one is your number?"

"The first one," she said. She pointed to the numbers

displayed on his phone, "And that's my number at my house, and I'm moving to Holly's soon, so, just in case, I gave you her number, too."

"Olivia Taylor." He smiled, her name felt good coming out of his mouth. "Jason Forrester." He put his phone in his pocket. The grin never left his face. "I'll call you!"

Holly entered Megan's home with great trepidation. The conversation with Megan's mother had been difficult. The memories that bombarded her at the sound of her voice—the years that they shared, the laughter and tears—had brought with them the realization that Megan would not be coming back. She was gone. Gone! The hole Megan left in Holly's life was enormous, but the sadness that her mother harbored was inescapable. She practically begged Holly to take care of Megan's belongings. She said it wasn't the illness that would hold her back, although it certainly would, it was the idea of seeing Megan's belongings, smelling her, knowing she wasn't there—the finality of it. She wanted no part of it. She had pleaded with Holly, and Holly had succumbed.

Holly stood on the landing at the bottom of the stairs, willing herself to walk up to Megan's room, to begin the process of wrapping up Megan's life. How do you wrap up a life? How do you fit a friend's life into tidy little boxes? How was she supposed to go through her friend's belongings without collapsing from sheer sadness?

Her heart raced as she looked up at the dark stairway.

A chill rushed through her body as an image of Megan's peaceful face, the morning after the ritual, lingered in her mind.

Holly turned away. She wasn't ready. She stared at the French doors in the living room. Settling her hair behind her ears, she walked slowly toward the door. Her legs shook. She stared out at the bonfire pit and was overcome with loneliness as she spied remnants of their evening—burnt embers, logs half black and charred sitting cockeyed on each other, and—what was that? A bit of color lay in the pit, tucked between two blackened sticks. She cocked her head and squinted, but could not define its shape. She opened the door carefully, as if the noise might make the item flee. She walked toward the colored object and bent down to inspect it more closely.

Tears sprang to her eyes as she opened the carefully-folded paper, burnt around the edges and brown in the middle. *A note.*

Slowly she opened the folds. The paper was stiff, the edges crumbled under her fingers. Once opened, she crouched down, resting her bottom on her heels, and stared at the handwritten note. *How did we not see this before?* She looked around, and everything else was just as she had left it, nothing changed, nothing rearranged.

Tears fell gently onto the paper and smeared the purple ink as she read.

Mom, where do I go from here?

I don't know what to do. I feel lost. Please come back to me. I need you. I'm sorry I was trouble to you. I'm sorry if you wanted to leave me. I love you. Olivia

Holly clutched the note to her chest, crying. Her hand shook. *Olivia.*

She tucked the note in between the two burned logs where she found it and felt her heart grow heavy with grief. *My poor girl.*

In Megan's room, Holly straightened the mess that Olivia had left. *I'll leave the clothes and go through them with Olivia.* She moved from the bathroom to the closet, the closet to the bed. She folded clothes and set things right along the way, as if in a trance. Her hands went through the motions, but her mind was in a fog. Holly reached down to pick up Megan's tie-dyed sleeping pants. They slipped through her fingers. Holly crouched to the floor and held the pants in her hands, running the soft cotton material through her fingers. *These were your favorite.* She smiled. A piece of paper peeked out from under the bed and caught her attention. She looked under the bed, taking the paper in her hand, and saw a small wooden box.

Instinct made her look around the room, like a child being caught snooping for Christmas presents. As her fingers grasped the box, she felt warmth spread through her body. *Nerves.* She slid the box out from under the bed and walked to the window seat. She sat with it in her lap. *I promise, Meg,*

I'm only looking for things you might not want Olivia to find. No judgments here.

The sun beat on her shoulders. She sighed deeply, again settling the stray hairs that had fallen into her face behind her ears. She lifted the lid of the box and was met with what looked like letters. She smiled. *Good for you, Meg. Maybe you did have a love life after all, you sneaky girl.*

Holly took out the letters one by one. Most of them were from Holly, written when they were little girls while Megan was at summer camp. Holly nodded, laughing to herself at how much she used to miss Megan while she was away. *I can't live without her!* she remembered telling her mother over and over, knowing that they could not afford to send her to camp, but feeling better by complaining all the same.

"Oh Meg," Holly said. She dug through the pile, and found a few from Peter, written, she thought, while he was away for summer vacations during college. There were two from Lawrence Childs, which Holly did not remove from the envelopes, though she was aching to know what they said.

As she closed the box, her finger brushed the inside of the top, where the cloth had come loose. She opened it wide again, and inspected the seam, immediately noticing a small envelope tucked between the material and the wood.

"Oh Meg. What do we have here?" She suddenly felt shameful, going through Megan's things. Her hands shook and she closed the box, spreading her fingers across the top and looked out the window. "Meg? What should I do?" She stood and placed the box on the bed. She turned and walked away. Halfway across the room, she turned back. Something inside her told her that the letter was vital, that she should read it. Just as loudly, a voice told her she was breaching Megan's privacy.

She walked back to the bed and stood over the box. "What the hell am I supposed to do?" With shaking hands she withdrew the envelope, which unfolded on its own as it was removed from the confines of its chamber, and two tiny photos dropped to the floor. She looked down, then closed her eyes, and let them remain there, scattered at her feet like forgotten crumbs. She scanned the document, and although she had known for a long time that what she was reading was true, her hand flew to her mouth, and a flood of tears streamed down her face. She folded the document as well as her trembling would allow, picked up the photos, which she glanced at quickly, and stuffed them back into the envelope. She put the envelope in her back pocket, and sat down on the edge of Megan's bed, trying to settle her nerves.

Stop it! You knew. You've known for a long time. Why are you so upset? Holly tried to reason herself out of her anxious state. She felt anger bubbling in her gut, mixed with sadness, regret, and...jealousy.

They don't know. What do I do now, Megan? How could you leave us with this type of burden? As the thought whipped through her mind with the force of a whole gale, the room filled with the scent of Megan, lavender and coconut.

The smell permeated her senses. Holly stood, feeling dazed and lightheaded. She looked around Megan's room. The smell overpowered her, as if she were standing right next to Megan. Her shaking doubled, her legs threatened collapse. Her voice trembled, "Megan?" she said.

There was no answer. *Of course.* Her eyes darted across the room, the pungent odor hung in the air like a cloud. "Megan?" she said a little louder, still just a trembling, forced whisper.

From above, Megan watched Holly. She didn't know what to do, how to lighten her burden. She had spent so much time protecting Olivia's father's identity that she hadn't prepared Holly. How could she have left this unsaid? How could she put Holly through that?

Megan looked down at her form, which, over the last twenty-four hours had started to fade into the air. She was certain she wouldn't remain in this place, this trap between two realms, much longer. Frustrated, she whisked her form around the room, invisibly circling Holly, trying to find a way to connect with her, to let her know she was sorry.

Holly was rooted to the floor. She was too scared to move, too shocked to find the strength to continue cleaning up. She willed herself to move toward the bedroom door. She moved slowly toward it, her legs felt weighed down with the knowledge she'd gained. As she moved, she noticed that the floral smell, Megan's smell, was stronger, as if it were trying to fill the space of the doorway, to block her way. She pushed through and rushed downstairs.

Megan was left with her own guilt wrapped around her body like a snake, squeezing her opaque form until she cried out in anger. Her hot tears streamed to her right, disappeared into the clouds. She watched them turn gray and heavy and felt her heart do the same.

Chapter Seven

Peter found himself floundering, as if out at sea with only a life preserver and no land in sight. He felt as though he were in a completely different place in his life without Megan nearby. It's not that he had seen her very often or had confided in her any more than he had his other close friends. Something had been happening to him, though, during the month since Megan's passing. There was an undeniable change occurring within his mind, his soul.

The realization of how quickly one's life could change made him rethink his actions, all of his actions. He had carried anger toward his mother for so many years that it had become part of who he was. It was a crutch that he relied on and rued at the same time—subconsciously, certainly, and on occasion, consciously as well. He'd felt it bubble beneath his skin when he was younger and was teased by his playmates about his mother leaving him. As he matured, and relationships would end, he always thrust the blame of his partner's leaving on his mother. How quickly he learned not to trust, not to fully give himself to someone else, not to put himself out there, in the open, splayed for the emotional beating that was sure to follow.

Megan's death changed how he viewed himself, how he viewed others. He felt a difference when he woke in the morning, seeing each day through more positive eyes, *Like Megan's eyes*, he thought.

He stepped onto the balcony and looked up toward the sky. As Cruz's arms wrapped around him from behind, hugging him close, he felt the strong pounding of his heart against his own back. Peter looked to the sky and thought, *Thank you, Megan*, and sighed deeply. Finally happy, finally able to try and give his heart, his whole heart, to his lover, he turned and reciprocated the embrace.

The kids around her laughed, passed notes, and flirted with one and other, just like normal kids did. *Normal kids. I'm nowhere near normal. Normal kids' moms don't die.* After four weeks' time, Olivia had thought she'd be ready to go back to school, face reality again, finish the last two weeks of school with everyone else—but in the halls, the other kids tried not to make eye contact with her and whispered, thinking she couldn't hear them. They thought she didn't know they were whispering about the "girl whose mother just died." Olivia wished she could be invisible. *Maybe it was a mistake to come back to school so soon.*

No one knew how to act around her. Her friends told her they were sorry and then quickly found excuses to rush away from her. She was just as confused about how to act around them. Everyone at school carried on as though nothing bad had happened. They went to school, went out on the weekend, and were carefree. *Why should they act any different? It wasn't their mother!*

Lunchtime was even more painful. Olivia sat at her regular table with the two girls she sometimes hung out with, but as she tried to laugh and joke, her loneliness slowly resurfaced. She struggled to smile and shrank back into her chair, engulfed in sadness. *What's wrong? Are you okay?* She told them that she was fine, but that her stomach hurt a little.

How am I supposed to act? What do you do when your mother dies? She won't be there when I get home. I can't call her to come get me. Olivia sat in the nurse's office with tears trickling down her cheeks.

Olivia spent the following morning going over her phone conversation with Jason from the night before. Jason understood so much of what she was going through that he was actually able to help her feel better. He really seemed to get her feeling of being abandoned. He said he had felt that way, too! *Don't worry, after a few weeks your mind will remember that it wasn't really her fault she had cancer. Then you'll be able to forgive her for leaving. It takes time, but it will get easier.* She knew he was right. She played that line over and over in her head, *it wasn't really her fault she had cancer*, and could already feel her body and mind accepting it in a way that she had been unable to the day before. She sighed and thought about how lucky she was to have found a friend like him.

At eight A.M., Olivia strode down the stairs two at a time, and bounded into the kitchen, surprising Holly, who had been thinking about how she could help Olivia through her pain—what she could and couldn't say. Holly was glad to see Olivia's rejuvenated spirit as she watched Olivia's pony tail bounce just above her shoulders as she prepared her breakfast, and instantly recognized the teenage splendor of a new relationship.

Olivia set cereal at the table and smiled at Holly. She hadn't been able to stop smiling, or thinking about Jason, since her mother's public goodbye ceremony. Jason. *Jason Forrester*. She sighed.

"You got it bad, girl," Holly teased.

Olivia lifted her eyes, smiled. "That's something Mom would say to me," she said.

"Oh, sorry."

"No, it's okay, really." Olivia ate her cereal, unable to hide her smile between bites. "I like that you remind me of her."

Holly leaned a little closer to Olivia, as if she were about to share a secret. "I was thinking, Livi, about moving your stuff over here. I don't want to push you." Her words rushed out of her mouth, much faster than she had practiced. She wished Jack were there, but he had a business trip and wouldn't be home until very late. "Whenever you're ready. I just wasn't sure how long you wanted to wait."

Olivia had tried not to think about the logistics of her

mother's passing. She tried not to think too much about her mother at all, lately. She found that when she did, she spiraled into a sadness that took control of her and she could barely break free from it. It was much easier, she decided, to go about her life, her daily activities, focusing on other things and keeping busy enough that her mind could not find the hole her mother had left.

She hadn't thought about when she should move *all* of her stuff. She was living with Holly and Jack, but her things, her mother's things, were back at Seaside Lane, where she and her mom lived.

She set her spoon in her bowl and sat back in her chair, knitting her hands together, her brow squeezed tight.

"I'm sorry. I didn't mean to upset you." Holly reached out to touch her arm.

"You didn't," Olivia said. She straightened her back a little so Holly wouldn't think she was really upset. She wasn't very upset. She simply hadn't thought about the timing. "What will happen to our house?" she asked.

"Well, we'll probably sell it and put the money away for your college," Holly said softly, eyeing Olivia, weighing her facial response, the soft tilt of her head. *Good.* Holly waited in silence.

Sell it. Sell it. I can't go there anymore. I can't see my mom through the French doors, or slam out of the house when I'm mad, or cuddle up next to her in her bed when I'm scared. She won't sit in my room anymore and watch me sleep.

Holly watched emotions run across Olivia's face, fear,

sadness, confusion. "Livi, we don't have to do this anytime soon. We can wait a year if you want."

Olivia shook her head, took her spoon in her hand, and slowly brought it to her mouth. The cereal was cold and crunchy. She focused on it. It felt good. It took no thought, no emotions.

Her mind reeled through the goodbye ceremony and found its way to Jason, his smile, his long arms and strong hand grabbing hers, her lips curled into a soft smile. *And Mom wasn't there. Life does keep going.*

"It's so weird, Holly," she said between bites. "I mean, Mom isn't here, but everything continues. The sun comes up each morning and goes down at night. School goes on. I look at everyone sometimes and think, 'Why can't they see how sad I am?' But then I remember that most of them don't even know Mom died, you know?"

Holly nodded, feeling the same way.

"It's like Mom was insignificant to so many people. She didn't even exist." Her eyes became glassy. "I don't want to forget her, you know?" Olivia pleaded.

"I know, baby. You won't forget her—ever. She lives in our hearts. She was very significant. She will always be very significant. It might be true that she didn't know everyone in your school or everyone you pass on the street, but those who knew her adored her, just like we do." Holly moved next to Olivia, hugged her, then leaned back and smiled at her.

"We don't have to do this now, honey. Let's just think

about it a while, okay?" Holly said.

Olivia nodded. "I'm sorry."

"Don't be sorry, Olivia. There's no need to ever be sorry. We love you and we want to know how you feel. I'll always be here for you, and if you want to go back to Dr. Cavelino, the therapist you and your mother saw together, we can do that, too. I'd even go with you if you want me to."

Olivia smiled. "Thanks. I'll let you know. I think I'm okay for now. I just hadn't thought about the house, that's all."

Trying to change the subject to a lighter one, Holly asked, "You seem a little…happier this morning. Have you heard from Jason?"

A mischievous smile crept across Olivia's face. She bit her lower lip and looked up at Holly through her long eyelashes. A hot blush rushed up her cheeks. She nodded.

Holly raised her eyes in question.

"He called yesterday. He wants me to meet him at the beach this weekend." Olivia carried her bowl to the sink. With her back to Holly, she closed her eyes tight and asked, "Can I?"

My first real decision. What would Megan do? Livi has a chance for a real friend. He seemed like a nice boy. What if she gets hurt. I know, Megan, you would say, "She's got to go through it sometime." Is now the right time? Oh, Meg, I wish you were here. Talking to Megan in her mind had quickly become a habit for Holly. It's as if Megan wasn't really gone but lived on and could help guide her. She took a deep breath, watched Olivia turn to face her, hiding what Holly knew were her crossed fingers behind her back.

"I guess," the words slipped out before Holly realized they had. Olivia rushed over and threw her arms around Holly's neck.

"Thank you! Thank you! Oh my God, I need to get my bathing suit!" True to her fourteen-year-old spirit, her thoughts quickly turned to excitement, and her mourning had been pushed aside—at least for the moment.

Standing on the beach, the sand warm between his bare toes, Jack remembered his night with Megan. He gazed out at the sea. He remembered the feel of her against him, the flecks of sand strewn across her naked stomach, the breathlessness of the moment.

Is she mine, Megan? Do I have a daughter? Damn it, Megan, how could you leave us like this? Jack knelt down, his head weighed heavy in his hands as fresh tears stung his eyes.

He reached into his pocket, took out the Yin necklace, and rubbed his thumb over its cold surface. *Meg.* He had thought of nothing else since the idea came to him that Olivia might be his daughter. It pained him to look at Holly, feeling his lie of omission of the past fourteen years like a dagger in his heart. He should have told her. Sometime during the past decade, he should have come clean. It just never seemed like the right time, and then so much time had passed that it seemed wrong to blurt it out.

Holly. Oh, poor Holly. If Olivia is my child, then Megan had the daughter that Holly never could. This would just kill her. Jack made a promise to himself, to the sea, that he would never mention it to Holly. He loved her too much to ever want to cause her pain—and this could very well be the worst pain of all.

Jack walked down the beach. He walked until the sun began to lower itself toward the sea, and in the distance, the sky became bright orange and pink. When he was able, he looked up and focused ahead of him, instead of staring at the sand. He was lost in a web of memories. He hadn't realized where he was headed. He found himself looking up at the towering lighthouse, the light just beginning to wink at the sea.

Jason peered out from behind the bushes, where he'd come to think about Olivia. Olivia. What a girl she was! So sad, but so nice—and talk about beautiful! She was prettier than anyone he thought he had ever seen in his life, even prettier than those girls in the magazines. And she was going to meet him at the beach! Who would have thought that someone like her would be interested in someone like him?

At first the guy coming toward the lighthouse looked like a typical tourist, walking the beach to enjoy the day, but when he was right in front of Jason, he remembered having seen his face before. He had been there that day with Olivia. *What was his name again?*

"Jack!" The word came out loud and fast, before Jason had time to stop it. *Damn!*

Jack turned at the sound of his name. He had told Holly he was on a business trip and was surprised to be recognized. His heart skipped as he looked around.

Jason climbed out of the bushes and walked toward Jack, forcing a smile on his face. "Hey. It was me—that said your name. It was me." Jason extended his hand. "I'm Jason Forrester, remember? I met Olivia the other day."

Jack eyed him cautiously. Surprised by the churning that ripped through his chest—a visceral feeling of protection, as a lion would protect its cub. He nodded and feigned a smile.

"I...I'm really sorry about Olivia's mom," Jason said. "Is she doing alright?"

Jack quelled the protective feeling that made him want to tell Jason to leave Olivia alone. "She's doing as well as to be expected."

"I was really sad when my parents died." Jason sensed the tension in Jack's voice and looked away. "It was kind of nice to talk to someone who was going through the same thing."

Jack's heart softened as he listened. Knowing his feelings were raw for Megan and Olivia, he quieted his thoughts and let them move to the boy who stood in front of him, the boy whose parents had died, the boy who found a friend in Olivia. Jack looked into Jason's eyes and allowed himself to see youthful kindness instead of a teenage boy vying for his daughter's attention. *Is she my daughter?*

"I'm sorry, Jason. I didn't realize that your parents passed away. This has all been a little overwhelming."

Jason nodded, "I know. I remember."

Feeling silly for being such a grouch, Jack reached out to Jason with a softer, kinder voice, "Who do you live with now?"

"My granddad. We live there." He pointed to the house on the hill. "I asked Olivia if she could come to the beach this weekend, but if you would rather she didn't, that's okay. I mean," Jason looked Jack in the eye, as his dad had taught him to do with adults, to let them know he was being honest, "I know you don't know me, and I don't really know Olivia, but, I mean, I just wanted to meet her as a friend. I'm not trying to…well…you know."

Jack remembered what it was like to be a nervous teen. A quiet laugh escaped his lips before he had a chance to stifle it. "I'm sure you aren't. I think it would be fine, but since she's been through so much lately, why don't we all meet you this weekend. I would feel better if we were here, too. I'm not really ready to let her out of my sight completely yet."

As the warm day turned to a gray, cool evening, Holly was unable to sit still. She felt like a caged tiger. Her old demons had come back to haunt her. The bringing of Olivia into her own home had dredged up her own secret that she had worked so hard to bury deep inside so many years ago.

Now, fourteen years later, it nagged at the forefront of her mind.

She couldn't settle her stomach which burned and immediately processed everything she put in her mouth, leaving her with a horrible case of the runs. Each time she saw Jack, she expected him to confront her, though she knew that was crazy, too. *He couldn't know. He wouldn't have waited all these years to confront me.*

Jack. She thought of all of the years they'd shared and of when they had first fallen in love. It wasn't an urgent love, but a love of comfort, security, and friendship. It was as if they had been married forever and just hadn't known that they were meant to be more than friends until Megan had gone away.

Usually, Holly took her Sunday run with Megan. But when Megan went to Italy for three months, Peter was busy building his interior design business, and Jack was next on her list.

Holly had found herself worrying about things she had never even thought about before with Jack, *Do I look okay?* She had realized that in all of the years she'd known Jack, she had never been alone with him. Somehow, with Megan around, they were a *group* of friends. Holly found herself flustered, giddy maybe—an unfamiliar feeling amongst friends.

They had met at Cockel Cove, in Chatham, and had planned to run along the beach. They hadn't run more than fifty yards, when Jack spotted a Golden Retriever coming toward them, and he slowed to a walk as they neared it. Holly noticed the way Jack eyed the man, and the way his face cringed as he bent down to pet the dog, and the dog cowered. Jack cocked his head to the side and furrowed his brow, *Much like Goldens do*, Holly thought. Once again, he bent down and tried to stroke the dog. Concern crept across his face as the dog cowered once again. Jack stood and spoke quietly yet firmly to the owner, gazing down at the dog before he walked away. Holly was taken with the way he protectively questioned the dog's reaction to being touched.

Holly read concern on Jack's face when he returned to her side. He wrung his hands and there was a quickness in his step. Holly had never seen Jack in anything but a jovial mood. "Is everything okay?" she asked pensively.

Jack stopped suddenly, took Holly's arm, and turned her around. He watched the man with the dog, and Holly remembered his face—a mixture of anger and concern—scrutinizing the stranger. He flinched when the owner pulled roughly on the leash in an effort to rush the dog. The dog moved slightly quicker, but not before it cowered its head briefly toward the ground.

The owner said something sternly and moved around the dog, kicking it from behind.

"I knew it!" Jack said through clenched teeth. With anger in his eyes, he ran to the scene and placed himself between the dog and the owner. "What the hell are you doing?"

"Mind your own business, dude," the young man said, yanking the dog's leash again. The dog folded into itself, hunching its back and pulling its tail between its legs.

"This *is* my business. *Do not* kick that dog!" Jack raised his voice as his hands instinctively clenched and unclenched.

"Move it," the owner said roughly. "It's just a fucking dog."

Jack's fist connected with the stranger's face before he had time to think.

"Jack!" Holly rushed to Jack's side, her hand on his lower back as he stood over the man, whose nose was bleeding. "Jack, stop," Holly said quietly.

Jack's breaths came in loud huffs. "How does it feel to have something bigger than you push you around?" he said in a deep and serious voice.

"What the hell?" the man said in a quivering voice. "It's a God damned dog! Take the damn worthless thing if you care so much. I don't give a shit!" The man got up and threw the leash in Jack's direction. "Fuck you!" he turned and quickly walked away.

Jack picked up the leash and moved to the dog's side, stroking it protectively. "It's okay, boy. It's not your fault."

Holly was both intrigued and intimidated by Jack's passion. "Jack?"

"I'm sorry. Animal activists, you can't take us anywhere." He smiled up at her, but his face quickly grew serious. He stood up quickly and put his hands on her shoulders, "I'm sorry, Holly. I didn't mean to scare you. I just can't let that happen to an animal."

Holly smiled and silently wondered why the touch of

his hands created a stir deep within her.

Holly remembered how she quickly had become aware of what a passionate man Jack was. It had taken her by surprise, the way they had melded together over the next three months, spending every moment together as if they had always been by each other's sides.

There was a part of Holly that wanted to admit her guilt to Jack, rush into his arms and tell him every sordid detail, to lay it all out between them—to be dealt with, cried over, and screamed about. There was a part of her that wanted to take Olivia in her arms and gush: *Olivia! My baby! You are my child, not Megan's. You are finally home!* Though she knew she could neither. At times she found she had to physically swallow the words before they escaped her mouth.

She went outside and paced the yard.

When Jack arrived home, he wrestled with keeping his day a secret, and yet, he couldn't fathom trying to keep another secret from Holly. He confessed his lie of a business trip and explained that he had gone back to the beach to think things through. He told Holly about his encounter with Jason. His memory of his night with Megan, however, stayed tucked deep within the borders of his own mind, silenced by his guilt.

Holly remained silent, growing more angry by the second.

"I know I should have told you. It's just…you are holding up so well, and I guess Megan's death hit me harder than I imagined," Jack said softly.

I'm tortured inside, and you're walking on a beach? Holly thought to herself. She wanted to yell at him, to scream that he was selfish! How could he do that to her? Leave her alone to wallow in her misery. It was she who had lost her best friend! Her! And yet, she could not bring a single word to her lips.

The next day, Holly awoke with purpose. She drove to the cemetery. The morning was chilly, and she wore a thick, brown sweater. Her jeans were loose and comfortable. The brown mules she wore picked up sandy flecks across the toes as she walked across the cemetery toward the tiny headstone.

Holly set the flowers next to Alissa Mae's grave. *Will your mother ever forgive me? Are you with her now? Does she know the truth?* She shuddered as she remembered the slick feel of the plastic ID bracelets as she had worked them off of the infants' wrists. Swallowing the acidic bile that had risen in her throat, she buried her head in her hands and cried frustrated, angry tears.

Fear, anxiety, and internal disgust were her constant companions. *If Megan knows, does she hate me? Did I do the right thing? Did I ruin Olivia's life? Megan's? My own?* she wondered. *Would Olivia have been better off with me, even if I hadn't been ready to be a mother, even if she hadn't been Jack's child?*

What would Olivia think of her now if she were to find out the truth? What would Jack think? *Oh, Jack. I'm so sorry.* Her body trembled as she thought of how her husband had supported her through Alissa Mae's burial and the awkward and heart-wrenching aftermath of her death.

Peter's gentle voice pulled her from her thoughts, "I thought I might find you here."

"Peter," she sighed as she wiped her tears and turned to face him.

The look in his eyes brought the guilt of their unspoken secret to the forefront of her mind. The turmoil from that confusing, steamy evening, fourteen years earlier, brewed inside her once again. All of her anxious and unsure feelings rose to the surface. She faced the same questions today, as she did back then.

What is with me? I love Jack. Why am I so scared?

She remembered that fateful day, so many years ago—packing their picnic carefully, adding each of Peter's favorite things—brie and crackers, fruit salad, and Jack Daniel's. As she had placed the bottle into the basket, she had thought of how ironic it was that she was bringing Jack with her in her mind. *Exactly what I'm running from!*

A picnic was just what she had needed—and Peter, of all people, would help her see that Jack was the right man for her, that she was doing the right thing and had no reason to fear their relationship. He would help her through her feelings of inadequacy. He would tell her to marry Jack! God how she had wished Megan were there. She was angry with

Megan for leaving for Italy so suddenly. She was angry with Megan for not taking her along. She was, in fact, jealous of Megan's carefree existence, her self-made career. Though her love for Megan was stronger than her anger or her jealousy, for she knew that had Megan been in town, Megan would have stayed up all night talking with her, helping her to figure out if she was moving too fast with Jack, if she was really feeling love and not something else. Else? What else could it be? Her stomach was tied in knots. Her head hurt, and she could not wait to get out of the house and clear her mind.

Holly had taken solace in the warmth of her drink as it trickled down her throat. A blush had risen and settled on her cheeks. The afternoon drifted seamlessly into evening. As she looked at Peter, she saw him through new eyes. He was handsome with his smooth tanned skin and wavy hair that had laid haphazardly across his forehead. She watched his chest move up and down with each breath and had felt a familiar stirring that she recognized but didn't understand. *Chill, girl. He's gay.*

She lay next to him, resting the right side of her body against his left side, and had felt his body tense, for only a moment, and then relax. For years, she and Peter had been close. They and Megan had shared hotel rooms, slept in each other's beds, and been like brother and sisters.

She hated to see him so sad, so tortured about his mother's abandonment, and yet, selfishly, she needed him to be strong. It was she who needed help that night! But she knew that was selfish–Peter had been battling his own demons. She leaned toward him, and tasted the sweet smell of the liquor as it rose with his breath, and pulled her racing mind away from her own turmoil to try and soothe his. “I’m sure she loved you, Peter. Mothers love their children. She had her own shit to deal with, that’s all.”

A tear slid silently down his cheek, landing on the blanket and spreading into faint, thin lines.

Holly placed her hand on his chest, and her fingers had brushed the edge where his unbuttoned shirt met his soft tufts of chest hair. Warmth spread from her chest to her belly and had awakened her senses deep within her center—senses that she knew were wrong, yet only made the heat of the moment that much more enticing.

“Peter, things are moving so fast with Jack. I’m not sure I’m ready.” Holly watched his reaction. His eyes remained still and closed. He didn’t move. She leaned her chest on his and whispered, “Peter? I need some help here. Am I making a mistake? Is it too fast?”

She felt a rise in Peter’s loins, as her hot breath had met his warm face. A look of confusion swept across his face. He remained still. Holly knew the sadness of his mother’s absence weighed heavily in his heart. She also knew the tears that fell from the corners of his eyes were born of years of pent-up hurt and anger. He reached up and pulled Holly close to him, hoping, she knew, to stifle the pain. Holly had the sense that the reason he clenched his eyes shut was to make what was happening not so real, as she’d done so many times in her own life. She knocked over the empty liquor bottle as she let Peter pull her closer, embrace her. Feeling his warm tears on her neck she bent her head back, and tried to both escape the heat that was growing and gather the strength to quell her desire for him. *You smell so good.*

He rolled her over as his mouth, sweet with alcohol and hot with passion, found hers. His tongue moved in hard, forceful strokes, drinking in the safety of her, and erasing his painful memories of his mother. Her anxiety about her relationship with Jack was set aside, as she gave in to Peter's desires—and her own?—and safely lost herself to one of her closest friends.

"Holly?" Peter's voice urged her mind back to the cemetery.

Holly looked at Peter as if she had forgotten he was there. "Peter?"

"Are you alright?" he asked. "You look really…I don't know, but not okay."

She smiled. "I'm okay. I was just thinking about the past."

Peter's voice shook just a bit, just enough for Holly to notice. "Yeah, me too," he said quietly.

Chapter Eight

Holly had been putting off the inevitable—Megan's final goodbye ceremony. She'd been telling herself that giving it time would be better for Olivia, but really, it would be better for her. Two months had passed since Megan's death and she was nowhere near ready for a final goodbye, wasn't sure what it would really mean, what it would do to her.

In the past few weeks, Holly had felt Megan's presence several times. She felt her when she was with Olivia, and when she was alone, thinking of her. She felt her when she was out running errands—or was that just her mind missing her? Wishing she were there with her? Would that stop once they held their final goodbye ceremony? Most of her hoped it would not stop. She loved Megan. She needed Megan. She missed Megan. But a tiny, selfish piece of her hoped it would stop. There was a part of her that was afraid of what Megan thought of her. She was terribly worried that somehow Megan would appear, angry and upset, hurt beyond repair, and wanting to hold Holly responsible for her sin.

Then Holly would know; she would know that she was never to be forgiven by her very best friend—and that, she could not bear.

At times when her guilt consumed her, she looked for Megan around every corner; her secret worked its way from her mind to her gut and back again. Megan never appeared at those times. That, too, scared Holly. *Is she staying away from me because she's so mad?*

Holly began making her list. At the top of the page she wrote, *Megan's Ritual*. Her hand shook as she wrote the names of the attendees: *Olivia, Peter, Jack*. She didn't need a list, she realized. These were the only people who mattered. These were the people who loved Megan and had been her world. Beneath the names she began to scrawl a list of necessities. After the third item, she put down her pen and held her face in her hands. *What am I doing? I can't do this!* Holly crumbled the paper and threw it on the ground.

"Holly?" Olivia was concerned when she walked into the den and found Holly with tears falling down her cheeks and trembling hands. "Are you okay?" she asked.

"Mm-hm," she managed as she wiped her eyes.

"What's wrong?" Olivia stood a few feet from Holly in her bathing suit top and shorts, not sure if she should move closer. "Is it Mom?" she asked quietly.

"No, baby, it's not your mom. It's me." *I was such a fool!*

Olivia stood in silence, unsure of what to do. If it had been her mother who was sad, she would have tried to pry out of her what was going on, but she wasn't sure what to do with Holly.

She didn't need to know. Holly stood up and said, "Are we ready?" as if she had been fine when Olivia found her.

"Sure. If you're sure it's still okay," Olivia asked, wondering if Holly was upset because of something she had done.

When Holly walked out of the room to find Jack, Olivia retrieved the crumpled paper and cautiously opened it. She could feel the air being sucked out of the room as she read, *Megan's Ritual*. Olivia knew it was coming and had wondered how soon they might do it, but somehow the note made it real. *You, huh? I knew it was Mom!* Her lower lip trembled—anger lay just below. Unable to deal with the flurry of emotions, she crumpled the paper in her fist, threw it back down on the carpeted floor, and ran out of the room.

Olivia sat angrily in the back seat of Jack's car, the air was thick with her attitude.

Jack eyed her in the rearview mirror. "You okay, Olivia?"

"Mm-hm," she said, tightlipped as she swung angry eyes toward Holly. Olivia didn't know what angered her more, the upcoming ceremony and what it would mean, or Holly lying to her about being upset over her mother—or maybe Olivia was just angry at herself for having ignored pressing thoughts of her mother for the past forty-eight hours. She didn't know, and she didn't care. She let her anger boil as she stewed in silence.

Oblivious to Olivia's anger, Holly was lost in her own world of guilt and confusion. She didn't even flinch when Jack nudged her with his elbow.

"When did things get normal again?" Olivia asked Jason as they walked along the edge of the surf.

Jason thought about that. "I don't know if things ever really get *normal* again. I was so mad for the first month or so, and my poor granddad had to deal with me. I was awful mean to him, but one day I realized that they didn't really leave me. It wasn't their choice."

"I know. You said that the other night—but then what? I feel so…so empty."

"Then, it sort of just happens. One day I realized that I wasn't just sitting around thinking of my mom and dad anymore. I was going out with my friends. I could watch TV without it always reminding me of how we used to watch together. It's hard to describe, really." Jason stopped walking and threw a rock into the ocean. "It just happened, like, one day I realized I wasn't so sad anymore. I guess I just accepted it."

Olivia knelt to pick up a shell. "But don't you miss them? I feel like I want to run to tell my mom everything that happens each day. I still look for her to walk through the front door of Holly and Jack's house or call on the phone. I mean, I *know* that's stupid, but I can't help it."

Jason sat down next to Olivia. "I still think about them a lot. I just don't…I don't know. I guess I just realize that they won't come back, so I never look for them anymore—but I used to. I used to run to the door, thinking the police or someone would come by and say it was all a big mistake, that someone else had died, but it wasn't my parents. I have my granddad, though, and he's really cool."

"Well, I can't wait for it to get easier. It just sucks. I know it wasn't really her fault she was sick, but she was the one who decided not to take her pills, so that was her fault."

Jason hesitated, not sure if Olivia really wanted to hear what he had to say.

Olivia noticed Jason turn away. "What? What is it?"

"It's just…well, I think she would have died anyway, right? From the cancer? And I bet that would have been more awful for her than dying sooner, or else she wouldn't have stopped taking her pills. I mean, you guys were really close, right? She wouldn't leave you unless she had to."

Olivia played with the sand, writing her name and thinking about what Jason had said. "Maybe…maybe it really would have been harder if she lived longer. Mom said she didn't want me to see her deteriorate."

"Geez, I wouldn't want to watch my mom die," Jason said, and then looked at Olivia, ready to apologize.

"It's okay," she said quietly. "I guess she did what she thought she should do. It's just so unfair that she had to die at all. I mean, I don't even have a father to turn to."

"Sometimes dads are a pain in the ass, believe me. Mine was strict and always harassed me about stuff."

"I thought you liked your dad," Olivia said.

"I did. I loved him, but he was still a pain in the ass."

"Well, I guess I have Jack now, so maybe he'll be a pain in the ass, too," She laughed. "Who knows, maybe I'll like having a dad, even if he is a pain."

The tension between Holly and Jack mounted as they stewed about their own pasts and the lies they were living. Holly lay in the sun watching mothers and their small children on the beach. *I couldn't have done it. I couldn't have been a good mother to Olivia.*

Jack yearned to be close to Holly once again. The distance that had silently crept between them saddened him. *I love you, Holly. I married you, not Megan. Even if Olivia is mine, I would have still married you.*

He covered Holly's small hand with his own, wrapping his fingers into her palm, and squeezing. When Holly squeezed back, he was relieved.

"Hol, I'm sorry," he whispered. "I've been distant lately and not here for you. I'm sorry."

She put her arms around him, unable to find the right words to say back. *I'm sorry, too* seemed too cliché, and *I love you* felt too simple. She really wanted to tell him what she had done and that she was ashamed of her actions, but she couldn't. Instead, she pulled her face back and looked into his eyes, placing a soft kiss on the edge of his lips.

"I want to help," Olivia said to Holly across the dinner table later that evening.

A confused look passed between Holly and Jack. Olivia had been distant from Holly since Saturday morning when they had gone to meet Jason at the beach.

"Help with what?" Holly asked lightly, glad for the break in her silence.

"Mom's goodbye ceremony." She shot her eyes from Holly to Jack. "I mean, I know we have to plan one, right?"

Holly cleared her throat and wiped her mouth with her napkin. "Yes, we should do that soon."

"I'm ready," Olivia blurted out. She turned to Holly. "If you were waiting for me, then I'm ready."

Jack reached out and touched Olivia's hand. "Are you sure, Olivia? We don't have to do it anytime soon. We can wait a while."

Holly interrupted, "You just started back at school. Do you want to wait until you are a bit more settled?" She looked to Jack for support.

"That might be a good idea," Jack said, shrugging slightly. Only Holly noticed.

"No. I'm sure. I'm ready. I mean, she isn't coming back, right? I need to say goodbye. Otherwise I'm stuck in limbo. I feel like I'm just waiting for something." Olivia began eating as if this were typical dinnertime conversation.

Jack raised his eyes toward Holly.

"If you're sure," Holly said. Holly was relieved that Olivia wanted to help plan the ceremony. The idea of planning it herself brought on such guilt that she had been unable to do anything productive. Olivia's wellbeing would give her something to focus on.

"I'm sure," Olivia answered.

Holly was reading when Jack climbed into bed, his warm legs brushed against hers. "Are you doing okay?" he asked tenderly.

"Yeah. Why?" she said.

"Well, this mothering is new to you. Fathering is new to me. I mean, does it make you sad?" Jack asked.

Holly laid her book down on her stomach. "It doesn't make me sad, really. It is a constant reminder that we can't have children, if that's what you mean, but we have Olivia." She looked at Jack, but saw Olivia's dimples. "She's our child now, Jack. I feel grateful."

"Good," he said as he hugged her. "I was worried about you. You've been a little distant lately." He felt Holly's body stiffen. "I have been, too. I'm sorry."

Holly picked up her book and changed the subject, "Jason was nice, huh?"

"Yeah. They remind me a little of me and Megan when we were young, at camp. They seem to be becoming good friends." Jack lay back on his pillow. "I think she needed a friend like him."

Holly looked away. *Did you love her then, too?*

Megan watched Olivia toss and turn, wishing she could make her feel better, give her warm cocoa, or even better, hold her in her arms. She hovered just above Olivia and whispered, *Your father loves you. I promise he does.*

Olivia opened her eyes with a start. "What?" she whispered. She looked around her room which still felt unfamiliar to her. Slowly, she made her way from her bed to the stairs, listening closely for Holly or Jack. Hearing nothing but silence, she crept downstairs and into Holly's den.

She saw the cardboard box in the corner and moved toward it, the box that Holly and Jack had been looking through in her kitchen. The one that had the stuff that her mother had with her the night she died.

She knelt in front of the box which was partially open. With her hands knotted in front of her, she peered inside. It was too dark to make out the contents. As she reached for the lamp on Holly's desk, she knocked over a small wooden box.

Olivia immediately recognized the handwriting on the envelope that fell out of the box. She reached for it. Her hands shook, her heart beat faster with each passing second. *Mom?*

She opened the envelope and reached inside. As she withdrew a folded paper, two small photos fell out. She picked them up and immediately recognized one picture that she had seen many times before. *That's me*, she smiled. The second picture looked just like the first, but it was a photo she had not seen before, and there was something different about it—what that something was, she could not pinpoint. *Who is this?*

Holly gasped when she saw the photo in Olivia's hand. "Where did you get that?" she asked in a soft, yet stern voice.

Startled, Olivia jumped up and put the photo and envelope behind her back. "I'm…I'm sorry. I wasn't looking for this. I promise. I was coming in to see what was in the cardboard box of Mom's stuff and I knocked over the lamp." The words flew out of her mouth fast and shaky. She turned toward the desk and righted the wooden box, quickly putting the folded paper and photos back in the envelope.

Holly saw the envelope and remembered the birth certificate. Her eyes grew wide as she realized that Olivia may have seen it.

"I'm so sorry," Olivia said again. She wrapped her trembling limbs around herself.

"What did you see?" Holly asked tentatively.

"My baby picture, but there were two. Are they both me?" she asked quietly.

A sense of relief washed over Holly. Holly looked down and sighed. "Sit down, Livi. It's okay."

"I'm really sorry, Holly. I wasn't snooping. I mean, not through your stuff. I promise." Olivia sat down on the sofa and folded her legs under herself. She held a pillow on her lap.

"The pictures that you saw, they were of you and Alissa Mae, my baby," Holly began.

"Your baby?" Olivia asked, confused.

"Yes, I had a baby girl the same day as your mother did. You two looked like twins, but, Alissa Mae—that was my daughter—died in the hospital," Holly's voice faded as she spoke, ending in a whisper. She took a deep breath.

"I didn't know," Olivia said in a quiet, concerned voice.

"I know. There didn't seem a need to tell you. She died the day after she was born of SIDS, Sudden Infant Death Syndrome, which really means that they don't know why she died." Holly shrugged, gloomily

"Is that why you don't have children?" Olivia asked.

Holly thought about how to answer her question. *Yes, because I was too scared to get pregnant again. I wasn't sure if I deserved to be a mother after what I had done.* She put her hand on Olivia's and said quietly, "I can't have more children, Livi. It just wasn't in the cards for me, but I do have a child. I have you." Even under the shady umbrella of pretense, she felt an inkling of relief as the truth was finally spoken.

Jason and Olivia had been talking on the phone every night since they went to the beach together. Each time Jason called, the butterflies no longer flew through Olivia's stomach, they were replaced by a different type of excitement. Olivia kept mental notes throughout the day of things that were funny or sad, interesting or weird, and couldn't wait to tell Jason about them later in the day. She loved to hear his "Hey girl!" when she picked up the phone. He was always happy to talk to her.

Jason was doing the same, looking forward to sharing his secrets with someone whom he'd felt connected to, someone who wouldn't judge him when he was sad, or think he was weird when he wanted to stay home at night with his granddad so he wouldn't be lonely. Jason loved the way that Olivia wasn't real girlie and giggly. She could joke like one of the guys or just be quiet and listen.

His granddad said she was his comrade-in-arms, and that he had needed one for a long time. When Jason asked what he meant, he replied, "She's your ally. She's going through what you've already been through. You two will tough out this storm together." Then he looked out the window and said, "You two need each other. It's fate, my boy."

"Why does it creep you out that Holly's baby died?" Jason asked as he wrapped the phone cord around his fingers.

"I don't know. I guess I feel guilty for being here or something—like it should have been Alissa Mae, and not me." Olivia listened to Jack and Holly in the den as they discussed her mother's ritual. She whispered into the phone, "Do you think she resents me? I mean, we were born on the same day."

"Hell, I don't know. That was fourteen years ago, and

you said yourself that you never heard her talk about it. She's probably long over it. Stop worrying about it."

Olivia smiled, "You're probably right." She lowered her voice to a whisper again, "They're in the next room talking about my mom's goodbye ceremony."

"I thought you did that already," Jason said.

Olivia wondered why she felt like she had known him forever, like he had known her mother and how much she had meant to her. The fleeting feelings she had of finding him cute had been easily replaced with another kind of attraction. *He's my friend, like Mom and Peter.* The realization made Olivia happy. *A real friend, someone who gets me!* "We had the public goodbye ceremony. This one is private—just for us."

Jason's stomach lurched. He wondered if he could be included, if he could be one of them.

Olivia woke with a start. The morning sun shone brightly through her curtain, spreading generous streaks of light across her comforter. She lay under the blankets, warm and secure. *Today is the day*—the day of her mother's goodbye ceremony. Planning it had not been as difficult as she had imagined. She and Holly poured over the details at first, as if it were a grand event. Eventually, though, they threw their hands up, wondering why it had taken them so long to realize what the ceremony should really be like.

They didn't need fancy foods and flowers. Megan was more practical than that, and that's what they both had loved about her. She wouldn't have wanted them to spend a lot of money and make themselves crazy over details. Her goodbye ceremony, they agreed, should be the beginning of their own annual ritual. They would give Megan the kind of ceremony that belonged to her, the one she had initiated so many years ago, the one she had left them with.

Olivia pulled the journal Holly gave her out from under her bed. She hadn't thought she would be able to keep another journal after—but she found that it helped her. She could write her thoughts without feeling guilty, without judgment, and that took a weight off of her shoulders that she hadn't realized was there just days earlier. She picked up her purple gel pen and began to write.

Dear Mom,
I know you can't read this, but I want to write it anyway. Today is your goodbye ceremony. I'm not sure how I feel about it. I mean, I know I have to say goodbye, but I don't really want to. I feel like if I say goodbye you will really be gone. I know you're gone, but, well, you know what I mean.

I wonder, Mom, do you still feel my pain? I hope you don't. That's not true, I kind of hope you do. I know that sounds mean, but I want to have some connection to you that is just ours. I feel you all around me all the time. I know you are somewhere out there. Is that going to change when I say goodbye? Are you going to really be going away then? If so, I wish you could tell me. I know you can't. But I wish you could.

Holly and Jack have been great to me. Holly is really sad about losing you. Sometimes I find her crying in the den or just sitting in her car alone, and I know she's thinking about you.

I found the letter, Mom. I'm not sure if I was supposed to or not, but I sort of tore apart your room after you died, and I found it in your mahogany box. I'm sorry. If you didn't want me to find it so soon, then I'm really sorry. But I'm kinda glad I did.

I know why you didn't tell me about Jack. At first I wanted to run and tell him that he was my dad, but every time I saw him and Holly together, I knew why you didn't tell him. I won't tell, Mom. I promise you that. I needed to know, but maybe he doesn't. I mean, he treats me like I'm his daughter anyway. So it really doesn't make a difference, does it?

I don't want to tell Holly that I know, either. I can't figure out if you told her or not, but she hasn't mentioned it to me, so I'm not going to mention it to her either. She loves me, Mom. I know you know that. And she's so much like you that it has made it a little easier for me. She's not you. Please don't think I could ever replace you. I miss you every second of the day. Sometimes I go, "Hey, mom!" and I expect you to be there to listen. I guess that will change sometime.

I have a new friend now, Mom. A real friend. His name

is Jason, and don't worry, he's not someone I'd date or anything. He's a friend. His parents died, too. He gets me. I like to talk to him. Holly and Jack like him, too.

I guess I have to face the day now. I hope you don't go away for real. I love you Mom. I miss you sooo much!

Love forever, Livi

PS: Mom, I haven't felt you around for days. Are you gone already? Have you gone away? If you are, I hope you know I love you. I won't ever forget you.

The day weighed heavily in Holly's heart. She had snapped at Jack when he had asked her what time the ceremony was scheduled to begin. Why had she snapped? She wasn't mad at him. Her guilt had still not settled.

Holly needed to be alone. Olivia was at home with Jack and she couldn't face either of them.

"Jack!" she hollered toward the den, "I'm going to the store to get some stuff for tonight. I'll be back later." She headed for the car without waiting for his response. She was worried Olivia might want to go with her, and she just couldn't handle being nice to anyone at the moment.

Once in the car, her stress lifted a bit. She was alone—finally. She headed toward the grocery store. On the way, she decided that she couldn't even handle being around people she didn't know. She turned the car around and headed toward the lake. Instantly, she knew she was going where she needed to be. The water calmed her.

She sat with her legs hanging over the edge of the dock and took in the beauty of the surrounding trees and small sailboats anchored just feet from the beach. She leaned back on her hands and let her head hang back, her face warmed by the summer sun. She inhaled loud and long, and let her breath out slowly. It felt good to be alone. It felt right.

Holly lay back on the dock, and closed her eyes. She thought back to that dreadful night, fourteen years ago. She had been eight months pregnant, resting on a cot in the room next door to Megan, who had given birth to her own baby just hours before.

"Hol! Wake up, Holly!"

Jack's voice had startled Holly. It had taken her a minute to remember that she was in the hospital. The pain in her belly, that she thought was in her dream, had been very real, hitting her fast and hard as she had tried to sit up. Jack's face, white with fear, had scared Holly.

"Jack? What is it? Megan?"

"Holly, you're bleeding!" Jack had run toward the door, then back to Holly. "Stay here," he had said. He had run into the hall and had hollered for a doctor. Within minutes Holly had been rushed onto a gurney and had disappeared down the hall.

The maternity ward was a happy place for most for

mothers, but not for Holly. It had brought all of her deepest fears to light. Giving birth was like lifting the lid of a compressed chamber, from which her anxiety came rushing up and out, enveloping her, consuming her thoughts, and sending her mind into an uncontrollable panicked spiral. While Megan slept peacefully, Holly's mind ran frantically in circles. Even the rocker where she sat with Olivia in her arms had made her nervous. The instability of the rocking motion made her feel uneasy. Olivia stirred in Holly's arms. A sweet cooing sound escaped her tiny lips. Holly turned toward Megan, happy for her best friend's blessing, and jealous of her ease and acceptance of motherhood—it scared the hell out of Holly. *Why did I agree to share a room?* She glanced in the bassinet next to her own bed and tried desperately to muster a loving smile for her own sleeping daughter, Alissa Mae. She willed herself to experience the emotions that every mother talked about—the feeling of being one with the child, wanting to protect it from everything, having loved it from the moment it was conceived.

Instead, she felt fear—and regret was quickly taking over. The lack of maternal feelings toward the little girl terrified her. Was she even capable of mothering? She was petrified that she had ruined her life, that she would ruin the baby's life. She became filled with desperation. *Alissa Mae, what have I done?*

Tears fell from her eyes. Her happiness for Megan became overshadowed by her anxiety. Carrying her secret made her lose confidence in herself, in her abilities. With the birth of the baby, how would she be able to continue lying to Jack?

Her hands began to shake. She closed her eyes and held Olivia tight, somehow wanting to protect her for Megan. *You can do this! You have to do this!* Her hands shook uncontrollably. She stood and paced the room, whispering to herself, "Get a grip on yourself. You are her *mother*." Olivia lay still. No cooing came from her little pink lips. No nestling into Holly's chest occurred. Through the jostling and worry, Olivia remained still.

Hearing the words had terrified her, *You are a mother*. "I can't do it. I can't. I can't do this. It's not right," she murmured through her tears. She sat again in the rocking chair, too consumed with her own fears to notice the limpness of the weight in her arms. She rocked hard, staring at the ceiling and wishing she could figure out what to do, wishing that somehow she could be transported back to eight months ago, wishing she could have never made the mistake she had.

Agitated, she rose and paced the room again. She carried Olivia in one arm, waving her other as she made her way through her thoughts. *How can I know? Paternity test, that's what I'll do. No! Then he'll know. He'll find out and then...Shit! Jesus Christ, what can I do?* Holly's heart pounded in her chest and she began to feel dizzy. She panted, as if she'd run around the room instead of having paced.

Guilt settled around her. She looked at Megan, her face peaceful and happy, even in her slumber. The sight of Megan brought her mind back to Olivia. The weight in her arms had become noticeably heavy. She lay Olivia in the bassinet next to Megan's bed. The baby didn't wriggle as babies do. Its mouth hung open, lips dry. Uneasy with the stillness of the baby, she lowered her head closer to Olivia's, scrutinizing her breathing. *Something is not right. Oh God!* She licked her trembling finger and placed it under Olivia's nose, hoping to feel the warmth of her breath. *Oh God! Oh God!* She moved it quickly in front of Olivia's mouth—nothing. Holly placed her hand flat against Olivia's chest, hoping for the comforting feeling of the baby's heartbeat. *Oh my God!* Fear ran through her body—her eyes darted around the room, *What do I do?* Her body began to tremble, and she realized that the mewing sounds she heard came from within her own lungs. She stood, picked up the baby and put it on her shoulder, pacing quickly around the room, patting her back, unsure of what to do. Surely the baby was fine, and she just didn't feel its breath. *Oh God! You're okay, right?*

As she paced, a thought came to her—a thought that was so treacherous, she couldn't believe she had it—and yet she could not dismiss it, either. *Should I? Could this be the solution?* She walked tentatively over to Alissa Mae's bassinette and laid Olivia's body next to Alissa Mae. The resemblance was uncanny—Holly realized that without the name tag, which noted the one ounce difference in the babies' weights, she could not tell the two babies apart—identical tufts of blonde hair sprouted like wayward grass under the edges of their caps, the same little pink lips, and remarkably, the same deep dimples. The only difference being that one baby's chest moved up and down with each breath, while the other lay motionless.

The sound of a duck landing on the water brought Holly's mind back to the present. Her mind swam with the inability to come to a decision about her past.

If she were to tell Jack what she had done, he would never forgive her. What about Olivia? Olivia's life would again be in turmoil if she learned the truth, and as it was, she was just barely beginning to come to grips with Megan's death. *Megan.*

She could never repair the damage she had done to Megan. She could only hope that Megan understood that she could not have raised her baby. *What would you have done, Meg? I didn't know if my baby was Jack's or Peter's!* Tears sprang from Holly's eyes.

Peter. Oh my God. What about Peter? What if Alissa Mae was his *daughter?*

She sat up abruptly. *Okay. That's it. I can't tell anyone. What's done is done. I can't tell Olivia, and Jack and Peter don't need to know. It would only hurt them. And what would they think of me? Of my deceiving them? It's better left unsaid.*

Holly played with her wedding ring. "Enough of this," she said out loud. "Megan is gone. I have to carry on. I have Olivia back—Alissa Mae—Olivia." She stood and brushed off her jeans.

She paced along the dock. "Am I right, here? Is this the

right thing to do?" Her arms moved as if she were speaking to an audience.

"Whatever I decide, it has to be right. It cannot be changed." She stopped. "Yes. Okay. This is right." She began pacing again, speaking into the warm air. "Megan, I am sorry I tricked you into raising Alissa Mae, but I couldn't be a mother. I wasn't ready. I didn't know if Jack and I would make it, much less if I could be a mother and a wife. I knew you could be a great mother—and you were a great mother. I did the right thing. I'm sorry you didn't get to mourn for your Olivia, but maybe I saved you some pain. And Jack, if I tell you now, I could lose you. I am not willing to risk that. Peter, well, Peter, I'm just sorry all around."

They sat solemnly around the fire, the air quiet and still save for the flames. Holly was glad that they had decided to do the goodbye ceremony in her back yard instead of Olivia's. She was worried that reliving the ritual in her own backyard would be too much for Olivia to bear.

Olivia had asked about including Jason in the ritual, though as she asked the question, she knew it was not the right thing to do. Holly told her that the decision was hers.

As Olivia looked at her mother's friends gathered as they had been the night of her death, she was glad she had decided to tell Jason that it was a family event, but that he did mean a lot to her. Luckily, he had understood.

She sat next to Jack and was glad that he was there, especially since he had missed her mother's last ritual. Peter and Holly had fawned over her all evening, asking if she was sure she was ready to do the ritual and say goodbye and assuring her that her mother had loved her. Olivia appreciated their concern, but found it harder to make it through with all of that attention. She was glad they were beginning the ceremony and that she was able to escape the microscope.

Olivia reached behind her for her mother's hippie bag, brought it to her face, and smelled the familiar scent of her mother swirling into her nose. She smiled, glad that she had remembered to ask Holly to retrieve it from the house.

She handed the bag to Holly and took it upon herself to take Holly's former position as the one in charge of the music. She pressed the Play button and hoped silently that with the music, her mother would appear.

Holly took the bag from Olivia with a heavy heart. She had been so consumed with making sure Olivia was alright and preparing the ceremony that she had lost sight of what they were really preparing for. With Megan's bag in her hands and the familiar group around the fire, her mind returned to the reason they were there—the final goodbye to her most treasured friend.

The circle of friends didn't feel right without Megan to lead them. Holly's voice caught in her throat as she tried to speak. Tears welled in her eyes. *How can I possibly live up to Megan's ability to lead our ritual? How did she start it again?*

Holly's mind drew a blank. She could not remember the words that Megan used to open the ceremony. Were they the same words each time? She felt insufficient. She was not worthy of this position of honor. The cool air pressed against her. Her heart pounded and cold sweat formed on her brow.

Jack reached over and laid his hand on Holly's arm.

"Hol? Are you alright?" he asked.

Her eyes were laden with sadness and confusion. Did he see fear, too? She tilted her head, as if she could not understand the words Jack spoke.

"Holly?" Jack asked again, rising slowly and moving toward her.

"I'm okay," she managed, breathing heavily. "I didn't expect—"

Olivia watched Holly and knew she was not alone in her fear of saying goodbye.

Holly closed her eyes and envisioned Megan. *Breathe. Breathe.* She took a deep breath, letting it out slowly. The music sifted through the air. *I can do this. I have to do this.* She opened her eyes and nodded toward Jack who was by her side. "I'm okay, really. I just got a little overwhelmed, that's all."

"It's okay, Hol. Do you want to wait?"

"No!" Holly and Olivia said at precisely the same time. Their eyes met, and a look of understanding passed silently between them.

"It's okay, Jack. I can do it now. I'm sorry." Holly patted Jack's hand. "We're good." She turned toward Olivia. "Right, Livi?"

Olivia nodded, the ends of her lips neared a smile.

Peter, Jack, Holly, and Olivia sat hand in hand and cross legged. Their faces warmed by the fire, their eyes closed.

"Thank you for bringing us together once again, oh Holy One," Holly began.

"Our circle has been…altered, as Megan is with You now. We are thankful that You took her peacefully, though her absence is felt in every breath we take."

Olivia wiped a tear from her cheek.

Holly held a purple flower in her right hand, against her heart. "Meggie, how much I miss you. You were taken too soon from us, and yet you are still here. I feel you. I hear you. I even talk to you, but you know that." She breathed a little laugh.

"Thank you for Olivia. Jack and I love her tremendously." Tears streamed down her cheeks. Her hands shook. "I love you, Meggie. You are my sister, and I miss you."

Four soft amens floated into the air. Holly kissed her flower and placed it in the fire.

Megan's view was blurry, as if she were looking through a very old glass window that had bubbled and warped with age. Her form had faded since her passing, barely visible. She felt lighter, not just in her physical being, but her mind seemed lighter as well. It was difficult for her to process thoughts. She understood what she saw, but she could control her cognition less as time wore on. She felt a little like she was able to view but was not able to think or feel.

Jack's heart beat faster as he thought of what he wanted to say. How could he consolidate his feelings for Megan, his questions about Olivia, and the emptiness he felt? How could he portray the chasm that Megan had left in his world without hurting Holly any more than what she already experienced?

His voice was just above a whisper, deep and solemn. "There are some friends who are always there for you, even when they are not present. There are others that are always present, and yet, somehow never there. You, Megan, were the queen of the first. You were the friend who touched one's heart, lifted one's spirit, and eased uncomfortable situations. You, Megan, were a miracle. I love you and know that when it is my turn to leave this Earth, you will be there, ready to fill me in on the goings on in heaven and show me a mural that only you could paint. Until that time, Megan, I say goodbye."

Jack placed his flower into the fire. Sparks popped lightly as they lifted toward the sky.

Peter took a loud, deep breath. The air escaped his lungs just as loudly as it had gone in. Tears sprang from his eyes when he opened his mouth to speak. He closed his eyes and thought of Cruz. *Be strong, Peter. You can do this.*

"I feel so much gratitude toward you, Megan, that it is really difficult to put into words. You always encouraged me to be myself, not to let others judge me, and to stand up tall with regard to my feelings, yet you didn't let me wallow in my mother's leaving me. You taught me that it was okay to let Cruz in." He began to sob. Jack and Olivia both reached out to him. He shook them off.

"I only regret that I didn't listen before you were gone. I was so selfish!" His voice grew louder.

Holly and Jack watched, helpless to comfort him from his guilt.

"You gave me the strength to love Cruz, and now… now…you aren't here to see how happy it made me. I'm so sorry, Megan." His shoulders and head bobbed as he sobbed into his hands. The flower he was holding dropped to the ground. "I'm sorry. I'm so sorry," he wept.

"Peter," Olivia's shaky voice brought his eyes to hers. "Mom knows how happy you are. She's here." She looked up toward the sky. "I can feel her. She's here. She knows."

The lump in Peter's throat kept him from speaking. He nodded, his sad eyes pleaded forgiveness from Megan's daughter. He hoped to someday have a child of his own—a child as sensitive and insightful as Olivia.

He took another deep breath. "I love you, Megan." He tossed his flower into the flames.

In unison, a relieved amen floated to the sky.

Olivia's stomach was on fire. Her head felt dizzy and tears streamed down her cheeks. She put her hand in her right pocket and pulled out a folded piece of paper.

Holly's heart jumped to her throat. Panic ran through her. *Is that—?*

The paper crinkled as she unfolded it, its blue lines and the three holes punched in the side revealed themselves.

Holly sighed. *Thank goodness!*

The paper shook in Olivia's fingertips. She stared at it, as if it might do a trick. She found her voice in a whisper.

"I wrote this for my mom. I hope you guys don't think it's stupid."

Her mother's friends smiled. Holly reached for Olivia's hand. It trembled in her own. She squeezed it, hoping to give her comfort and strength. "Go on, baby girl."

Olivia read, her face wet with tears, her shoulders trembled, and yet her voice did not waiver.

"Dear Mom." She lifted her eyes and saw the other faces watching her with eager anticipation and support—lots of support.

"I don't know why you are gone. I don't know why God took you so early, when I needed you here, but I think he must have needed you more than he thought I did."

"I don't want you to worry about me. I'm okay. We are selling our house but not because I want to, I sort of have to. Otherwise, I can't think of anything other than being there and waiting for you to come back." Olivia's throat began to close as a sob escaped her lips. She sucked in air, spitting out her words quick and strong. "I'm okay. I can do this."

"Anyway, Mom, um, I will do well in school and make you proud. I don't know what I want to be when I grow up, but I know I will do something that you would approve of and be proud of. You taught me to think outside of the box." She looked at Holly. "I hated when she used to say that!" She flashed a crooked smile, then bent her head to read.

"I'll be good for Jack and Holly who already feel like parents to me." Heat rushed up her cheeks as she said, "Jack is like my real dad."

Holly covertly eyed Jack, who sat teary eyed and silent, watching Olivia speak with his heart on his sleeve.

"And Holly is like you, Mom. She's not you. God, no one could be you, but she's like you."

"I'm sorry I went through your room. I understand things now, Mom, things we didn't talk about. It's okay. I get it. I think you were right to keep it to yourself."

Holly's heart skipped a beat. She looked questioningly from Olivia to Peter, who shrugged, and Jack, who lifted his eyebrows.

"I love you, Mom." Sobs wracked her trembling body. She covered her face, the note slipping from her fingers to the ground.

"I can't say it!" she yelled between her fingers and tears. "I can't say goodbye. I can't! I don't want to!"

Holly was quick to wrap her arms around Olivia. "Baby, it's okay. You don't have to. You have said enough." She turned to Jack.

"Maybe we shouldn't have planned this," Jack said.

Olivia broke out of Holly's arms, shaking her head. "No! We had to! I have to do this!" She picked up the note and stood on quivering legs. Holly was by her side, confused and hurting for Olivia.

Olivia stared into the fire, crying openly. She looked at Peter who nodded at her.

She held her letter over the fire, looked to the sky, and said, "Goodbye, Mom. I love you." The letter slipped from her fingers into the fire. Red and purple flames engulfed the fragile paper. Olivia's face grew so warm she had to take a step backward.

Olivia felt something push through her body with such force that she swayed forward then back, her neck suddenly jerked upward, arched toward the sky. She gasped. Her arms trembled violently at her sides, then, as if lifted by unseen hands, they were drawn up, as if reaching for the clouds. Her body thrust forward in one great push, the arch in her back painful, as a wail escaped her lips.

Holly scrambled to her side, grabbing hold of her body and fearing the unseeing look of Olivia's eyes. Jack grabbed Olivia's other side, steadying her.

"What the hell?" Jack asked.

"Olivia?" Holly's voice shook frantically, "Are you okay?" She looked to Jack, pleading.

Peter pulled them back, away from the fire. "Let's get her inside."

Olivia blinked repeatedly. Her legs were weak, and yet her body felt cleansed, lighter, as if something had been lifted from within. "Mom?" she looked around, dazed, and suddenly her eyes flew wide open. She looked around, her face a mixture of panic and excitement. She struggled against those that held her up.

"She's delirious," Jack said, his voice rising in panic.

"Mom? Mom?" Olivia broke free of the shackling arms and ran to the fire, looking up toward the sky. "Mom!" she yelled. "I love you! I felt you!" All at once her body shook, and she sobbed. She began to lose her balance, her body teetering limply.

"Oh my God!" Holly rushed to her just in time to lower her gently to the ground. "Olivia?" She patted her face.

"Peter, get some cold water," Jack ordered.

Peter rushed inside, feeling completely inadequate and helpless. He brought a cold glass of water for Olivia, and handed a cool, wet cloth to Jack, who patted Olivia's face.

"Livi? Honey?" Jack said.

Olivia's eyes rolled around. She blinked several times. "Mom. She's gone," she said confidently, yet softly. "Mom's gone."

Holly cried, wiping Olivia's sweat-beaded hair off of her forehead, "Yes, baby, she is."

"No. I mean, she's really gone now, Holly. I felt her. She went right through me." Olivia wrapped her arms around her belly.

Holly, Jack, and Peter exchanged glances.

"Really, Holly," Olivia insisted. "I felt her. I felt her!" Tears rolled down her cheeks. "It's okay." She looked around for her mother's urn, spotting it on the table on the deck.

Olivia leapt toward the deck, as if she had renewed energy. "We have to do this, Holly. It's okay. I know that now." She grabbed the urn in her arms and held it close to her chest.

She stood next to Holly and smiled. "C'mon." She tilted her head toward the fire. "Peter, Jack, c'mon."

Bewildered, they followed her lead toward the fire. Olivia, her face radiating the heat of the flames and her tears glittering like moon sparkles, knelt down by the fire, settling the urn between her knees. Peter, Jack, and Holly knelt, shrugging and confused.

"Olivia, are you sure you're okay? I mean…" Holly said.

"Yes! I'm more sure of this than anything in my whole life!" she leaned toward Holly, letting her body rest against her for just a second or two. Then she sat upright and asked, "How do we do this?" Her tears had dried. She wore a smile—a real smile.

"Um, okay, well, I think we should say something," Holly offered.

"I am sorry, you guys. I'm sorry I was such a knucklehead before. It's just that Megan—" Peter's eyes filled with tears. He squeezed them shut and placed his thumb and index finger over them. "I'm sorry."

"It's okay, Pete," Jack said, his hand rested on Peter's back. "We know how you feel."

Jack looked at Olivia and asked gently, "Liv, I'll do this, okay?"

She nodded, and handed the urn to Jack, holding it with him for an extra moment, then she released it and nodded, rolling her lips tightly into her mouth.

Jack wrapped his large hands around Megan's urn, removed the lid, and held it up toward the sky. He looked at Olivia, who smiled and nodded.

Jack's voice boomed into the night, strong and firm, "Megan! We release you!"

Suddenly, Holly's mind cast back to the cobwebs of a memory—a memory of a soft, confident voice she could hear but could not place, *One will be released, and returned after death.* She turned toward Olivia and stared in disbelief. *Returned after death.* "Oh my God," Holly said in a voice too low to be heard by the others. Her legs buckled, and she barely caught herself from complete collapse as she fell slowly to her knees. All she could do was raise her head and her eyes to the heavens, seeking Megan's spirit, seeking forgiveness and understanding.

Jack looked down at her, smiled, and nodded, misunderstanding her intent. He pushed the urn higher toward the sky, "Soar like the wind, Megan! Paint like there's no end to your canvas! We will see you again one day. We love you!" Jack tipped the urn. Megan's ashes floated through the cool night air, landing in the roaring fire. Crackles of yellow sparks flew into the sky, feet above the flames. Red, yellow, and purple flames swirled high, reaching toward the clouds. The flames reflected off of each of the love amulets that hung around their necks—and the Buddhist chant, the one that could not be changed, played on.

Acknowledgements

When I think of whom I would like to thank for their support, many people come to mind: my mother and family, first and foremost. Mom, thank you for loving my characters and hating my premise. Thank you for reading and correcting, crying and laughing. Thank you most of all, Mom, for always supporting my creative outlets and for pushing me to do my best and to keep going.

Thank you, Les, my amazing husband, for your undying desire for me to do the things that make me happy, and for your unyielding excitement over each character developed, each twist in the plotline, and each scene as it unfolded. Without your support, I could not write a single word. You are my treasure.

I'd like to thank all of my children for their patience and understanding, but most of all, I'd like to thank Jess and Jake who, as my youngest, have borne the brunt of my efforts. Thank you for allowing Mommy to spend countless hours writing and for accepting my "Mm-hmm" responses. Thank you for helping me come up with the title, and for being so very excited about *Megan's Way* coming to print. You are my biggest fans!

There are too many friends to call out, but one I cannot miss. Thank you, Beth Grimmett for reading, rereading, and enjoying my manuscripts. Thank you for being honest with your feedback and for pushing me to continue. To my other early readers, Michelle Belski and Jen Lo Turco, thank you for plodding through what was not yet a finished manuscript and for supporting my efforts.

Dominique Agnew, my editor and friend, without whom *Megan's Way* never would have found a shelf, you are a godsend to me. Thank you for fine-tuning *Megan's Way*, indulging my stubbornness, making me see the other side of things, and helping me see that together, anything is possible! *Megan's Way* would not have flowed as smoothly without your input.

Lastly, to all my sisters from The Women's Nest, of which there are too many to list: Govtmule, Tabitha, Clare, Cara, Davesgrl, Sweet_Escape, Jacklynr, Bekah_shrinks, Gardengrl, Kerri_Draper, Nel361, Riverspirit, Shadowrose, and everyone else who has stood by me, motivated me, and cheered me on. Thank you!

A conversation with Melissa Foster

Q. *What was your inspiration for* Megan's Way?

A. Many years ago, my mother went in for surgery that I was told was for several benign cysts on her ovaries. It wasn't until a year later that she told me that there had been an oncologist in the operating room because they had thought she may have cancer, and that she had already determined that had they found cancer, she was not going to undergo treatment. This was over ten years ago, when treatments were not as advanced as they are now. My heart sank when she told me, and I hung on to that feeling and mulled over what it would have been like for both of us—I could not let it go. That's how Megan's Way was born.

Q. What was the underlying theme you sought to impart to your readers?

A. There are so many. I think it is important that we do something in life that we enjoy, and that we make decisions based on what we feel is best in our own individual circumstances, rather than what others think is best. In this case, Megan thought that prolonging her death would, in the end, be more treacherous to Olivia than her passing on sooner and more quickly, and her decision was made. Forgiveness, belief in one's self, the depths of friendship, and cherishing each moment as we live it—that's what I was going for.

Q. Did your own lifestyle influence the book in any way?

A. In some ways, yes. I paint, and therefore wanted Megan to live a very artful lifestyle, hence the art shows and flea markets. I think instincts are overlooked far too often, and that's why I gave Megan a sixth sense with Olivia. If we are open to them, I believe these lines can become strong within our own minds. I cherish the few close friends that I have, and felt it was important to show their feelings toward Megan's death.

Q. Do you believe in life after death?

A. This will either turn off my readers or entice them. The truth is: yes, I do believe in a certain type of life after death. I do believe one has a certain amount of time to reach out and touch our loved ones. Weird, I know—but that's me.

Q. With six children, when do you find time to write?

A. I had to wait until my youngest was in school full time, and then I wrote for six hours each day, but *Megan's*

Way wasn't my first novel. My first novel was *The Knowing*, which has not come to print yet. Megan knocked on my door, and I had to let her in and set down *The Knowing* for a bit. The Knowing for a bit. I continue to write while my children are in school and after they go to sleep at night, or while they are doing homework or are otherwise busy.

Q. What are you working on now?

A. I am working on my second novel, *The Knowing*, a mystery with a paranormal twist about Tracey Potter, a seven-year-old girl who is abducted, and one woman's desperate search to find her. Molly Tanner has had visions all her life, but never have they been this horrifying, unveiling images of a young girl being held captive. Guided by her visions, she weaves her way through the secret cavities of people's lives, creating upheaval in the small town when dark secrets are exposed.

Q. May readers contact you? Are you available to speak with book clubs?

A. Absolutely! I love to meet and chat with readers. They can contact me through my website(s):

www.megansway.com
www.thewomensnest.com

Questions for book club discussions

1. Megan struggles throughout the book with guilt over her decision to stop her medications and treatments. Do you think she did the right thing?

2. Megan didn't decide to disclose who Olivia's father was until the night she died. Why do you think it took her so long? Do you think she should have disclosed the information to Olivia and/or Jack sooner, or not at all?

3. Holly implies that she knew Megan's baby was Jack's. Why do you think she never approached the topic with Megan? For that matter, why did she avoid discussing the possibility with Jack?

4. Olivia progressed from self-inflicted pain to meeting someone she chatted with on a prohibited website, putting her own life in danger. Do you think this is typical teenage

behavior? Should Megan have seen that coming?

5. Do you believe in life after death?

6. It appears that Jack knew Holly was right for him when they began dating, do you think it ever occurred to him that he may have fathered Megan's baby, or was he simply in denial?

7. Peter is greatly affected by Megan's death. Why do you think his relationship with Megan, rather than his relationship with Holly, brought his inability to commit to a relationship to a changing point?

8. What themes do you see throughout the book?

Breinigsville, PA USA
24 March 2010

234783BV00001B/48/P